COYOTE'S CALLING

The McKenna Brothers: Coyote - Book Three

MARIELLA STARR

Published by Blushing Books
An Imprint of
ABCD Graphics and Design, Inc.
A Virginia Corporation
977 Seminole Trail #233
Charlottesville, VA 22901

Mariella Starr
Coyote's Calling

eBook ISBN: 978-1-64563-972-5
Print ISBN: 978-1-64563-973-2
v1

Chapter 1

Riley McKenna awoke to the sound of the bus door being slammed shut. He instinctively rolled over to grip the padded metal bar surrounding the exterior bunks on the touring bus. He'd been thrown from a bunk many times in his lifetime. The bar was not there, and he smiled, realizing he was home. More to the point, he was at his parents' home in San Antonio temporarily.

His house, vehicles, and nearly everything he owned had exploded and gone up in flames. You wouldn't think a modern lighthouse-shaped tower built with a lot of concrete over a boathouse would burn, but it had. The voltage of a lightning bolt had destroyed his house, the boathouse under it, and the six boats housed there, along with his beloved Jeep and a nearly new truck. It had taken him almost a year to build his dream house. It had been reduced to ashes in less than thirty minutes. Lesson learned. When you lived forty miles from the nearest fire department, and a bolt of lightning hit your place, it was toast. As one of the roadies had said, and he'd quoted a few times. *'He was damn lucky he was on tour at the time. Otherwise, he would have been a roast.'*

The fire department had been able to keep the fire from spreading into the surrounding forests. The flames hadn't torched the nearby homes belonging to older brothers Micah and Sully.

His home, music studio, instruments, and vehicles were gone. Riley was still thanking the overall technology universe. Everything he wrote or created was stored on offsite servers and the mysterious '*cloud*'.

Physical belongings were replaceable, but the time he'd invested in designing and the actual construction wasn't. He'd been hands-on in building his home. From helping to pour concrete to installing the tin roof, he had enjoyed every part of the experience. Construction was different from the years he'd spent in academia. Riley still didn't know what to do with the degrees packed away in a safety deposit box. They didn't have a lot to do with the idea he'd been toying with and mentally rejecting for several years.

When he would find the time, or if he was going to replace his house, Riley had no idea. He was thankful no one had been hurt. He was also grateful for his habit of sending his awards to his parents. They enjoyed displaying the Grammys and Music Awards, won by himself and his brothers. They were all still loosely connected by their band I-35. They were more connected as brothers, tight, and only a phone call away. Careers, marriage, and growing families had a tendency to keep them apart.

Riley had bitched at the high cost of insurance, complained it was extortion, but he was glad now he'd paid the sky-high premiums. Or rather, his business manager had paid them. He showed little interest in his finances, except checking the balances and stopping at an ATM for cash. Most people thought he was careless about such matters. He wasn't. What they didn't know was he could balance the books, without the aid of calculators, spreadsheets, or programs, in less time than it took to input the numbers into a computer. There was no way he would be ripped off by an *expert* cooking the books and trying to play dirty with his money. It had happened to far too many of his friends in the business.

He stretched his arms and legs to their full six-foot five-inch length and smiled at his feet hanging over the end of his childhood bed. He'd had a custom-built bed at his house to accommodate his height. It was gone. After the shock had worn off, he'd spent a couple of days staring out the window of the tour bus, wondering what was next. In his muddled thoughts, he kept asking himself, did it really matter?

Rolling from his bed and looking through the window, he saw one of his band's technical crew carrying a bucket and broom and heading toward the tour bus.

Easy Bishop was a roadie, who had worked for I-35 in its heyday, and now worked in his crew. Riley and Easy had arrived outside San Antonio the night before. They had rolled into the driveway of his parents' property long after midnight, but they had been welcomed with open arms.

Today, he and Easy would unload the bus. They would locate all the things hidden in every nook and cranny of the 48-foot touring bus. Promoting his third album in two years had exhausted everyone. Several days earlier, they'd dropped his backup musicians and technicians at the airport to return to their homes and families. Riley and Easy were the only ones left.

Once the bus was returned to the rental agency, Easy would head for the airport. Aging into the mid-fifties, Easy was the *old man* of the crew. When Easy wasn't checking mikes and wiring on tour, he was somewhere in the world where the waves were breaking high.

Riley looked around his old bedroom in his parents' house. Nothing had changed much since he had left home at nine-teen. He had claimed, at the time, that living on campus made it easier for his studies, but it hadn't been the truth. What he had needed was to cut the parental strings of his over-protective tight-knit family. He loved his family, all of them, but he required space. He'd witnessed his older brothers' struggles to break free to become adults. At nineteen, he had already charted a music career with his brothers. On top of his musical accomplishments, he'd earned two Bachelor's degrees. Before he'd hit the road again, Riley had been working toward his master's in a subject that wouldn't further his career, but he found it challenging.

His older brothers, Micah and Sully, had formed a band as young teens. He'd joined them at age nine when he'd discovered music made sense to him. He had been only twelve when their first album had hit the charts. Riley had been talented enough to be a member of the band. For the most part, though, he'd gone along to get along with his brothers. He loved music, but his interests were broad, scattered, and in some instances secret.

They had been the only children of Carole and Daniel McKenna when they had launched their careers. Several years later, his parents had adopted the four children of a distant cousin of his mother. All of his siblings were referred to as first-set, second-set. He was first-set, and he'd been the youngest when there was only one set. Teased by his older brothers, he'd been nicknamed Coyote, a name he'd loved as a kid but hadn't been able to shake as an adult. He'd released his first single album under his real name Riley, and he'd stuck with it since.

Riley had been filling stadiums for the last couple of years on his own, while his brothers' careers had continued to skyrocket in different creative and family venues. Oldest brother Micah had won an Oscar the previous year for a soundtrack in a blockbuster movie. He and his wife Tess had increased the size of their family to three kids. They were waiting for the paperwork to adopt a baby girl. They'd only been married three years, but they weren't wasting time.

The second oldest, Sully, was cranking out movies and awards. Only six years older than Riley, Sully and his wife, Karina, were in the production of baby number six. Both of his brothers were deliriously happy as married men. By comparison, Riley felt like he was coasting or drifting. He could never tell which.

The McKenna I-35 hadn't disbanded. They simply couldn't align their schedules enough to write and release another album. He and both of his brothers were writers of music and song. Some people might assume the McKenna brothers had faded from the music scene. They had no idea how much of their music was still charting. Creating music was part of their DNA.

Riley had to admit the constant touring had lost its appeal, again. He was fully aware of his fan base. As a Texas boy, he'd been raised to be polite and well mannered. On-stage he was funny, loud, and professional. Off-stage he was quiet, and as he aged, had become more reserved and careful of his friends. Riley avoided conflicts of any kind. When a guy had his height and build, the blame would fall on him regardless of who started it.

Lately, Riley had been feeling empty, and it wasn't a feeling he liked. The guys in the band thought he needed to get laid, but it was far more than that. Women liked him, although not always for the right reasons. He liked women, but he had been raised to believe in monogamy and commitment. The women he met on the road wanted one-night, no strings attached, and bragging rights. Most men his age and most of his backup musicians and crew thought easy sex was a perk of being on the road.

Although the sex was usually enthusiastic and generous, all it did was scratch an itch and melt away a bit of lonesome time. Then there was the guilt. Riley knew his prowess around women, but he hadn't been raised to be a man-whore.

It had been two-and-half years since Riley had taken a break, and he needed one. He was going to be off the radar for a while. Award shows, nominations, and wins had helped establish his solo career, but the music business was fickle. You had to stay on top to be on top. He'd lost his edge and his drive to strive for more. He'd reached those goals so many times already, in music and in academia. Still, there was a hole inside him, and he couldn't explain it. He hadn't found what he needed to fill it. He'd thought he had, but he'd been wrong, and that particular failure still hurt.

Riley dressed and went to help Easy. The pile of leftover stuff was boxed and separated by the owner. He would ship it to the guys.

Easy nudged Riley and nodded toward the gate. "She's back. Third time since I started cleaning the bus this morning."

Riley walked over to the entrance gate to the property. He didn't open the gate to her but walked over to the car.

"Do you need something, Leigh Ann?" he asked.

"I wanted to thank you for the donation," the woman said.

"I believe in your work," Riley said.

She nodded. "I know I went too far, but can't we take a step backward? We were good together."

Riley shook his head. "I can't be what you need. I won't become what you need."

"You could destroy me, my church, and my work," she said.

"I won't. I'll continue to support your efforts," Riley said. "All I ask is, you let me find what I need and leave me alone."

She swallowed hard, and nodded. "I had to try. I won't bother you again."

Riley returned to the garage, and he didn't look back at what he'd once thought would be part of his life and future.

"Is she the reason you've been living like a monk?" Easy asked.

"I haven't," Riley denied.

"Close enough," Easy said. "Are you going back to the studio, or are we done?"

"I don't know," Riley said honestly.

"When you figure it out, give me a call," Easy said. "I have expensive habits and ain't none of them illegal. We only live once, kid. A lot of people think I'm nuts because I live for the next big wave to break. If I die in the next big one, I'll die happy. You need to find what makes you tick. You've been looking for it for a while, but you haven't found it yet. You'll know when it's right. It usually hits like a lightning bolt, straight between the eyes."

"My life has already been hit by a bolt of lightning," Riley said.

"Hell, kid, that one missed you by a thousand miles. You'll know when the real one hits! Jump on it and ride it for all it's worth!" Easy slapped Riley on the back.

Riley watched as his friend drove away, and he knew one more phase of his life was ending. He didn't know what was going to replace it.

His parents, Carole and Daniel McKenna had called for his help, and he wasn't going to refuse. Several years earlier, a medical scare had shaken the entire McKenna family. There had been several misdiagnoses before Riley's mother, Carole, had been diagnosed with Hodgkin lymphoma. She'd been treated with chemotherapy, radiation, and finally a stem cell transplant. It had taken a long time for her to stabilize, but her doctors were currently claiming she was cancer-free.

Daniel had planned a three-month cruise to celebrate his wife's restored health. Daniel had known Riley was due to finalize his tour, and one of the second-set kids was screwing with his father's plans.

Riley knew he had lived a charmed life so far. He wanted to milk it for every opportunity he was given. An end-of-tour vacation of wilderness camping, whitewater rafting, and rock climbing was now canceled. The next three months were about payback, and he owed his parents a lifetime of it.

Noah, the youngest and only brother of the second-set, was supposed to spend the summer with Riley on his vacation. Those plans were now shot to hell.

Juvenile irresponsibility, mixed with underage drinking, and teenage entitlement, had sent Daniel McKenna into a rarely seen wrath. His youngest son had been fined a thousand dollars, and he was on a year's probation to be monitored by his parents. Noah had celebrated his seventeenth birthday inappropriately and had spent the night in a juvenile facility. Daniel McKenna decided his son needed a lesson in real-life responsibility.

Riley's plans had been scuttled along with his younger brother's. Noah was being sent to their uncle's ranch outside of Yuma, Arizona.

"Why there?" Riley had asked his father.

"Why not? You and your brothers sent Noah to Frank's ranch when he needed a kick in the pants when he was nine, and your mother and I were in Europe. He was fine, and he got a taste of reality. I think he needs another dose. Frank called, and he's closed the Boy's Home temporarily. He's building an extension on his house, and he fell off a ladder. With a dislocated shoulder and three broken ribs, Frank needs help," Daniel explained. "I was planning on sending him money so he could hire additional help. Now, I'm sending the money and Noah. Your brother is going to learn there are consequences for his actions!"

"He screwed up," Riley agreed. "Other than hanging around with crappy kids, no one was hurt."

"He could have been injured or killed," Carole said with a worried tone in her voice.

"Could have," Riley interjected. "The only thing he's guilty of is using bad judgment in picking his friends."

"Son, I am not letting your brother get away with this kind of behavior," Daniel warned. "It's not going to hurt him to swing a hammer or muck out the barns! He's been there before. He should remember what is expected of him."

"He was only nine when he pulled that stunt," Riley said. "Uncle Frank is a tough old guy. He's gruff and opinionated. Without Aunt Katherine around to smooth out his rough edges, I imagine he's a bear to be around."

"My brother is tough. He has to be to maintain the kind of order he needs to run a foster home. He is also injured, and he needs help. It's a done deal. If the timing was different, I'd go myself, but I do not intend to disappoint your mother. I'll send Frank some money. He can always use it for the kids, but I'm also sending Noah. Frank needs someone who can do physical labor, and Noah needs to work off the fine."

"Dad, Noah could pay the fine by working one gig. During the summer months, there are a lot of bands who need backup drummers," Riley said.

Daniel McKenna gave his grown son a look that still made Riley feel like he was guilty of something. "You're missing the point. He could pay it out of his bank account now, but that's not going to teach him a lesson. Noah can either hate it or do what is right! I am not raising a spoiled brat!"

Riley didn't have a comeback. He'd heard those words before, and once his father decided on something, it was a done deal. Now, they would spend the summer in Dry Rock, Arizona, working on his uncle's ranch. Frank McKenna needed able-bodied muscle, and they were going to provide it.

"You aren't part of this," Daniel said. "This is about Noah learning responsibility for his actions. I'm fairly sure at this point in your life you're not making stupid decisions!"

Riley shrugged, and he wanted to retort, *Do you want to bet?*' but he didn't. "It's not like I have a home to go home to. All I had to look forward to was a pile of ashes, and knowing Micah like I do, he's already had the mess cleaned up."

"Something is bothering you," Daniel said intuitively.

"Yeah, but I'm not ready to talk about it," Riley admitted, and both of his parents nodded. They knew he would talk to them when he was ready.

"Did you talk sense into Dad?" Noah demanded as soon as Riley entered his old bedroom. The kid was waiting for him.

Riley didn't answer. He went to his closet, and he came out holding an old pair of cowboy boots in his hand.

"No," he admitted to his younger brother. "You and I are going to spend the summer in Dry Rock, Arizona!"

Jessica Harper pulled her car over to the curb. She looked in all directions carefully before using her remote for the garage opener. Before driving into the garage, she looked again and closed the door. Opening the backseat door to her older model Toyota Camry, Jessica unhooked Jake from his safety seat.

Jenna Harrison joined her on the other side of the car and released Jackson from his seat. As the twins scampered inside, she went to Jessica and gave her a hug. "Are you okay?" Jenna asked, giving the younger woman an inquiring look.

"I'm okay," Jessica said with a wan smile. "Take care of my boys."

"Like my life depends on it," Jenna said seriously.

"I'm counting on it," Jessica said. "I'm going to go to

Braxton's department store during my lunch hour. Star Wars sheets are on sale. I have a little bit of extra money since I have been working overtime. I want to treat the boys for their birthday."

"Mixing practical with what they really want," Jenna said with a smile. "I'm sending Dave over to the toy store to get them a few things. He's been into Star Wars since he was about eight-years-old, and he's still into it. He'll know what will interest the boys. I gave him a budget, but I don't know if he will stick to it. What is it with men and their toys? Dave is fifty. You would think he would be over it by now."

Jessica laughed. "If he buys too much, feel free to return whatever you think is excessive." She kissed her friend on the cheek. "If I get the opportunity for overtime, I'll call."

"Don't worry about it," Jenna exclaimed. "I enjoy the twins. I would still be coddling my boys, except they got this strange idea that just because they're grown men, they don't need their momma hovering over them anymore!"

Jessica left the house smiling. She didn't see a car parked behind a thick hedge. Even if she had, she would have never suspected he had rented a vehicle from a company called Rent-A-Wreck.

The driver of the 2000 silver sedan pulled into traffic several vehicles behind her. Like so many silver look-alike vehicles, he was able to blend into traffic. It was easy. His bitch of an ex-wife wasn't going to get away. She belonged to him.

Chapter 2

Riley pointed ahead and tapped his brother on the arm to get his attention. To keep from arguing over the music, they had agreed on devices and earbuds. Noah took one of his earbuds out. "What?"

"Town," Riley said. They were traveling over the southwestern part of the state of Arizona. When they had left Texas, the temperatures were in the high eighties; crossing New Mexico, the temperatures had risen into the high nineties. It was getting hotter and dustier every day. The Sonora Desert with giant saguaro cactus was a majestic sight. Plastic saguaro had been used in so many western movies most people thought they grew all over the southwestern states. It wasn't so. There were only four places in the world, and one of them was the Sonora Desert.

Riley drove off the highway and onto a packed dirt and sand parking lot. He parked in front of the gas pumps and took stock of their surroundings. The GPS hadn't identified where they were. There was an icon of a gas station showing, but where they were wasn't considered a town, as far as Google was concerned. It was a settlement. There was a gas station/grocery store/restaurant combination and a building with a sign over the door stating it was a hardware/leather/silver jewelry repair shop.

There was a cinder block building painted white and had a sign in the front stating it was a *Church of the People*. About three hundred yards from the grocery store was a small stable-like building and a corral. Across the road was a shack of a building labeled simply Bar with a hand-lettered sign. Next was an Old West Antiques Shop. It looked to be a dumping site for anything old, rusted, and broken.

"Yet, another armpit of America," Noah quipped sarcastically.

"Cut it out!" Riley said automatically. "I'll get gas. Go inside, and see if you can find us something to eat."

Noah jumped from the truck.

"Noah," Riley stopped him with a warning. "Don't give them any money," he nodded his head towards a group of men loitering around the front door of the store. "It only encourages them to be pan-handlers."

"What if the money I give them is what makes them change their lives?" Noah asked.

"More than likely, they will pool those dollars and buy booze as soon as we leave," Riley warned.

"When did you become a pessimist?" his brother demanded. "You've always been a soft touch!"

"I'm a realist," Riley corrected. "You haven't spent any time in major cities recently." He watched his brother weave his way through the men blocking the entrance. It was something he saw every day on the streets of every city and nearly every town he visited. It was something they had witnessed again and again. Still, there didn't seem to be anyone interested in solving the problem.

Where many were in need, there were also con artists. When Riley suspected the signs were valid, he still gave. He looked at their shoes or jewelry. Two-hundred-dollar sneakers, gold teeth, jewelry, and expensive cell phones were a sure sign of a con. Maybe he was getting jaded, but he'd seen a woman with a baby dressed as a homeless person, picked up in a Lexus. He followed them to a swank neighborhood and realized he'd fallen for the con.

His younger brother's sympathetic nature had cost him almost all the spending money he had brought with him. Noah tried to hide that part of his personality under teenage bravado, but Riley knew. He knew because he was a soft touch. Over the years, though, he'd learned to channel his donations to food banks and shelters where he knew the money wasn't being siphoned to pay for high dollar publicity and salaries.

Riley washed his windshield and grimaced. He'd bought a used truck, and it wasn't unusual in his family. They could afford new, but why pay thirty-to-fifty percent more? A vehicle was four wheels, and its purpose was to get from point A to point B. It had taken him all of six hours to find a decent truck, with low mileage, good tread on the tires, only two-years-old, and still under warranty. It was six hours well spent, and he'd had a family friend who was a retired mechanic check it out before writing the check.

The metallic dark green paint job was covered with road dust and bug splatters. Now it was a nasty shade of brown. The last car wash he'd seen was a hundred miles away, and by the look of the vehicles in the parking lot, clean vehicles were not a high priority in this part of the country. He drove his truck from the gas pump to the parking lot in front of the store. None of the men standing outside looked to be con men.

Inside the store, he looked around for his brother.

The cashier, a pretty, black-haired, dark-eyed beauty,

noticed him. "If you are looking for a teenage kid, he's over behind the row of shelves, sitting at a table."

Riley looked to see her glancing at a curved mirror that gave her a distorted but clear view of the restaurant section. "Thanks. Can you tell me if I'm anywhere near Dry Rock?"

"You found it," the girl answered. "Have you been here before? You look familiar."

"It's been a while. I'm looking for my uncle's ranch."

"You two must be Frank's nephews," the girl said.

"Yes," Riley responded. "I'll give my uncle a call."

"You needn't bother," the girl exclaimed. "John Henry will be here within the hour. He works for your uncle, and he'll show you how to get to Frank's place."

"Thanks, but I had better make the call anyway," Riley said, and he bought a phone card to use on the public phone outside since his cell was showing only one bar. Using the public phone, he spoke to his uncle briefly and reentered the store. When the young cashier looked at him questioningly, he shrugged and grinned. "My uncle told me to wait for a man named John Henry."

The girl smiled. "It's a small town, and we all know each other's business."

"Our lunch is ready," Noah said to his brother.

Riley joined Noah at one of the four available booths in the small restaurant part of the store. He looked at his plate and gave a sigh. "Noah..."

"It's not my fault," the teenager protested. "Everything they have here is deep-fried."

"No sandwiches or vegetables at all?" Riley questioned, knowing his younger brother's preference for fried food.

"Everything is deep-fried. Even the bread here is called Fry bread," Noah claimed. "Since when did you become a health nut?"

"I'm not, but I do like a change from fried food once in a

while," Riley said, appraising what looked like a fried wedge of something. It was zucchini, it was good, and he ate the rest of it but pushed the onion rings and fries aside. "We've found Dry Rock, and I've already called. We are supposed to wait for a guy named John Henry to show up."

Noah stared at his plate. "I remember him vaguely. He came around occasionally when I was sent to Uncle Frank's before. He's a cop, sheriff, or something to do with law enforcement. You don't have to be here. You could be rock-climbing or rafting by now."

Riley shook his head slightly. He pushed his lunch around on his plate without much interest. On tour, fast food was sometimes the only food available late at night. He hadn't realized his culinary tastes had changed. They hadn't, not much, he still liked a good burger and slice of pizza, but he'd learned about other cuisines.

"I still think it's cool that you came here with me," Noah said earnestly.

Riley cracked a smile. "Don't sweat it, kid. I need a notebook. Don't wander off."

"Yeah, like I'm going to take off, hiking across the desert or something," Noah cracked.

"Don't," Riley mumbled, already distracted.

Noah watched his older brother walk off, and he pulled Riley's plastic basket of food over in front of him and added more ketchup to the fries. Riley had a *spaced-out* look all his brothers got when they were writing music. Riley was already composing either music or lyrics. All three of his older brothers were weird like that.

It was great having older brothers who were superstars, but it could be a bummer too. He didn't get to spend much time with his older siblings. They had careers and families, and they never seemed to be in one place very long, except Micah. Noah couldn't figure out why Riley had launched a single career using his real name and not his cool nickname of Coyote.

Riley went over to the grocery store side of the business, selected several apples, grabbed a Dr. Pepper from the cooler, and returned to the checkout counter. Looking over his shoulder, he could see Noah finishing both of their meals.

"I'm going outside. When John Henry arrives would you tell him we are here," Riley asked the cashier.

She took his money and looked into the mirror to see Noah still sitting at the table.

"He'll recognize you," she said with a smile. "You're strangers, and we don't get many around here."

Jessica Harper checked the lobby before she stepped from the elevator. She'd worked in the same building for six months. It was the longest time she'd spent in one place for a while. Caution was a way of life now. It was after six, and most of the employees had gone home. The few hours of overtime gave her a little extra money. She waved at the front desk guard and used her employee ID to open the front doors.

Everyone had warned her. Going underground would be the most difficult thing she would ever have to do. For her, it wasn't only difficult. It was dangerous. It had meant complete abandonment of everyone she knew. She'd done it, and seeing her boys happy every day of their young lives was worth it.

She tightened her grip on the Braxton shopping bag she carried. The boys would be thrilled with the Star Wars sheets. The linens had been on clearance because they were from the previous movie released, not the current one. At four-years-old, the twins wouldn't care. She glanced around the parking lot and skipped down the stairs in a good mood.

When she started to cross the parking lot, she stopped as a

Porsche was coming toward her. She recognized it as a Porsche 911 Carrera, a vehicle costing well over a hundred thousand dollars. Her ex-husband's Porsche was metallic red. He wanted people to notice and envy his wealth. This Porsche was dark silver. The car drove past her, screeched to a stop, and reversed. She froze.

The driver leaned over and shoved open the door.

"Get in!"

Run was her first thought. A gun pointed at her made her hesitate.

"Get in!" the order was demanding. The Braxton's bag was snatched from her hands and thrown into the backseat. "Don't make me use this!"

"Did you think I wouldn't find you, *Jessica Harper*?" Gregg Novak mocked as he drove through the city of Irvine, California. "There isn't anywhere you can hide from me! I'm your husband, bitch!"

"No, you're not. I divorced you!"

A vicious backhand snapped her head around and slammed her face against the car window. His hand ripped the wig from her head, and the glasses from her face.

She sat stiffly in her seat, ignoring her bleeding lip and her pounding heart. She clutched her small backpack to her chest and began repeating a silent mantra. "I have to get away! I have to protect my babies! I have to get away! I have to protect my babies!"

"Thanks." Riley took his bag of apples and looked in the mirror at Noah one more time. Three days in the full-time company of his younger brother had proven his father's point. Noah was smart and talented, but his early success as a drummer had gone straight to his ego. His younger brother was arrogant, and he had an attitude of entitlement.

Sometimes the eight-year gap between them was enormous. Riley hadn't recognized those traits before, not living under the same roof or spending a lot of time with his younger brother. Truthfully, he hadn't spent much time with any of the second-set siblings for the last couple of years. He'd either been in college full-time or on tour.

The first-set of brothers hadn't been allowed to become spoiled from their early successes. Daniel and Carole McKenna wouldn't have allowed it. His parents had eased those strict rules for the second-set. Parents of large families tended to get more lenient with their younger children. When Carole had fallen ill, Daniel had refocused his attention entirely on his wife's health.

Riley headed outside, stopping at his truck. He pulled a leather-bound notebook from the door pocket. He looked around for a quiet place to sit, and the most deserted area was over by the corral. He didn't mind desert heat, preferring it to the high humidity of the east coast.

Taking a seat on top of a wooden box, he leaned against the corral fence boards. He opened his lined music paper notebook, propped it on a raised knee, and started scribbling musical notes as fast as he could write them. He was writing with his left hand, balancing his notebook, and eating an apple with his right.

Oblivious to the surroundings, he was lost in his world of music. Riley forgot the apple in his hand as he scribbled notes quickly, organizing the structure as he *heard* the music in his mind. He ignored the hot blasts of air at first. They were coming from behind him, and he moved away from them slightly. Suddenly there was a loud snort accompanied by a blast of hot air. Riley jerked around to discover himself face-to-face with the head of a black horse. The snorts and the gusts of hot air were from the horse breathing on him.

Startled by the massive animal, he almost fell off the box. The horse tried to bite the apple from his hand, and he dropped it. The horse jerked its head back and backed away from the fence.

"Sorry about that, big guy," Riley apologized, appreciating the beauty of the magnificent stallion. He didn't know anything about horses, but he could distinguish male from female. Digging another apple from the bag, he offered it to the horse. The horse eyed the apple but snorted and threw its head upward.

"Okay," Riley said, reasonably. "So you don't know me. That's okay. But, if you want the apple, you have to play nice and come and get it." He placed the apple on the top of the corral post.

He stood perfectly still and watched as the black horse eyed the fruit with interest and eyed him with distrust. He continued to stand motionless. Finally, the horse moved forward cautiously, nuzzled, and bit the apple with one daring chomp of its teeth. What was left of the apple fell on the outside of the corral fence. Riley bent slowly, picked up the remainder of the fruit, wiped the dirt on his jeans, and placed it on the top of the post. The horse backed off, but when Riley didn't move, the horse came forward and ate what remained. He had the horse's attention.

Having already received a sweet treat, the magnificent animal was interested. Riley set another apple on the top of the post, but he didn't back away. He waited patiently with his hand outstretched. The horse nervously moved forward, and when it was close enough to bite the apple, Riley touched it gently on the neck. The horse jerked and moved slightly, but Riley continued to gently stroke his fingers in the coarse mane. He spoke in the same gentle manner he used to console his bass guitarist's baby girl. It worked with the baby, and it was working on the black horse. Riley petted the horse for a while, and the horse was content to let him.

"You have a way with horses," a deep voice stated behind him. The horse's head jerked upward at the sound, backed away from the fence, and raced to the other side of the enclosure.

Riley turned to face a man who matched his deep voice exactly. He was of Native American descent. The man equaled Riley's height but was older, in his late thirties, maybe mid-forties. He had chiseled sharp features, and he looked dangerous. Dark-skinned, with long black hair pulled away from his face, he was wearing a khaki uniform complete with a holstered gun on his hip.

The officer offered his hand, "Chief Deputy, John Henry Walker."

Riley took the firm handshake. "Riley McKenna."

The deputy gave him an assessing look and nodded his head. "I figured you must be one of Frank's nephews." He motioned toward the black stallion prancing around the corral.

"He's a wild one and usually dangerous. I don't think he has let anyone else get close to him. Are you good with horses?"

Riley laughed and shook his head. "I know the front end from the back-end, and I can tell a he from a she. That's about it."

The deputy gave him a long stare, and he grinned. "Those are good things to pay attention to," he said wryly. "Where's the kid who got into trouble?"

Riley lost his smile. "That's my younger brother, Noah. He is usually a good kid. He made the mistake of not bailing when his friends were drinking and driving. Our dad overreacted a bit."

"Maybe," John Henry agreed. "But, I would rather see a parent overreact than not react at all. I see too much apathy in my business. It won't hurt your brother to work for Frank for the summer. Your uncle is a good man. We've been working together for a long time, and I've been worried about him."

The two men started to walk across the dirt parking lot towards the store. "Do you work for my Uncle Frank besides being a deputy?" Riley asked.

"Chief Deputy. I'm in charge of the Fort Yuma Indian Reservation. We are the Quechan People," John Henry explained. "I'm responsible for the law on the reservation. I report to the Tribal Council. I am also the liaison with the Yuma County District Sheriff's office.

"The reservation is mostly peaceful. We get a few fights on Saturday nights, domestic calls. I get a couple of calls a week from the Casino. Usually, a uniform is enough to calm people down. In one way or another, I am related to most of the families on the reservation. I work with Frank several afternoons during the week. He knows my job has to come first."

Riley and John Henry walked around a group of four men standing outside of the store. They were milling around eating hamburgers and drinking coffee or sodas.

"Good afternoon, Rainey," John Henry said to the girl at the cash register.

Riley found Noah at the back of the store playing a video game.

"Noah, we have to go."

The teenager didn't take his eyes away from the video screen. He looked at the score and continued to blast his way through warriors on the video screen. "I'm almost there," he mumbled.

Riley looked at the score and turned to the man who had walked up behind them. "He has almost beat the game. It's one of his favorite things to do."

"Not favorite," Noah exclaimed with a triumphant fist cheer. He typed his initial and last name into the machine's registry, and his name went to the top of the list. "It's fun!"

"Noah, this is…"

"John Henry Walker," the deputy interrupted, offering his hand to the teenager.

Noah grinned and shook it. "Noah McKenna. We met a couple of times when I was nine years old. I heard you work for Uncle Frank too. We're going to have something in common."

"We're going to have a lot in common this summer," John Henry promised. "Blisters, backaches, and sore thumbs, to name a few. Are you ready to go?"

"We were waiting for you to show us the way," Riley answered. "We have visited a few times, but my older brother usually flew us in on a kite, he claims is an airplane. He's a pilot, and he thinks flying is fun."

On the way outside, Noah stopped at the cashier and gave her a twenty-dollar bill, and she gave him a few coins in return. The pretty girl named Rainey smiled at him.

Weaving their way through the men, several of them thanked Noah.

Riley looked over at his brother with a frown.

"What?" Noah demanded. "You said not to give them money. I didn't. I gave them burgers." He motioned over his shoulder at the cashier. "She gave them the coffee for free."

Deputy John Henry slapped Noah on the back, maybe a little harder than the boy would have liked.

"It's okay, kid," John Henry chuckled. "I buy cigarettes, and I don't smoke." He called out the name, "Charlie Bitter-root," and tossed the man a cigarette pack. The down on his luck man could be seen passing them around to his friends.

Riley followed John Henry from the small settlement of Dry Rock. He turned from a paved road onto a rutted dirt road, bouncing them around even though they were strapped in with seat belts. After a long, slow, and very dusty drive of fifty minutes, they followed the Yuma Reservation Chief Deputy into a group of farm buildings. There was a gray, wind-beaten ranch-style house with a large addition under construction. There were two barns and many outbuildings, feed elevators, and windmills.

Frank McKenna was six years older than their father. He was a hard-looking man, his face wrinkled and leathered from living and working in the desert. Daniel claimed his brother had returned from a stint in the army and war, a changed man. He had initially lived in a small town on the outskirts of Austin.

Twenty years earlier, he, and his wife had sold their hardware store and moved to Dry Rock. Frank and Aunt Katherine had opened their home to children in the foster care system. Aunt Katherine had died of a heart attack five years earlier, but Frank had continued their work.

John Henry pulled his vehicle to a stop in front of a porch, and Riley parked beside him.

Frank McKenna was hammering boards on the new structure, a large extension with many rooms. He laid his hammer aside and came to meet his nephews. He was moving slowly. His shirt was unbuttoned, and they could see his ribs were wrapped in bandages.

Despite his broken ribs, Riley and Noah were caught in bear hugs, and they were surprised. The hugs did cause their uncle discomfort because of his shoulder and rib injuries.

"Look at you two," Frank exclaimed, trying to catch his breath. "You have both grown. Riley, you've filled out with muscle, and Noah, look at you! You were this high the last time I saw you!"

Noah grinned and moved his uncle's hand upward. "More like that. How have you been, Uncle Frank?"

"I'm not at my best, but I'll heal. I'm sure going to appreciate the help," Frank exclaimed. "I wish the rest of the family could have come. I have missed all of you."

Riley and Noah exchanged glances. This Uncle Frank was friendlier than they remembered. Maybe the next several months weren't going to so bad after all.

Chapter 3

Tossing a pitchfork full of horse manure, Riley grabbed the handles of the wheelbarrow and lifted. Stall cleaning was one of the nasty jobs attached to keeping horses. He wasn't used to the smell, and sometimes he still gagged. He did like the smell of the fresh straw he laid in the stalls each morning.

Riley rolled the wheelbarrow towards the dumpsite, but he stopped and climbed to the fence's top rail. The sun was about to break over the horizon. Sunrises and sunsets in the Arizona desert were glorious to watch.

Frank McKenna joined his nephew and handed him a cup of coffee. Riley took it, but he didn't take his eyes from the horizon. They watched the gentle rays lighten the distant mountains and the sky change from pitch black to an incredible show of colors. The transformation took six or seven minutes, and every color of the rainbow spectrum was present. When the sun had established its dominance, the sky settled into a cloudless blue.

"I never get enough of that glory, every morning and

evening. I thought this was Noah's job today," Frank said, nodding his head at the wheelbarrow.

"It is, but I thought I would let him sleep," Riley said. "He's worked hard these past couple of days. He's not used to it."

"Neither are you," Frank said. "And, you sit on the porch half the night, writing in your book. Sleeplessness is a sign of PTSD. Are you still seeing a therapist?"

Riley hesitated before he answered. This was private— something he rarely discussed outside of his immediate family and occasionally with a therapist.

"Dad's got a big mouth."

"Don't be pissed at your dad. He needed someone to talk to, someone who would understand," Frank said. "How you guys kept it out of the news was amazing."

"That was with the cooperation of the FBI, and the streaming service. A small town convenience store robbery and hostage situation didn't draw a lot of attention. I've become friends with the FBI agent, Shawn Williams who was the computer guy who saved my life.

If losing a little sleep is the worst of it, I'm okay. After..." he stumbled and continued, "How do you get over someone holding a loaded gun to your head for the better part of six hours? I was in the wrong place at the wrong time, and the bastard was determined to kill. He was whacked out, but he was filming it on his phone for social media! Luck was on my side. One of the platform filters caught it, and the FBI was called. He kept saying it was his day to kill someone, and he was going to be famous."

"You survived," Frank said.

"Only because he flipped his nut and turned the gun on himself."

Frank gripped Riley's shoulder with his good arm. "PTSD is a bitch!"

"All three of you first-set kids have had to deal with wackos. Sully was kidnapped, Micah and Tess were attacked by his crazy ex-girlfriend, and you were in the wrong place at the wrong time. You were dealing with a deranged man. If it hadn't been you, it would have been the next man who walked in. You were a random victim in a scenario where he was the only one in control because he held the weapon. The most important thing was you survived."

"Do you know what's weird?" Riley said. "It was six hours, but it has affected me every day since."

"It might for a long time," Frank warned. "I spent two tours in Iraq, over thirty years ago. It affects me to this day."

Riley didn't want to accept that piece of insight. "I want to get over it!"

"You won't, but you will learn how to live with it," Frank said. "I learned to bury it. Your Aunt Katherine understood. Now my grief is about losing her. If you ever find the right woman, and you know she's the one, grab on and don't let go. It's the making of a man. Your mom and dad have always been a great support system."

"Dad was busy dealing with Mom's cancer, so I didn't feel I could tap into that," Riley said. "I didn't even tell them for a long time. Micah and his wife Tess were a lot of help, and so was Sully," Riley said, and he decided to change the subject.

"So why are you building a big-ass extension on the house?" Riley asked, changing the subject. "I overheard you and John Henry talking about it. He called it a dormitory."

"Jason Gobel," Frank said grimly, and his nephew frowned in surprise. "He was fourteen years old. The kid walked into his middle school, shot seven kids, and turned the gun on himself. He had parents, but they were so involved with their problems, they couldn't see they were losing their kid. Too many kids are falling through the cracks. Your Aunt Katherine and I couldn't have kids of our own, but we wanted to help kids, and we did. With the addition, I'll be able to take in more kids who are tittering on the cusp of doing right or wrong. To do that, I needed more space for them."

"Apathy," Riley mused. "That's what John Henry said the other day when we were talking about Noah."

"John Henry is a big part of this," Frank explained. "We were certified to take five kids at a time. We ripped off the back bedrooms to the house, and when we are finished rebuilding, I'll be able to house ten to twelve kids. I've already hired a qualified assistant who will live here. With John Henry's background in law enforcement, me, and the new assistant, well, we hope to make a bigger difference. Taking a nosedive from a twelve-foot ladder wasn't in my plans. It has delayed the building progress."

"You should be proud of what you've accomplished here," Riley said.

"I am when we can turn a kid around and steer them in a different direction."

"Is Noah your *guinea pig* for this new project?"

Frank laughed. "No. Daniel sounded like he was exasperated, and he's had a lot on his plate for the last couple of years. I know your parents have done a fine job raising their kids. By the way, how are the girls?"

"Macy is living in London again, and she's moved into the First Position, ballerina position. She's worked hard for it, and she's happily married to a great guy. I don't think we'll ever get her or her husband in the states permanently. Lily is spending this summer with her and training. She's determined to be like her big sister, only the folks aren't ready to let her flap her wings too far away yet."

"What about Allison?" Frank asked.

"We're still trying," Riley said sadly. "But how many times do you keep repeating the same help only to have it thrown back in your face as interference? She's been in rehab for most of the last three years. We think she's clean, the doctors agree, but as soon as she leaves, she's hunting for a dealer. She was released in January was home for two weeks, and poof, she was gone again. She's been AWOL since."

"I guess you keep trying until it takes," Frank said. "Drugs are everywhere, even here. I've had kids who think using drugs is normal because that's what they've seen all their lives. I wouldn't wish it on any child. Well, come on, boy. We're wasting daylight."

"You know, if you set up this Boy's Ranch as a foundation, I could help more," Riley offered. "My business manager is always looking for tax shelters."

"Is that one of the problems of being rich and famous?"

Riley looked to his Uncle, trying to decide if he was kidding or not. He decided Frank was trying to be funny.

"Well, when you get in my tax bracket, you have to do whatever it takes to keep part of what you earn. Otherwise, you become a highly paid government worker. I'd much rather give to good causes than letting the government spend my money. The interests of politicians and my interests never seem to jive."

"That's one way to look at it," Frank commented. "However, it's not a problem I have ever had to deal with, personally."

Riley laughed. "We were so young when we started; it never occurred to us either. Dad took care of the finances when we were young. It was a big responsibility. Even this last venture of mine, going solo, surprised me. My accountants keep track of everything."

"Isn't that your responsibility too?" Frank asked.

"Yes, sir, and I pay very close attention. Finances may not be my favorite thing to deal with, but Dad didn't raise us to be idiots. I've seen too many artists cheated by managers and so-called advisors. I'm far more interested in the creative side of things, but I'm not a fool," Riley griped good-naturally."

"Well, how about using your creative side to cook breakfast," Frank suggested. "If you haven't noticed, cooking is not my specialty."

"I noticed," Riley, grumbled. "Let me finish this job. My cooking skills extend to using a microwave, and I have noticed you don't have one. Other than that, I can make toast, and you do have a toaster. Noah, on the other hand, makes an excellent scrambled egg fry.

Frank grunted and looked thoughtful. "I think I'll go put your brother to work cooking breakfast."

Another day went by quickly, as they did when you were kept busy. In the middle of the night, there was the sound of a thump. Then a mumbled curse, followed... "Ouch!"

Noah rolled over and peered into the darkness of the room.

"Bro?" Noah whispered. "Are you okay?"

"No," Riley groaned. "I smacked into the wall. I'm not used to sleeping in a bed made for munchkins."

Noah smirked. "I wouldn't know since I'm still a foot shorter than you!"

Riley's only response was to grumble as he rolled over, causing the bedsprings to squeak. "I think Uncle Frank must have bought these beds from a World War II surplus auction."

"Riley?"

"Yeah?"

Noah faced his brother, although he couldn't see him. "It's not as bad here as I thought it would be. When Dad said he was sending me here, I was really ticked off. When I was sent here before, I was only nine. It was okay because Aunt Katherine was here. Uncle Frank is not as bad as I thought he would be."

"Yeah," Riley agreed. "He's more easy-going than he used to be. Maybe having all those kids around has mellowed him."

"Riley?"

"Noah," Riley whispered in an exasperated tone. "You are screwing my chances of grabbing a couple of hours of shuteye."

"Sorry," Noah mumbled.

"Okay," Riley mumbled.

"Riley?"

"Humm..."

"Thanks for coming with me," Noah said, and he rolled over to face the wall. He thought his brother had fallen asleep, but he felt a jolt as Riley booted him in the ass with his foot.

"You're welcome, now, shut-up!" Riley ordered gruffly.

John Henry parked Frank's ranch truck beside the barn. Frank had an old truck and a decrepit truck, and both were used for ranch work. Only his better truck was legal to drive on public roads. John Henry left the ranch truck wearily, as did Riley. Both of them had worked a long day of replacing fence posts. They were tired, sweat-drenched, and filthy.

John Henry got into his Deputy truck and gave a slight wave as he drove off.

Riley climbed the four steps of the porch wearily and sat on the edge of porch flooring. He looked at his younger brother, who was sitting on the swing with a glass of iced tea in his hand, looking cool and clean.

"Noah, do you notice something wrong with this picture?" Riley asked. His younger brother gave him a cheeky grin and handed over the glass of tea. Riley drained it in one long drink.

"You're getting a great tan," Noah remarked tongue-in-cheek.

Riley looked at his arms, and he would have agreed, except all he could see was the dusty red grime clinging to his skin. "You get in trouble, and I'm being worked to death!"

"I'm still a kid," Noah said, grinning. "I can only work so many hours a day and I've got blisters." He held the palms of both of his hands in the air as proof.

Riley gave his brother a dirty look. It should have terrified him, but as usual, it had no effect at all. "I'm hitting the shower."

He reappeared a half-hour later, clean and feeling only slightly revived. He wasn't used to manual labor either, but at least he'd had the common sense to wear leather gloves. Frank and Noah were sitting at the kitchen table, ready to eat dinner. As soon as Riley joined them, Frank bowed his head, voiced a quick thanks, and began to pass around the simple fare.

Frank's cooking skills consisted of steak and beans, hot dogs and beans, bologna, spam... always something resembling meat with beans. If a bean had a name and came in a can, it was in the food pantry.

It was also served hot, and all Riley longed for was something cool. He'd never been a salad eater, but he was beginning to dream about them. Emptying another full glass of iced tea, he picked at his meal. It was too hot to eat, and he was too tired to try.

"Not hungry?" Frank asked.

"It's too hot," Riley said simply.

"You'll have help tomorrow," Frank said. "John Henry is going to bring a couple of guys with him, who need the work."

Riley nodded his head. "I think I'm going for a swim."

"Me too," Noah agreed.

Frank set his fork on his plate. "You know, a swim sounds good to me too. Why don't we go for a swim now and eat later?" Three heads nodded in a joint decision, and their chairs scraped back in unison. Frank and Riley headed inside to change into shorts. Noah headed for the door pulling his shirt over his head as he went.

There was a reservoir tank behind the barns. It was sixteen feet wide and eight feet deep with a solid steel cap over the top to prevent evaporation, and it was equipped with a filtering system. It made a perfect swimming pool. The top was on a hydraulic lift, and with a flip of a switch, the cap lifted. Once the cap was raised and locked into position, there was enough light in the tank so they could swim comfortably.

When Noah walked through the barn, he didn't pay much attention to the smells that had made him gag a few days earlier.

Frank and Riley changed into shorts and were about to open the backdoor when Noah burst inside, gasping for breath, his eyes wide with fright.

"There's a dead body by the tank!" Noah croaked.

Frank and Riley ran. Noah, already out of breath, tried to keep up, and he was only a few feet behind. Frank came to a stop at the reservoir tank, looking around, but he didn't see anything. Noah pointed to the wooden box, sheltering the electric pump. Frank and Riley saw the body.

Riley knelt and turned the body slightly. It was a woman. She was small and dressed in blood-splattered pants and a blouse torn to shreds. Her head was covered with a tee shirt. It was stiff from blood seeping through the fabric. The sleeve of her blouse was caked with dried blood from a long cut. He could see a long thin gash running from her shoulder to elbow. He pressed his finger against her throat, got a pulse, and watched closely to see her chest rise slightly.

"She's still alive," Riley stated bluntly. "She's breathing. Frank, bring your truck over here."

Frank turned to his younger nephew. "Noah, run to the

house and call Doctor Andrews. His number is written on the wall by the phone. Tell him to get over here fast."

Noah turned to run but stopped. "What's the address?"

"Tell him to come to the McKenna ranch. He'll know," Frank yelled.

Frank followed the boy, moving a little slower to get his truck.

Riley left the woman for a moment, removing a tin cup hanging on a hook and filling it with water from a spigot. He returned, lifted her head gently, and dribbled the water into her mouth. She swallowed. The tee shirt over her face had holes ripped open for her eyes, but she didn't open them.

Frank parked the truck and got out, ready to help.

"I'm not sure about moving her," Riley said. "They say never move an injured person, but she's been moving, or she wouldn't have made it here. I don't see any signs of broken bones."

"She either walked or crawled here," Frank said. "She's been assaulted and exposed to the sun for a couple of days by the looks of her."

"Drop the tailgate," Riley said decisively. "You can't lift her with your bad shoulder and ribs. I'll lift her into the bed and hold her, and you can drive us over to the house."

Riley lifted her carefully, and she moaned. He hated to hurt her, but it couldn't be helped. He laid her into the bed of the truck and jumped to sit beside her so she wouldn't roll out. Frank slid behind the wheel, driving slowly to the house, parked, and ran ahead, opening doors as Riley carried her into the house.

"Take her into my room," Frank said. "Noah, when did the doctor say he would be here?"

"He's on his way, but he said his ETA was at least an hour," Noah reported.

Riley stood by the bed, appraising the woman. "Uncle

Frank, have you had any medical training?"

"Only the first aid classes we are required to take to become a foster parent," Frank admitted.

"Okay, I took a medic course a couple of years ago, and I have paramedic accreditation. You two go wait for the doctor, and I'll try to help the best I can. Noah, get the first-aid kit from my truck."

Frank hesitated, and he motioned for Noah to leave the room. The boy returned with a large first-aid kit and passed it to his brother. Obviously, Riley intended to undress the woman to assess her wounds and treat her before Dr. Andrews arrived.

"Shouldn't you wait for the doctor?" Frank asked.

Riley was pulling on rubber gloves. "Sometimes, a minute can make the difference between life and death. If she's been shot or stabbed, we might have to get help flown in here before the doctor can arrive. I'm going to need clean towels, washcloths, and a basin."

Frank nodded and followed directions while Riley addressed what he deemed necessary. The woman winced and moaned as Riley disinfected cuts and scratches while waiting for the doctor to arrive. Frank was sure some of the cuts would need stitches. When he left the room for another clean pan of water, he saw Noah sitting in the hallway.

"Why did Riley take an EMT course?" Frank asked.

"He was the first person at a car accident scene, and it really bothered him that he didn't know what to do. He said he didn't ever want to be in a position where people could die because he was an idiot. He took a paramedic course, and he passed the tests."

Frank made several trips in and out of the bedroom. Each time he came out, he looked shaken. Noah had moved into the kitchen. He kept watching and waiting for the trail of dust announcing the doctor's arrival.

Chapter 4

R iley stayed in the bedroom, watching over the woman. When Dr. Andrews arrived, he was directed straight into the bedroom. Frank and Noah waited what seemed like a very long time for both the doctor and Riley to come out.

"Frank, do you know this woman? I've never seen her before," Dr. Andrews asked.

"No, we found her by the water tank," Frank said.

"Well, she didn't get here by herself, and if she was dumped, this is a matter for the police," the doctor said.

"No," Riley countered. "She regained consciousness for a few seconds, and she very clearly said, '*No police.*' Then she fainted again."

"Which probably means the police should be involved," Doctor Andrews argued.

"If you call the state police, they will post her description. Maybe she has reasons she doesn't want to be found," Riley argued. "What if the person who hurt her isn't satisfied and wants another go at her. By calling the police, we might be putting her in more danger."

"We don't know what happened to her," Dr. Andrews said.

"Exactly my point," Riley said. "Don't report it, and we'll talk to John Henry in the morning. I've worked with a friend of mine, a minister, who helps women get away from abusive situations. We have a law enforcement officer coming here every day."

Both Riley and the doctor looked to Frank to make the decision.

"Technically, this land is leased to John Henry, and we are on the reservation. That makes it Tribal Police business, under his jurisdiction," Frank said. "John Henry has a lot of contacts with the state police. He should be able to nose around for a reported missing person. You said she is not in any immediate danger. It will take a couple of days for her to recover enough to talk to us. She doesn't represent a danger to us."

"It will take weeks for her to fully recover," Doctor Andrews countered. "Thank God, she had enough sense to cover herself, or she would have been burnt to a crisp. She should be awake tomorrow or the next day. I want her brought to my clinic as soon as possible for X-rays. I don't think anything is broken, but I want to make sure. Facial fractures are hard to diagnose."

"I will bring her in as soon as she is able," Frank promised. "Keep quiet until she can tell us what is going on."

"Frank, I know you," Dr. Andrews warned. "Do not make this woman another one of your rescues."

"Anyone I have ever helped needed it," Frank objected. "I'm taking my lead from Riley. He's the one who has been in there with her and talked with her. I'm willing to give her the benefit of the doubt."

"Sometimes, all a person needs is a little help to change a bad situation," Riley said. "We don't want to add to her distress."

"All right," Dr. Andrews agreed, reluctantly. "She wasn't

shot, so I'm not required by law to report this incident. I'll keep quiet, provided John Henry has full knowledge of her being here. If I'm out this way, I'll stop in. Be careful. Just because she's a woman does not mean she can't be dangerous."

As nightfall came, Riley said he was going to watch over the woman. They carried a comfortable, overstuffed chair from the living room and set it beside the bed. Riley settled in for a long night. He spent hour after hour watching the woman and wondering what had happened to her. He'd had to soak the bloodied tee shirt to loosen it from her face. Blood had dried, and the fabric was stuck to her skin. He suspected she was a pretty woman. Now her face was swollen, cut, and bruised but not severely sunburned.

When Dr. Anderson had arrived, he'd taken over the job, and Riley had assisted. The worst had been the nine-inch cut on her arm. It was deep, but it didn't look infected.

The doctor had stitched a few of the cuts on her face, neck, arms, and hands. Her legs were spared the damage because of the jeans she had been wearing. Her feet, only covered in thin-strapped sandals, were cut and blistered. Riley changed the bandages on a few still seeping cuts.

Riley understood being a victim. People became victims for many reasons, most of them not voluntarily. He didn't understand why or how someone could mistreat another human being so badly. Dr. Anderson said the cuts on her neck were likely done by a knife. It was a miracle the carotid artery hadn't been sliced.

This kind of abuse was beyond his understanding. He believed in a man being the head of his home and family. He'd been raised believing in domestic discipline. His belief in D/D relationships was as anchored as his belief in God. Giving a woman a well-deserved spanking was not the same as deliberate abuse and cruelty.

Riley was awakened by his uncle, but he sent him back to bed when he wanted to trade places. Frank was recuperating from an injury himself. Riley continued to watch over the woman and gradually drifted into sleep himself.

He must have fallen asleep because when he jerked awake, the bed was empty. Jumping to his feet, he only had to go as far as the kitchen. The woman was leaning against the refrigerator. She looked like she was going to collapse at any second.

"You won't get very far," Riley warned gently. "Even if you manage to get outside, you will probably faint or collapse."

Startled by his voice, she lost her balance, stumbled, and sank to the linoleum floor.

Riley went to her and slowly offered his hand to help her up. She looked at him, studied him for a long moment, and finally nodded. She was visibly shaking, but she allowed him to help her to a chair.

"We won't hurt you," Riley said gently.

"We?" the woman whispered.

"My uncle, my younger brother, and myself. My brother found you," Riley answered. "We won't hurt you. I promise."

Supporting most of her weight, he helped the woman walk the hallway. When they reached the open bathroom door across the hall, she indicated other needs. He waited patiently, and when she opened the door, he assisted her back into bed. When the woman was settled, Riley left the room and returned a minute later with a warm cloth, a glass of cold water, and several pills.

"The doctor said you could take these."

"Doctor?" the woman questioned in a croaking voice. She looked terrified.

"It's okay. Dr. Andrews won't tell anyone you are here," Riley reassured her. He handed her the pills and waited until she had taken a drink of water. He rolled the warm wet towel and placed it on her forehead. "If you want a cold compress, I'll get it, but when my mom was sick, she said warm compresses made her feel better and relaxed her."

"It feels good," the woman said softly.

"If you think you can keep it down, I'll get you a piece of toast and a cup of tea. The doctor mentioned that you are dangerously underweight."

"Why?" the woman whispered, and tears began to flow onto her cheeks. Her eyes were glassy with shock.

Riley took the woman's hand and gave it a gentle squeeze. "Why what?"

"Why are you helping me?"

"Because you need it."

The woman tightened her grip on his hand. "Who are you?"

"Riley."

"Thank you," the woman whispered. "I'm Marissa."

He barely caught the name before she closed her eyes to pain and exhaustion.

Riley checked her pulse and took his vigil seriously. He continued to apply warm compresses to the woman's forehead and cooler ones to her swollen face and neck. Sometimes she would stir slightly, and he talked to her gently. He hated to see anyone hurt or sick.

Sometime in the early morning, the woman started thrashing around. She was obviously reliving her nightmare experience. Riley remembered his nightmares, and he didn't want her to hurt herself further. He slid into the bed and curled his arms around her, being very careful to keep the blanket's fabric between his gentle touch and her skin. He held her, rocked her, and crooned to her calmly.

"You're all right. No one is going to hurt you. I'm not going to let anyone hurt you, again," Riley whispered. He continued to reassure through fits and spurts of awareness. He tightened the blanket around her, having read of the calming effects of heavy blanketing on hysteria in one of his sister-in-law's medical magazines.

He crooned to Marissa using what he considered his *'baby'* calming voice, and it was working. She stopped fighting and fell into an uneasy sleep. He had to repeat his actions several times, and after she calmed, he returned to his chair.

Noah finished the early morning chores and returned to the house to meet his uncle coming out to do the same.

"You should have woken me," Frank exclaimed.

"Riley says you're doing too much now. Is she awake?" Noah responded.

"I don't know. Your brother is still with her," Frank said, turning to the task of cooking breakfast.

"I'm here," Riley said, coming into the kitchen. "I want scrambled."

"Is she awake?" Frank asked.

"Not now, but she was earlier. Her name is Marissa, and I think she was going to try to run away. I think I convinced her she wasn't going to make it very far. She's asleep again."

"Did she say anything?" Noah asked.

"Only her name," Riley reported.

"Someone is going to have to stay with her today," Riley said, looking over at his uncle as the obvious choice. Frank was temporarily disabled himself.

"I think she might sleep a good portion of the day, and we can take turns," Frank said. "I need to talk to her as soon as she is able. You two need to understand there is as much a chance of her being a criminal as being a victim."

"I'm not a criminal." A soft-spoken but firm voice made all three of the McKennas turn and face the woman. She was leaning heavily against the doorframe. She was wearing one of Riley's tee shirts and a pair of boxers of Noah's. Both were too large, hanging loosely from her too-thin frame.

Frank slid the frying pan off the burner and turned to assist the frail woman, but Riley got to her first.

"You shouldn't be on your feet," Riley scolded. "You should be resting!"

"I need to leave. I don't want to bring trouble on you," the woman exclaimed nervously, slurring her words around swollen lips as Riley helped her to a chair at the kitchen table.

"Why don't you tell us what kind of trouble you are in, and we will decide if we want to be involved or not," Frank suggested.

The woman shook her head vehemently. "No, I have to leave as soon as possible. If he finds me here, he will assume the worst. At this point, I don't know what he's capable of doing."

"He, being your husband or boyfriend," Riley guessed.

The woman shook her head and clamped her swollen lips shut, although it looked like it hurt her to do so.

"Marissa, you can trust us," Riley coaxed gently. "This is my Uncle Frank and my brother Noah. We only want to help."

"You can't help. I need to leave so you won't be involved or in danger!"

"In danger from what?" Frank demanded. "You might as well tell us. I'm not going to allow you to leave in your current condition unless it's to take you to the clinic to see the doctor. I'm also not going to allow you to endanger my family."

"I don't want to put you in that position either," Marissa exclaimed tearfully. "If you could take me to the bus station, I'll disappear."

"You won't be able to disappear so easily," Riley said. "I'm not trying to be rude or mean, but you look like a woman who has been assaulted. Someone will take notice, and they'll call the police."

"Besides, leaving Dry Rock isn't easy," Frank remarked.

"No, kidding!" Noah agreed sarcastically.

Frank looked over at his nephew with a reproving look, and Noah grinned. He opened the refrigerator freezer to remove a frozen can of orange juice.

"My nephew is a smart-aleck, but he's right. The bus only runs once a week, on Tuesdays. This is Wednesday, so that's six days from now. Besides, if you wanted to take the bus, we would have to call ahead to Wolf Springs bus station to tell them to send it here. Dry Rock isn't a normal stop or a town. We are strictly a rural route. The reservation is recognized, and it's our postal drop. In a place the size of Dry Rock, or Wolf Springs, a stranger would be noticed."

Riley joined his brother in finishing the breakfast preparation.

Frank talked gently to the woman while Noah and Riley finished cooking breakfast. Noah scrambled the eggs while Riley stirred the frozen orange juice and loaded bread in the toaster. They set their plates on the table, and Riley slid a plate of food in front of Marissa.

The McKenna's ducked their heads quickly in thanks and began to eat. Riley motioned for her to eat. The woman looked around the table. In his mid-to-late sixties, the older man was fierce-looking with his thin, drawn face and thinning gray hair, but he had a gentle voice and an equally gentle manner. He had brown eyes and was non-threatening.

The man named Riley was in his early to mid-twenties, very tall, good-looking, with the same brown eyes and brown hair. He looked familiar, but she couldn't place him.

The teenager was shorter, with a lanky build. His eyes were blue, and his hair was buzzed short. He was still somewhat baby-faced and had the eagerness, dimples, and the quick smile of a youngster.

"So, are you going to tell us what happened?" Noah blurted out.

"Noah," Frank said in a warning voice while Riley stomped on the toe of his younger brother, causing him to yelp. Noah threw a piece of toast at his brother's head.

"Noah," Frank repeated sternly.

"What?" the teenager demanded. "We all want to know!"

"I can kick the brat out of the room," Riley offered to the woman with a glare at his brother.

The woman watched the effortless interplay between the boy and the two men, and she shook her head slightly. She tried to smile, but it hurt her swollen lips. She laid her fork aside, although she had eaten very little. "You have a right to know, but I can't tell you."

Getting dressed for church in a small western town was simple. As tradition decreed, fancy clothing was not required. A clean shirt, polished boots and combed hair were church attire. Church services were also a long affair, starting with an early morning Sunday service segueing into an eleven o'clock service lasting until one or two o'clock in the afternoon. Pre-warned, Riley had decided to drive his truck and leave between the two services.

He hadn't felt comfortable leaving Marissa by herself, but Frank had insisted. She hadn't left the bedroom very often for the last couple of days, only when it was necessary.

Frank had taken her to Dr. Andrews' clinic for the X-rays the physician had demanded. The film had shown no broken bones. The doctor had prescribed tablets for pain and a light sedative, allowing her to rest better at night. Riley was still sleeping in the chair beside her bed. She had to be rescued from nightmares several times a night.

The McKennas found a pew, joined in on hymn singing, and settled in to listen to the sermon. The minister had begun a loud fire and brimstone sermon when Riley excused himself and left the church. After a few minutes, Frank McKenna leaned over and whispered into Noah's ear. "Where did your brother go?"

Whispering back, Noah tried to explain. "Riley doesn't think expounding on the negative things going on in the world is the way to spread the word when the good things people do are ignored."

Frank nodded, but he sat back to listen to the preacher who had founded the small church thirty years earlier.

Riley went outside and sat on a bench. He found the quiet outside the building more spiritual and peaceful than what was going on inside.

The grocery store/gas station was open. Frank had told them the preacher hadn't approved, but many locals came long distances to attend church. They could fill their gas tanks and complete a few errands between services. The only activity going on outside the church was across the parking lot at the corral. Several men were milling around the corral.

He waited impatiently for the first services to end. He wanted to tell his uncle he was going back to the ranch. He stood over by a fence, alternately watching for his relatives and watching the men in the corral. Whatever the men were doing, the horse was not happy about it. It was kicking, snorting, and making a screaming noise. Riley hadn't known horses could scream. The fence slats blocked most of his view, so he couldn't see what was going on.

Finally, Uncle Frank and Noah appeared at the doorway and looked around to find him. Frank made no mention of his leaving the services. The hour or so between church services was a social gathering. Long-distance neighbors talked to one another while the children ran around, played, and ate ice-cream cones from the store. The children only got to see their school friends once a week during the summer months.

"Hey, bro, let's go get a soda," Noah suggested. "You're buying."

"Why? Don't you get an allowance?" Riley asked, following his brother.

"My allowance disappeared when Dad sprung me from the police, and I got a whopping fine to pay," Noah grumbled. "Dad paid the fine, but I have to pay him back. At $50.00 bucks a week at Uncle Frank's place, it's going to take all summer to pay half of it. I have the money in a bank account, but he wouldn't let me use it to pay the fine. What's the good of having money in the bank and not being allowed to use it when you get in trouble?"

"You would have to talk with Dad about that, and I dare you. Paying Dad back isn't about the money. It's about taking responsibility," Riley said. He didn't envy his younger brother. Daniel McKenna had been their biggest fan and indulgent with his help to launch I-35. Nevertheless, during their teenage years, he had cracked down on his boys. He'd heard the statement *'I'm not raising a spoiled brat!'* more times than he could recall.

Riley dug into his pocket and removed a couple of bills. "Get me a Dr. Pepper or a Coke and something for Uncle Frank. It looks like he is heading over there to see what is going on."

"Okay," Noah agreed, and he hurried inside. He was only inside a couple of minutes, and then he jogged to catch his brother, who was following their uncle.

Suddenly there were loud terrified screams from the horse and shouts from the men inside the corral. There was a crashing sound of wood splintering. Noah choked on his upturned soda as he saw the black horse racing towards them. Riley heard a woman scream, and in the fraction of a second it took to shift his eyes, he saw two children directly in the horse's path. Without thinking, he jumped between the horse and the children.

Riley heard Noah yell at him, but he was too preoccupied to hear. He stood still in both panic and disbelief at his stupid reaction. The horse was running straight at him, and he raised his arms because he thought the horse might change directions and go around him. Instead, it stopped directly in front of him, reared on its hind legs, pawing at the air like a scene from an old western movie. It screamed threateningly.

Again, not thinking but reacting, Riley grabbed the tie ropes and jumped back. Surprisingly, the horse's front legs came down, the hooves barely missing him. The stallion stood snorting, pawing, and looking at Riley with wild eyes. The muscles in the horse's body were trembling with fright and anger. A saddle was leaning precariously sideways, which seemed to be the cause of the animal's distress.

"Whoa, fellow, remember me," Riley crooned softly.

The sound of his voice seemed to settle the horse, so Riley kept talking. He slowly worked his way closer to the horse by pulling the rope through his hands. He kept talking, and finally, he was standing within inches of the horse blocking its view. Holding one hand firmly gripped on the rope, Riley used his other hand to stroke the horse's forehead, all the time crooning to him.

The men from the corral had come running. They were now circling the horse and Riley. John Henry was among the men.

"Riley, uncinch the saddle," John Henry advised quietly. "Move very slowly, and keep talking to him."

Riley moved his free hand slowly. As soon as he touched the saddle, the horse shifted away from him. Riley continued to croon softly, moving slowly to try again. This time he got a grip on the girth strap and pulled it up and over the pin. As soon as the saddle started to slide, the horse jerked, reared, and dragged Riley. He didn't lose his footing, but he skidded twenty feet before he could firmly replant his feet. He started crooning again to calm the animal. Riley looked over his shoulder and discovered John Henry, his uncle, and other men watched. The saddle and blanket were lying in a heap in the dirt.

John Henry motioned for the men to back off. Frank was saying something to the deputy.

"See if you can lead him to the corral," John Henry advised. "Keep a firm grip on the lead rope."

Riley followed John Henry's instructions, and he began to lead the horse towards the corral. He saw the deputy bend, and retrieve the saddle and say something to someone behind him. A man stepped forward and took it.

He kept walking backward, talking, and pulling the horse towards him gently. John Henry and the other men were following them but not close. They were also making sure the other people were keeping a safe distance. Riley walked backward to the corral gate, and the horse balked.

Someone ran to John Henry and handed him several apples. John Henry motioned for Riley to stop.

"Turn the stallion to my right, and I'll place these apples where you can reach them," John Henry offered.

The deputy deposited several apples on the top of the tack box, and he backed away. Riley led the horse over to them and, raising one of the apples, offered it as an enticement to get the horse to follow him.

"Keep the apple slightly out of his reach," Frank warned behind John Henry.

Riley did as he was told until he was inside the corral. Several men moved quickly and closed the broken gate. Now he was inside the corral with the horse, and he could see the faces of several men watching through the open slats. He continued to pet and talk to the horse.

"Okay, John Henry, how do I get out of here?" Riley asked in a slightly louder voice.

"Push him around to face the stable. Set the apples on the ground, and move away from him. Stay out of the range of his hooves."

Riley followed the instructions. As soon as he climbed over the fence, John Henry was slapping him on the back."

"Damn, good job!"

His words seemed to be the consensus of most of the men who were standing around. They were nodding their heads in agreement, and some were already hammering on the broken gate to fix it.

"Wow, Ry," Noah exclaimed. "When did you learn how to handle a horse?"

"I haven't," Riley snapped.

"Considering no one else has been able to get near him, I think some would disagree," Frank concluded. "Good job."

"The stallion has chosen you."

Riley turned around to see John Henry standing beside a short, older man who could have been eighty or a hundred. He had spoken, and he was obviously of the Quechan (Yuma) Tribe. Riley knew as he had done his research on the internet before leaving San Antonio. The older man had dark wrinkled skin and a broad nose. His hair was pure white, in two long braids trailing over his shoulders and chest.

"Chosen me for what?"

"To be his spiritual guide into man's world," the older man said. He turned and walked off.

"What the heck does that mean?" Riley asked of John Henry.

"I think he means the stallion has chosen you to be his trainer," John Henry said.

"Is he nuts?" Riley demanded.

John Henry stiffened, and suddenly he looked dangerous.

"Jefferson Ironheart is not crazy. He is our tribal leader and Chief of the Tribal Council. When he speaks, we listen. We may not understand at first, but his wisdom will be known and respected. He is also my great-uncle."

"I'm sorry," Riley apologized. "I didn't know."

"Accepted," John Henry, said bluntly and he walked away following the footsteps of the older man.

"I didn't mean to insult him," Riley said to his uncle.

"Which one?" Frank asked.

"Neither of them."

"They're fine. If they weren't, you would be flat on your butt and nursing a sore jaw," Frank warned.

"Ry, I think it was cool, the way you handled the horse," Noah exclaimed.

"It was sheer stupidity on my part," Riley said. The church bell rang, and most of the people milling around started walking toward the church. Frank said something to Noah, and they joined the exodus.

Chapter 5

R iley hadn't planned to stick around for the second church service. The first ten minutes of the sermon made him wish he hadn't come. He had a bad feeling as he drove toward the ranch, with Marissa on his mind. They were trying to allow her the privacy and time to heal from her injuries. She'd been with them for five days, but she stayed in the bedroom and barely spoke to anyone. He recognized the symptoms and thought Frank did, too.

Marissa was retreating into herself, barely answering when spoken to, and pretended to be asleep when he or anyone else knocked or entered the bedroom she was using.

She was closing off her emotions, and he knew from experience, it wasn't good for her. The young woman was going to have to face what had happened to her. Hiding from the obvious didn't work. He knew that well enough because he'd tried it.

Riley turned onto the ranch lane when he saw something moving in the desert, and it wasn't an animal. It was Marissa, and she dodged between fence rails and began to run.

Riley pulled to the side of the road carefully, vaulted the

fence, and ran after her. He didn't know where she expected to go or run to. There was nothing but sand, sagebrush, and cactus for miles. There was nowhere for her to hide. It didn't take him long to catch her.

"Whoa," he said when he caught her.

"Let me go," she screamed, backing away from him.

"Go, where?" Riley demanded. "There's nothing but desert. You are not even heading in the right direction to Dry Rock. Beyond that, it's almost a hundred miles to a place large enough for you to disappear without being noticed. Are you trying to kill yourself?"

She turned and stumbled in the sand, almost falling into the spikes of a cactus.

"Stop it!" Riley ordered, grabbing her by the arms.

"I can't stay here," Marissa screamed.

"You can't go either," he yelled. "Damn it, woman, look at yourself! You're wearing men's underwear, and you are still covered in bruises and scabs. You might as well be wearing a sign saying, *'Call the Police!'*. I'm taking you to the ranch!"

"No!" she swung at him, but there was no strength behind her fight.

Riley bent over and tossed her over his shoulder.

"Let me go," she cried.

Riley tightened his grip around her knees and smacked her bottom with the other hand. "One more word, and you are going across my knee," he warned. "If you're going to behave like an irrational child, I'll treat you like one!"

He carried her to the truck, dumped her in the passenger seat, and opened a cooler. He handed her a bottle of cold water. "Drink!" he ordered.

She drank the water, and her fight was gone.

Riley got behind the wheel and started the engine. "You know, I expect foolish behavior from my younger brother. He's in the throes of teenage obnoxiousness! I don't expect it from a grown woman!" He started the truck and drove to the ranch in silence. When he parked in front of the house, she didn't attempt to get out. He gave a sigh.

"Marissa, we are trying to help you. You can't get away until you can stand on your feet long enough to keep moving. You can't get away from the people who hurt you until you are strong enough to fight them. I'm willing to help you, but you have to trust me enough to let me.

"Now, I'm not going to tolerate any more nonsense. You're going into the house, and you're going to bed until you are well enough to stand on your own two feet again. I don't want any arguments about it."

"You threatened me," Marissa whispered.

"No, I didn't," Riley exclaimed, looking puzzled.

She looked at him with accusing eyes. "You did!"

Riley shook his head in frustration and slammed the driver's side door, and went around to open her door. "Okay, I threatened you with a spanking! That's nothing, and it wasn't a threat. It was a promise! If a man can't get common sense through to a woman by talking to her, sometimes a sore bottom works better. It's faster and settles the matter! Now, out!"

She scrambled from the truck and made sure she stayed a few feet ahead of him until they were inside the house. He pointed to the bedroom, and she obeyed.

Riley returned to the kitchen and went to the back porch, and opened the large chest freezer. He set several steaks on the kitchen counter to thaw. Their guest hadn't eaten enough for them to determine what she liked or disliked, but the McKenna men were carnivores.

He fixed a pot of coffee, wandered through the rooms

until he found his notebook, and returned to the kitchen to scribble a phrase of words he might be able to use in a song.

He raised his eyes as Marissa came into the kitchen and timidly sat in one of the old dinette chairs.

Marissa hated prying eyes, but she didn't feel threatened. Instead, there was an almost palpable sympathy from her rescuers, all three of them. She'd been hiding on the ranch for nearly a week, and the men had been remarkably patient with her. It was time to be honest, although she didn't know where to start.

"You should be resting," Riley said.

"I've awakened several times at night, and you've been holding me," she said.

"You have nightmares, and you thrash around," he said. "When I hold and talk to you, it seems to relax you. You have enough bruises, and you were hurting yourself. I didn't mean to frighten you."

"I was at first, but I'm not now. Thank you," Marissa whispered.

"Who did this to you?" Riley asked gently, motioning with his hand toward the dark bruises. He went about the kitchen, cupboard, refrigerator, and breadbox. He carried the makings of peanut butter and jelly sandwiches to the table.

She watched him assemble two sandwiches and lay them on paper towels. He returned to the refrigerator and poured a glass of milk before filling his mug from the coffee pot. His way of dealing with the simple, everyday task was somehow reassuring.

"My ex-husband," Marissa answered in a whisper. "Well, partially. Some of this damage was caused by my jumping from his car and wandering around lost in the desert. I kept running, and it was dark, so I couldn't see where I was going."

"You jumped from a moving vehicle?" Riley asked.

She made a confused movement of her head, first a nod

and then a shake. "He was forced to hit the brakes," Marissa said haltingly. "When he laid the knife against my throat, I knew he'd lost his mind. When he raised the gun again, I knew he was going to kill me. All I can remember thinking was: *He's going to kill me this time!* He took his eyes off the road for a few seconds, and a herd of javelinas was crossing the road. There were lots of them. He slammed on the brakes, but he hit several of them. I opened the door and jumped. I rolled down an embankment and into the desert. I don't know why there was a bridge, because there wasn't any water. I heard a crash, and then I heard him screaming and firing the gun.

"He said I couldn't get away. He screamed, 'I own you!' He's insane! I ran, and I kept running until I couldn't hear him screaming anymore."

"I take it the divorce wasn't amicable?"

Marissa gave a harsh sound as Riley took a bite of his sandwich and motioned for her to do the same.

She raised the triangle to her lips and took a bite. She raised her eyes to the man sitting across from her. She didn't know why, but it was vital for him to believe her. "The words amicable and my ex-husband don't belong in the same sentence. We divorced almost five years ago, and he's made my life a living hell since."

"Why didn't you move away?" Riley asked. "Or get a restraining order or have him arrested for harassing you?"

"Because my ex is Gregg Novak and he's a District Attorney in Las Vegas. He's a very powerful man. He knows all the wealthy movers and shakers in the city. He knows people who have connections to both the law and the syndicates, mafia, and drug cartels. He was working for, and with those people, friends with many of them.

"My ex-husband is a control freak. He doesn't really want me. If he can't control me, he doesn't want me to have anyone else in my life. He's pathologically possessive and controlling. When I first met him, he wasn't. I would never have married him if I believed him to be like that. I don't suppose any woman would marry if she knew in advance that she was involving herself with a man like him. He was very good at hiding his real personality, or maybe I couldn't see it. The possessiveness and temper started within the first month. If I didn't comply, he became a monster.

"I did try at first, mostly because he was claiming that I was the one being unreasonable. I finally realized it wasn't going to get better. When I left Gregg, I thought I could get away and start a new life. He went along with it, at first. I found out later, his mistress moved into our house three days after I left it.

"Divorce is quick in Nevada, and I was divorced before I realized I was pregnant. It didn't matter. I wasn't going back to him. When he discovered I was pregnant, that's when the real harassment started. Even before the twins were born, he filed papers in court to keep me from leaving the state. I have two beautiful boys, twins. Their birthday was three days ago, and I missed it!"

Marissa's face crumpled, but she tried to pull herself together, although a few tears escaped. She wiped them away and took a couple of deep breaths.

"My ex-husband doesn't want his sons. He has never wanted them. My babies are a weapon he uses against me. He's manipulative, and he gets revengeful when he doesn't get his way. We were only married for ten months, and I have been fighting him for almost five years. I finally realized I couldn't fight him. He knows the law, and he knows how to manipulate it and the judges he must be bribing. He knows how to use the law and his friends in power to his benefit."

Marissa rose from the table slowly and paced a few feet nervously. "Eight months ago, I answered a knock on my front door. A social worker and a policeman handed me a piece of paper and took custody of my children.

"Somehow, Gregg got full custody of my boys without my even being aware of what he was doing. I pleaded, and I begged, but it didn't matter. He made it very clear if I wanted to see my children again, I would have to remarry him. I refused.

"I was stupid, so stupid! I actually thought if I took him to court, I would get my boys back. I was granted limited, supervised visitation rights. If I violated their rules, I could be thrown in jail. He violated the orders repeatedly. No matter what I said, the judges ruled in his favor. He filed abuse charges against me. One way or another, Gregg Novak gets what he wants."

"Where are the boys?" Riley asked.

Marissa swiped at her tears again, and she faced him. "I told you I am not a criminal, but that's not true. If you call the police, there is an outstanding warrant for my arrest for non-custodial kidnapping."

"Where are your boys?" Riley asked again.

"I won't tell you," Marissa said quietly, defiantly. "I won't. My children are safe. I know they are being cared for in a loving environment with someone I trust. They can lock me up. They can throw away the key, but I will not let Gregg Novak get his hands on my babies again!

"If I can't be with them, I know they are safe. I was in an underground network for abused women when Gregg found me. He was holding a gun on me when he forced me into the car."

"Did he do this to you often? Did he abuse the kids?" Riley demanded.

She shook her head. "No. He wouldn't be that obvious. He would pinch me, trip me, or shove me into something. If anyone mentioned a bruise, he claimed I was a klutz. If he has hurt the boys, they have never admitted to it, and I have looked for bruises. His abuse was total control of every second of my life. When I was with him, he picked my clothing, hairstyle, my makeup, and manicures. He controlled what I ate and what I did every minute of the day, even who I spoke to.

"He hired a nanny for the boys and would only allow me to be with them if I was *good*. He ignores them, except when he wants to play the perfect daddy in front of someone he needs to impress," Marissa said. "He sees my children as tools to gain control over me again. His anger has been getting worse, and I knew it was only a matter of time before he turned it on my babies. I did what I had to do to keep my boys safe."

Marissa sank into the kitchen chair, and she seemed to collapse both physically and emotionally. She began to sob.

Riley went to her, pulled her into his arms, and let her cry. Then he guided her to the bedroom. He gave her a pill Dr. Andrews had said would make her rest, and he stayed with her until she had gone to sleep.

When Noah and Frank arrived home, he informed them of what she'd told him.

"Is she okay?" Noah asked.

Frank wasn't pleased with her confession. He stuck his hands in his back pockets and rocked back on the heels of his boots. "Guys, I don't like this. By her admission, she has broken the law. She has admitted to kidnapping."

"They're her kids," Noah objected.

"Kids belong to both the father and the mother," Frank said. "The children have been removed from her custody by a court of law," Frank said. "This could be bad stuff."

"She is also a victim," Riley said. "She didn't get those cuts and bruises on her by accident, although she admits the physical abuse was somewhat limited before she divorced him. This time he flipped out. Have you looked into her eyes,

Frank? We know what terror looks like, and I believe her. Marissa is telling the truth, and she is being victimized by her ex-husband and a corrupt legal system. Her ex-husband is a jerk. He has used his position in the law to work the system against her."

"We can't abandon her!" Noah exclaimed. "She needs our help."

"I can't take that risk," Frank stated bluntly. "Daniel would have a fit if I put you two in a compromising position with the law."

"I'm beyond the age where I need Dad to speak for me," Riley interrupted. "I can also promise you that Dad would not walk away from a person who needed help. He didn't raise us to bail on people when they need you the most. Call Dad, you'll see."

"I say we keep her," Noah voted.

"Marissa is not a stray cat, Noah," Frank admonished, shaking his head. "I think we should help her too, but it might become complicated. If there's any chance of this becoming a tell-all in the tabloids, you guys can't be involved! If this is played the wrong way, it could ruin your careers!"

"If we don't do something to help her, we're cowards," Riley said. "If this guy is a corrupt control freak, he's not going to want the truth to come out."

"Dad always taught us bullies are cowards, and generally, they are cowards who don't want to be caught. Face them, and they will tuck their tails and run. Call, Dad, but it might take you a while to make contact. They are somewhere in the Atlantic by now. Clear things with him about Noah. He may want Noah clear of this, and that's his prerogative. I make my own decisions, and I'm throwing my weight behind Marissa because I believe she needs help. I have a friend who can make inquiries and discover the truth."

"Shawn?" Noah questioned, looking over to his brother, and Riley nodded.

"Shawn?" Frank questioned.

"Shawn Williams was the FBI computer hacker who tapped into the surveillance system in the convenience store," Riley explained to his uncle. "The convenience store was in the middle of nowhere, but it had a sophisticated security system. The cameras on display were destroyed, but there were other hidden cameras. Once the owner of the store was contacted and Shawn was briefed on the surveillance system, he was able to reverse the programming and enable the police and the FBI agents to know exactly what was going on inside. He saved my life with his computer skills."

"I'm not a computer expert, and would never make that claim. Shawn is and just about everything is done on computers now. It's a matter of finding the right lead and path to follow. If anyone can discover the truth, I trust Shawn to do it," Riley explained. "I consider him a friend, and there's not much he can't do with his computers."

"Regardless of how it's done or who we trust, this situation could go sour," Frank said. "I could lose any chance of being re-approved for foster care. John Henry would be a better bet for working inside the law. I'm sure he has plenty of contacts. How do you know your friend won't report her to the authorities?"

"If I ask him to keep his inquiries to himself, he will," Riley said. "Shawn is a hacker, and he loves his job, but he's also a professional. He works within the law."

"Okay," Frank agreed. "We will ease into this cautiously. My gut says she's telling the truth, but I have to use a bit of caution, just in case."

"Yes!" Noah exclaimed with a smile and a fist punch into the air. "We get to keep her!"

Chapter 6

"**N**oah, how do you like your steak?" Frank asked, laying three large and one small steak on the grill.

"Well done for both of us," Noah answered from his comfortable position on the porch swing.

Noah was bored, but there wasn't a lot he could do about it. Uncle Frank's television was an old set dating to a prehistoric age before flat screens. His uncle had cable and internet, but the TV was only turned on for news as far as he knew. Noah had already been warned to stay off the ancient computer. He hadn't been given the passwords.

The teenager's cell phone and his electronics had been confiscated after his father picked him up from police detention. It was part of his punishment.

Out of sheer boredom, Noah had resorted to plucking chords on his brother's guitar. Noah was a drummer. He wasn't a guitarist. Besides, Riley hadn't liked his messing with one of his favorite guitars. It had survived the fire only because it had been on tour with him. He suspected his brother was writing a song from the intermittent sounds of notes played in the living room. All three of his older brothers wrote and composed music.

"Uncle Frank, can you teach me how to ride a horse?" Noah asked.

Frank looked surprised at the question. "Boy, you were born and bred in Texas, and you don't know how to ride? What's wrong with my brother?"

"We live in San Antonio–a city," Noah reminded his uncle. "I've been on a horse a couple of times, but I'm not real good at it. I figure since I'm here, it's a good time to learn."

"It's an excellent time to learn," Frank agreed. "Can Riley ride?"

Noah laughed. "No, baseball and football were his sports in summer leagues and college. The first-set didn't go to regular school. They were homeschooled."

"Well, I guess riding lessons are on for both of you."

"Cool," Noah responded. He looked at a cloud of dust moving along the ranch lane. "Are you expecting company?"

Frank looked at the dust cloud and shook his head. "No, that's John Henry's vehicle and Gillian Taliwood's truck. Go tell Marissa to stay inside and lock the bedroom door."

The old truck, that had seen better days, and John Henry's vehicle stopped in front of Frank's house. John Henry and the older man he had identified as Jefferson Ironheart got out. Three more men stepped down from the other truck.

Frank turned the gas down on the grill. "Noah, keep an eye on the steaks."

Noah took a position in front of the grill as Frank went to greet his friends. He invited the men onto the porch. The only one who took a seat was the elderly man.

"Frank, Jefferson Ironheart would like to speak to Riley," John Henry explained.

Frank was puzzled, but he opened the front door and yelled for his nephew.

Riley appeared in the doorway. "What?"

Noah turned off the grill so he could listen.

John Henry stepped forward. "Riley, I would like you to meet my Uncle Jefferson Ironheart and Tribal Council Members Gillian Taliwood, Mike Saganey, and Joseph Stoneman."

"He's the one?" one of the men asked of their elder.

"He's the one," Jefferson Ironheart confirmed.

"The one for what?" Riley asked.

"Jefferson Ironheart wants you to train the black stallion," John Henry said.

Riley laughed. "I can't do it."

"You are the chosen one," Jefferson Ironheart repeated.

Riley swallowed his humor. All three men were looking skeptical. John Henry and Jefferson Ironheart looked solemn.

"John Henry, I told you, I don't know anything about horses," Riley protested. "I have never been around them. I've only been in a saddle two or three times. I don't know how to ride, and I don't know anything about training horses."

Jefferson Ironheart spoke directly to John Henry in his native tongue. The other three men listened and joined the conversation. Riley looked to his uncle, who only shrugged.

The old man barked out what sounded like orders, and all three grown men listened intently. Finally, John Henry turned to Riley.

"I know you don't understand this, Riley, but my Uncle believes you were chosen by the horse. The tribe has had the stallion for months, and no one has been able to get close to him. We've tried breaking him with various methods, but nothing is working. So far, two men have been injured, not seriously, but still, they were hurt. My uncle believes you can reach the horse. Jefferson Ironheart says you are a... well, for no better word, a horse whisperer. That's someone who can connect with horses. We were considering hiring a professional, but you have made a connection with the stallion. He believes you can train the horse."

Riley looked at John Henry in disbelief. "I'm not a horse whisperer. I saw the movie, and I don't have a mystical connection with animals. I fed the horse apples, and he connects me with getting something he likes to eat! I don't know anything about horses, except they are big and can stomp the crap out of me."

"You have a point," John Henry said. "But, you have made a connection with the stallion, and we've seen it. No one has been able to get past the stallion's fear of men. When he broke free this morning, you were able to control and lead him to the corral. It was an impressive achievement. The stallion would have tried to kill anyone else. We would have had to use much rougher methods to break him. Using those methods would have only made his distrust of men worse."

"You're asking me to do something I don't know how to do," Riley said. "I'm a musician! My brother and I are here to help Uncle Frank with the construction of his house. I know how to build because I was taught by professionals while working on my house. Come September, we're out of here."

"I will teach you," Jefferson Ironheart said solemnly. "John Henry and I will show you the *old ways*. You have a gift, and we need you to help us. We have invested a great deal of money on this horse. We need to train him so we can race him. We need your help."

Riley looked over to his uncle for direction.

Frank took the cue. "I would like to speak to Riley for a minute. Why don't you men go inside and help yourself to a beer or a soda from the refrigerator."

John Henry and Jefferson Ironheart exchanged looks and went into the house. The other men followed.

Frank motioned Riley to follow him. When he noticed,

Noah hovering close by, he motioned for him to join them. They walked to the edge of the road before he faced them.

"Riley, I don't know what to make of this any more than you do. I do know the Quechan tribe honors Jefferson Iron-heart. If he believes you have a special gift or connection with the horse, they'll go along with his ideas. The Tribal Council has invested a lot of money in this stallion. They believe if they can get this horse broken by the time the riverbed races start in the late fall, he will be a winner."

"Riverbed races? You mean they want him to be a race-horse?" Riley questioned.

"The tribes run races in the dry riverbeds in the fall. It's a source of income and a source of pride to have the best horse. Jefferson Ironheart isn't doing this for petty cash Riley. A winning horse on the circuit can make a lot of money," Frank explained.

Riley looked at his uncle and his brother. Frank was waiting for an answer.

"Okay, but you have to make these guys understand we're only here for a few months. Noah has to return to school. I have to go back to my life, and I don't know how to do what they're asking of me!" He pointed to Noah. "You have to keep your mouth shut to Mom and Dad! I don't need Mom freaking out!"

Frank, Riley, and Noah entered the kitchen, and everyone looked to Riley for an answer.

Frank spoke first. "Riley has agreed to this, but I have a few stipulations. First, when Riley said he doesn't know anything about horses, he means it. My nephew doesn't know enough to keep from getting hurt, so it's your job to make sure he doesn't. He was raised in San Antonio, and he's a city kid. I don't want to send him home broken!"

"Thanks, Uncle Frank, but I'm not exactly a kid anymore.

I do agree I don't want to be sent home in pieces," Riley said, and the men smiled and chuckled.

"I will teach you what you need to know," Jefferson Ironheart promised.

"John Henry, you need to bring the stallion to the ranch. Riley still has chores and work. The training can not interfere with the jobs needed to be done here on the ranch," Frank said.

John Henry nodded his head in agreement, and he looked to Riley for a sign of agreement.

Riley looked around the room of work-toughened men, and he knew he was out of his element. Daniel McKenna had raised his sons with what his father called *necessary man skills*. What he hadn't learned from his father, he'd learned from other men. He was not qualified in any way to do what they were asking of him. Still, he did like a challenge.

"I can only promise to try. But, if you get me maimed or killed, there are going to be a lot of people pissed, me included!"

Riley paused in front of a section of cosmetics at the convenience store in Dry Rock. He looked at a package and hung it on the hook.

"Can I help you?" the young cashier asked. Rainey Two-Trees had been watching him for the last five minutes in the overhead mirror.

Riley looked around with embarrassment. "Uh, no," he said, and looked around to see if anyone else had noticed what he was looking at.

Rainey grinned. "Do you want to buy a particular cosmetic? We don't carry much."

"No!" Riley backed away and turned.

"Riley, it's okay," Rainey said, leaning toward him and lowering her voice. "I know about the woman who is staying at Frank's place."

Riley looked startled. "What?"

The teenager shrugged. "John Henry asked a few of us to keep our eyes open for out-of-state license plates and an ear open for anyone asking questions."

"So much for secrecy," Riley grumbled.

"You don't need to keep secrets from us," Rainey exclaimed. "We're not the enemy. In fact, the people here at the crossroads are probably your friend's best defense. We would be the ones to raise the alarm if someone did come around, asking questions. We protect our own."

"We are part of Dry Rock's *our own*?" Riley asked.

Rainey nodded her head. "If John Henry says she needs protection, yes. We will do whatever is necessary to protect her."

Riley nodded his head and smiled. He loved the idea of simple acceptance of the townspeople based on one man's word.

"Okay, if you know about her, tell me something else," Riley asked.

Rainey lifted an eyebrow and waited.

"Where can I buy her some clothes? She's wearing hand-me-down clothing from my brother and me. She hasn't complained, but I know it must be bugging her. She needs girl clothes."

"There's no place here to buy new clothes," Rainey said. "We either shop online, catalog, or we go to Murdock or Yuma. You could try over at Max's Antiques. Mrs. Moonbeam has a room in the back for used clothing. It's our version of a thrift shop."

"Moonbeam?" Riley questioned.

The young cashier laughed. "Yes, Max and Loretta Moonbeam. She's in her eighties, and so is Max. They started the antique store in the 1960s when their van broke down, and they couldn't go any further. They're still the only hippies around. Don't be put off by how the outside looks. The inside is reasonably clean, and sometimes they really do have nice things."

Riley smiled at Rainey. "Pick an assortment of the best of what you have available here. You know, things women use... nice smelling shampoos, creams, and make-up. She's a pretty blonde with green/hazel eyes. I'm sure she will appreciate it. She's a lovely woman, and you are very nice to help her. I'll be back in a few minutes to pay for it."

Rainey got the message. The nicest looking young man who had come into their community for a long time, and he wasn't interested in her. He was obviously interested in the mystery woman who was living at the McKenna ranch.

Riley turned to leave but turned back. "She's about the same size as you, maybe a little smaller. What size should I get?"

"I wear a medium in most things," Rainey said. "If she is smaller, go with a small or medium. Jeans would be a size five, six, or seven. It's used clothing, so it might have shrunk."

"Thanks, I'll do the best I can," Riley said.

Loretta Moonbeam was an aging hippie, and so was her husband. Wearing a bright orange and purple tie-dyed caftan, she was more than happy to help Riley search the backroom stacks and hanging clothing.

Tee shirts and shorts with elastic waistbands were plentiful. So were used jeans. Tattered and torn jeans were in fashion. Riley knew his sisters paid good money for jeans that looked like they were already worn out. Why, he didn't know, but they did. He usually was pissed if he ripped his jeans.

Mrs. Moonbeam found a pair of white jeans with the original tags on them and a few other items with very little wear.

He had to guess at used sandals, and Loretta asked about height and told him to buy the same sizes as the jeans but with adjustable straps. There was only one pair in a smaller size.

Riley left the antique/thrift store with two bags of clothing, and he carried them over to his truck, dumping them in the passenger seat. He returned to the store and waited until Rainey completed a transaction with a customer. She handed a bag over the counter to him, and he paid for it, not bothering to look inside.

The teenager took a phone call, hung up, and swore under her breath. She looked upset.

"Problem?"

"Yes, I had the early shift today, and it's over. My mom is busy and can't come to get me," Rainey said. "Now, I'll have to wait around for hours for my cousin Dillon to pick me up, and he's a flake! He won't remember. He never does!"

"I can take you home," Riley volunteered.

"It's in the opposite direction," she said.

"I owe you," Riley said. "Call whoever, and tell them you have a ride."

"Thanks!" the teenager exclaimed. After her phone call, she directed him toward the Fort Yuma Indian Reservation.

Riley was surprised at the size of the enormous casino they passed. Rainey said it employed most of the reservation population, and it was a tremendous draw for tourists.

He was guided into a housing development similar to most suburban areas. The houses were single-story bungalows. Many of them were neat, while others looked like no one had tried to do any maintenance for a while, typical of all suburban housing areas.

There was no such thing as grass for the yards, considering the desert conditions. Like most of the southwest, yards were gravel. Rainey pointed to her home, and he parked outside the fenced yard.

There was a BMW parked alongside a section of fence.

"Mr. Duquette is here," Rainey explained. "He buys a lot of arts and crafts from our artisans. Would you like to meet my mom?"

"Sure," Riley responded.

Rainey led Riley into her house. It was clean in appearance, but large macramé wall hangings and woven pieces were draped over every piece of furniture in the living room. Riley looked at several of the art pieces, and he was impressed.

"Wow, these are amazing."

Rainey smiled. "They're okay. Mr. Duquette sells them at tourist shops. It's not traditional weaving, but they sell."

"These are beautiful," Riley protested. "They would sell like hotcakes in the galleries."

Rainey laughed. "Not really. The most Mr. Duquette gets for these seems to be about a hundred dollars. Mom tries to keep the designs original. I'll be back in a couple of minutes."

Riley was introduced to Mr. Duquette. He was wrapping the art pieces with protective coverings and carried them outside to his car.

A woman he assumed was Mrs. Two-Trees came into the living room. She and Mr. Duquette were discussing the prices on several of her larger pieces. She wanted more for them, but he claimed he couldn't market them for more. Rainey's mother was obviously upset, and she left the room.

As a principle, Riley tried not to prejudge people. Still, his hackles rose as the man argued with the artist. He had met his share of shady, wheeler-dealers. He recognized Duquette as a man who worked most opportunities to his benefit and not the person he was supposed to be representing. Maybe he was assuming, but Riley took an instant dislike to the art dealer.

Riley looked at the signature of Glenda Two-Trees. When the dealer carried an armload of her art outside to his car,

Riley took photographs of the signature and several larger pieces.

A few minutes later, Rainey returned and handed him a bag of clothing.

"I'm sorry, but my mom is busy right now with Mr. Duquette. I've outgrown these, and my mom said I could give them away," Rainey said. "I threw in a pair of flip-flops. I have several pairs."

"I can't thank you enough," Riley said.

He drove to the ranch and carried the bags inside, and dumped them on the kitchen table.

"What's all this?" Marissa asked.

"Secondhand, but it's the best I could do in Dry Rock," Riley admitted.

"These are new," Marissa said, removing a pair of white jeans from a bag."

"The woman who owns the antique shop found those, and I didn't know your size, so things might be too small or too big," he said.

Marissa opened the bag from the convenience store and gave him a strange look."

"What?" Riley asked.

She removed a box of tampons.

"Oh, crap," Riley exclaimed, and his face flushed. "I didn't buy those! Well, I paid for them, but I didn't pick out the stuff. The cashier did, her name is Rainey Two-Trees, and I told her to pick out some female stuff. I didn't..."

Marissa laughed at his denial and reaction, so typical for a man. "It's okay. I appreciate the thought, and I'm equally sure I'll need them."

"You probably should wash everything," Riley said, motioning toward the bags. "Mrs. Moonbeam said she washes everything, but who knows how long they've been in the antique shop."

"Mrs. Moonbeam?" Marissa repeated.

He grinned. "Loretta is an eighty-two-year-old hippy and proud of it. Her husband, Max, is eighty-five. They are very cool old people! They were at the original Woodstock, and they have photographs plastered all over the shop of what they called *the good days*. She was a hottie back in the day! I'll leave this to you. I need to get to work."

"Tell him I'm going to try to cook tonight," Marissa said. "I found a recipe box. It must have been his wife's."

"He'll appreciate it," Riley said. "So will we!"

Marissa walked over to Riley and motioned for him to bend to her level. "Thank you for everything," she said, briefly kissing him on the cheek.

"Hang tight with us. We're going to help you," Riley responded. "And, for the record, I like being kissed by a beautiful woman."

Marissa dropped her eyes and stepped back. She raised her hand to her face to cover the bright red scars.

Riley closed the space between them, laid his fingers gently under her chin, and tilted it upward to face him.

"You are beautiful, Marissa. Those little scars don't take away from your beauty, and they will fade with time. Those little outside scars aren't the ones you're going to have to worry about. It's the ones inside and up here," he tapped his head. "Those will do the most damage. Those are the ones that you will have to guard against ruining your future happiness."

"How do you know that?" she asked.

"Because a man intent on killing held me at gunpoint for five hours," Riley admitted. "I survived it, the same as you will survive and thrive once we discover what we need to pay your ex back for what he's done."

"I'm not sure that's possible."

"I believe it is," Riley said. "If you have doubts, you can

lean on me for strength. I have something else for you." He pulled a cell phone from his pocket and handed it to her.

"This is a pre-paid phone, and I maxed the minutes on it. You have my word of honor that you can use it safely. No one can trace the calls because no one but you and I know about it. I would suggest not taking incoming calls unless it's an emergency. Call your boys, and make sure they're okay. They, and whoever is taking care of them, need to hear from you as much as you need to hear from them. When you've used the minutes, tell me, and I'll buy more."

Marissa's eyes filled with tears.

"Don't do that," Riley exclaimed. "I was trying to do something nice. I don't know what to do when women cry!"

Marissa's tears overflowed into heartbreaking sobs.

Noah slammed the back door and stopped dead in his tracks when he saw Marissa in tears.

"What did you do to her?" he demanded.

"Nothing, I didn't do anything," Riley exclaimed.

"He didn't," Marissa sobbed.

"Then, why are you crying?" Noah demanded.

"Because I'm happy," Marissa cried.

"Happy?" Riley and Noah questioned at the same time.

Marissa nodded her head. "Yes, happy," she repeated. She swiped her face furiously with her hands. She turned to Riley and kissed him squarely on the lips, and said, "Thank you!" She turned to Noah, hugged, and kissed him on the cheek. She grabbed a napkin, wiped her eyes, and ran down the hallway to the bedroom.

Riley and Noah looked at each other in bewilderment.

"What was that all about?" Noah asked. "She was laughing and crying at the same time!"

"How am I supposed to know?" Riley demanded. "Women are strange creatures. Even at your age, you should know that by now!"

Chapter 7

Riley watched as John Henry and Jefferson Ironheart were trying to remove the stallion from the horse trailer. It was a clear case of man against beast, and the horse wanted no part of what they were trying to force it to do.

"Riley, talk to him," John Henry ordered. "He responds to your voice. It will calm him."

Riley climbed the trailer slats and spoke in a soft, soothing voice. Sure enough, the hooded horse stood still listening to him. He talked, and John Henry maneuvered a rope around the horse's chest. All that did was cause the stallion more distress.

"Can you turn him around?" Noah asked. "Maybe he doesn't like backing up."

"No horse *likes* to back up. It's too tight inside the trailer to turn the stallion around unless he cooperates," John Henry explained, backing further away from thrashing hooves.

"He might follow me," Riley suggested, and he swung a leg over the top slat of the trailer and dropped down inside.

"For God's sake, Riley, get the hell out of there!" Frank ordered.

"No, let him try," Jefferson Ironheart disagreed. The old man climbed on the trailer slats to issue his orders. "Be careful! Get a grip on the hood and use it to steer him around. Push your weight against his shoulder. Don't let him pin you against the side of the trailer." Jefferson Ironheart offered a continuous stream of advice as Riley spoke low and encouraging.

His married friends teased him about his ability to calm their babies. There was no hesitation to hand off their offspring to him. This horse was one giant of a baby, but he responded and turned as Riley pushed his weight against his flank and talked to him.

"Lead him down the ramp. Keep a tight hold on the hood because as soon as he is on the metal ramp, it's going to scare him," John Henry advised.

Riley moved in front of the horse, pulled, and had to step quickly to stay in front of the high-stepping front hooves. He could feel the fear in the horse as its muscles trembled with fright. It dissipated when they were on solid ground again.

"Good boy," Jefferson Ironheart exclaimed.

Riley turned. He didn't know if the elder was talking to him or the horse.

"Try to lead him into the second stall," Frank said. He blocked Noah with his arm to keep him clear of the powerful animal.

Riley led the horse into the barn and into the prepared stall. He and Noah had cleaned and laid fresh straw in it earlier.

John Henry closed the stall gate and hooked the latch. Noah climbed on the gate and peered over the top.

Frank handed a bucket of oats over to Riley. He stretched to get it but missed getting a tight grip on the handle, and the bucket rattled when it hit the straw-covered floor. Before anyone could react, the stallion gave a mighty kick, slashing its back hooves against the gate's second slat and shattering the wood. The force of the blow slammed into Noah's chest and knocked him onto the barn floor.

"Noah!" Riley shouted, distressing the horse further.

"Calm down, Riley!" Jefferson Ironheart ordered in a gruff command. "Talk to the horse. Settle him, or you'll be next!"

Frank and John Henry ran to assist the fallen boy, who was deadly silent for a few seconds before he began to gasp for breath. Frank leaned over his nephew.

"Noah! Where are you hurt?"

The boy looked wild-eyed for a few seconds while he was gasping for breath. Frank yanked up his tee shirt and inspected his chest.

"How is Noah?" Riley demanded.

Jefferson Ironheart looked over his shoulder briefly. "He's fine. Keep talking to the horse and try to work your way over here to the gate. Bring him around with you, and before you slip out, I want you to remove the hood."

Riley did as he was told, and with one foot outside of the stall, he removed the hood. Jefferson Ironheart shouted and waved his arms to distract the stallion as they locked the gate.

Riley ran to his brother, who was still lying on his back.

"Are you hurt?" he demanded.

"No," Noah croaked.

"I think it knocked the wind out of him," Frank exclaimed. "Let's get him to his feet."

"I'll fix the gate, and I'll be in," John Henry said as he watched his best friend and mentor help the teenager walk toward the ranch house.

"Old man," John Henry said, turning to his uncle. "How

many more will get hurt before you realize this horse cannot be tamed?"

Jefferson Ironheart held his ground stoically. "The boy wasn't hurt. He only had the wind knocked from him. The stallion doesn't fight the older one. He is the chosen one, and if the horse can trust him, it can be trained."

Frank helped Noah into the living room and laid him on the couch. Riley had stopped at his truck, and he was removing his large medical box. He carried it inside and proceeded to take his brother's vital signs. Noah was breathing normally, and his color had returned. There was a red welt on his chest from being hit by the board.

"I'm okay," Noah insisted. "Stop messing with me," he protested.

Marissa edged into the room and over to the couch, looking worried.

"You need to go back to the bedroom," Riley warned. "You said you weren't ready to meet John Henry, and he might be in here at any second."

Marissa looked conflicted, but she was also frightened. She disappeared down the hallway, and they heard the door close.

Frank ordered Noah to lie around for a couple of hours and to report any pain immediately. Noah did as he was told. There would be no training for the stallion on his first day at the ranch. Riley and John Henry left in Frank's old pickup with a load of fence posts to repair fences. Jefferson Ironheart left to return the horse trailer, and Frank went to work on the house addition. After a couple hours of lying around, Noah joined him, and both of them were moving slow.

When Riley awakened in the middle of the night, he traced his mind for details of a flashback. Bad memories were usually the culprit of his waking from a deep sleep, but not this time. He heard a raspy choking sound. Leaping from the bed, he turned on the lights. Noah's face was pale, and his eyes were squeezed tight with pain.

"What's wrong?"

"Hurts to breathe," Noah rasped out.

Riley laid his hand on his brother's forehead. Noah was clammy, and his pulse was racing. Riley ran into the living room, turning on the light. He shouted to wake his uncle, who was sleeping on the couch.

Frank sat up and demanded, "What?"

"Noah's having trouble breathing. We have to get him to an emergency room!" Riley ordered.

"Right," Frank answered, sitting up on the couch and grabbing his jeans in one motion.

Riley returned to his brother, helping him to sit up. He got Noah to his feet and into the living room.

Marissa joined them. "Maybe we need to call an ambulance."

"The closest ambulance service is forty miles away," Frank explained. He went to the phone, and after waiting through repeated rings, he spoke to Doctor Anderson and told him they were bringing Noah to see him.

"Riley, get dressed," Frank ordered. "We'll take your truck, with your first-aid kit, just in case."

Riley ran into the bedroom, grabbed Noah's clothing from the day before, and helped his brother get dressed. "Marissa, stay inside the bedroom and lock the door from the inside. No one knows you are here, so you should be safe. I'll call you as soon as I can, and we'll be home as soon as possible."

Riley drove. They had barely passed the barn when Riley looked over his shoulder sharply.

"What?" Frank demanded.

"I forgot to shut the front door," Riley said, and he was surprised when his uncle laughed.

"As long as the screen door is closed, nothing will get in," Frank said.

"At home, we are more worried about locking everyone out," Riley admitted. He saw a woman's silhouette in the doorway, and the door closed. "Marissa closed it. I'll bet it's locked too!"

"She might not be there when we get back," Frank said.

"What do you mean?" Riley asked.

"She has clothing now, and my truck is there with the keys in the ignition. She knows there's cash in the empty oatmeal box in the cupboard," Frank said.

"She won't run," Riley said. "She's still skittish, but I don't believe she would steal or run."

"She did before," Frank said.

"She was running in a blind panic before," Riley said. "She knows us now, and she doesn't fear us." He turned to his brother. "Noah? Are you okay?" At his brother's nod, he turned his attention to the road. "How far is the nearest hospital?" he asked of his uncle.

"We're going to Dr. Anderson's Clinic in Wolf Springs. It's forty miles."

"Jesus!" Riley exclaimed.

"This isn't San Antonio or Austin," Frank said gruffly. "We're lucky we have a clinic. Before Dr. Anderson came here, we had to go to Yuma." He turned his attention to Noah, who was sitting between them. "Are you hanging in there okay, son?"

Noah nodded and closed his eyes.

Riley felt incredibly helpless as he watched his younger brother struggle to breathe. He'd thought of adding an oxygen tank and mask to his kit. He had also countered his own caution by telling himself that while he was a licensed EMT, he wasn't affiliated with any rescue service.

Noah wasn't complaining, but Riley knew from experience

how awful it was to be at the mercy of something beyond your control. The recently turned seventeen-year-old liked to think he was grown, but he still had a bit of growing up and maturing to do. The boy took after his natural father. He was small for his age and looked younger than his age.

When they arrived at a single-story adobe building, the light was on, and Dr. Anderson appeared in the doorway. Noah was taken into an examining room.

Frank explained what had happened while Dr. Andrews began to examine his patient.

"Hi! Who's that?" a little girl asked. She was about six or seven years old, dressed in an oversized sleeping tee shirt.

"Scarlett, go back to bed," Dr. Andrews said over his shoulder.

"Awww," she complained.

"Scoot," Dr. Andrews said sternly, and the little girl flounced away.

"What's wrong with Scarlett?" Frank asked as the little girl left the doorway.

"Chronic asthma. It's unusual for this climate. I'm keeping an eye on her for a few days until I can get an extra oxygen tank shipped in. Her folks live too far out, and it takes too long for them to get her to me when she's having an attack," Dr. Andrews explained while he was examining Noah's chest and back. He inspected the bruise across his chest.

"You two need to go in the hallway, so I can take an X-ray," the doctor suggested as he pulled a portable machine over. Frank and Riley moved outside to the hallway.

A few minutes later, the doctor opened the door. "I'm a one-man shop, so you have to wait until I get this developed."

Noah was breathing better with the help of oxygen. The doctor reappeared with the X-ray film, clipped it to a light board, and studied it.

"Well, there are no broken ribs and no fluid on the lungs,

so I am left to believe this is swelling caused by the impact. I'm going to hook you to an IV, and a dose of antibiotics will reduce the swelling. You should be right as rain by morning," Dr. Anderson told the teenager.

"Frank, leave him here for the rest of the night. I'll keep an eye on him, and you can come to get him tomorrow unless I have to head in your direction. If I do, I'll call and save you the trip."

Noah pulled the mask from his face and looked to be in a bit of a panic.

"Hang in there, bro. It's only one needle, and it won't hurt. Don't look, and it will be over in a second," Riley reassured him in a whisper. "Remember when I was a chicken-shit about needles? I was scared silly of them. They're not so bad."

Noah nodded and tried to smile.

The doctor returned, and he assisted Noah from the examining room into an open wardroom. The room had five beds with curtains between them. He guided Noah to one of the beds and clipped the oxygen tube to his nose. The doctor prepped him for the IV and had it inserted before Noah could protest.

"Okay, I'm going to give you a slight sedative to help you sleep tonight," Dr. Andrews promised. "You're going to be okay."

Riley looked around and spotted a vinyl and chrome chair, and he carried it into Noah's cubicle. "This will work for me tonight," he said.

"You don't have to stay. Noah will be fine here. I'll only be in the other room," the doctor explained.

"We have this brother thing going on," Riley said. "I'm staying."

Frank gave Riley a nod and turned to the doctor. "Okay. Doc, I'll be coming through town in the morning, is there anything you want me to pick up?"

"Yes, swing by the post office. I should have a package there by morning. If you don't mind stopping, I'll call in an order for groceries too. I'm not used to feeding a kid, and my cupboards are getting bare."

Frank smiled. "No problem, I'll see you when I get here."

Dr. Andrews walked Frank from the Clinic, and he turned off the outside lights. "You can sleep in one of the other beds," he said to Riley. "Extra blankets are in the closet. Scarlett is using the extra bedroom in my living quarters so she won't bother you. I'll set the alarm and check on him in a couple of hours. With any luck, we won't be disturbed again tonight."

"Thanks," Riley said.

"All in a day's work," the doctor said.

Three hours later, Riley was awakened by Dr. Andrews.

"What? Noah?"

"He's still sound asleep and doing fine," Doctor Andrews said quietly. He disconnected the IV from Noah's arm. "I have to go and hopefully deliver a baby. My cell numbers, and my patient's number, are written on a notepad by the kitchen phone. Landlines are more reliable. If you need me, call. Keep an ear open for Scarlett and your brother. If Noah has trouble breathing, turn his oxygen up to level three. If Scarlett has an asthma attack, hook her to oxygen the same as Noah, she knows the drill and can help you. Put that EMT training to work."

Riley agreed.

"I'll be back as soon as possible," the doctor promised.

"What do you normally do if you have to go out, and you have patients?" Riley asked.

"I don't have many overnighters, and I've been dropping Scarlett off with a retired nurse who helps me," Dr. Anderson said. "If I have a patient I can't move, Mrs. Pascale can be here in six minutes. Her number is listed on the pad too. Medical emergencies do tend to come in the middle of the night. Baby arrivals are prone to early mornings too. It's one of the many quirks of nature. You are in charge."

"That's not real comforting," Riley mumbled to himself as he watched the doctor's headlights disappear.

Noah was sleeping peacefully, so Riley stretched out on the bed he was using and drifted into sleep himself. He woke a few hours later when he felt a tug on his arm. He opened his eyes, and he was facing the little girl, Scarlett. She put a finger to her lips to silence him and then crooked her finger at him to follow her. Riley looked over to his sleeping brother, and he followed the little girl into the private home part of the building and into the kitchen.

"I fixed cereal, but Doctor Anderson says I can't take hot food from the microwave," the little girl complained.

Riley opened the microwave and removed the hot bowl of instant cereal.

"Hello, you must be Scarlett. I'm..."

"I know who you are," Scarlett interrupted.

"You do?" Riley questioned, expecting to be recognized for the first time.

"Uh-huh," the little girl nodded. "You're Mr. McKenna's nephew. Jefferson Ironheart says you are going to train the black horse. Everybody knows about you. Do you have special magical powers like Harry Potter?"

"No, I don't have any special powers at all," Riley denied as he searched the kitchen cabinets for coffee. He assembled an old percolator and measured several spoons of ground coffee. He found a loaf of bread and dropped a couple slices into the toaster.

"Hey," Noah said, wandering into the kitchen, looking sleep tousled and tired.

"Scarlett, this is my brother, Noah," Riley said.

The little girl and the teenager looked at each other, and she returned to eating her breakfast.

"What is dying?" Noah asked, turning around as the old percolator emitted a low moaning sound.

Scarlett giggled, and Riley motioned towards the coffee pot. "I hope it doesn't die before it finishes perking."

"Me too," Noah agreed, and he shook his head when his brother offered him a piece of toast.

"Are you okay?" Riley asked. It wasn't in his brother's character to turn down food at any time.

"I'm okay," Noah said quietly. "My chest is sore, but I'm breathing okay."

Riley poured two mugs of coffee.

"Me too!" Scarlett exclaimed, perched on the edge of her chair.

"Aren't you too young to be drinking coffee?" Riley objected.

"He got some!" the young girl exclaimed, looking at Noah with reproachful eyes.

Noah raised his eyes from his concentrated stare into the dark liquid and blinked.

"So he did," Riley agreed with a chuckle and a smile when his younger brother glared at him.

"Does your mother let you drink coffee?" Riley asked.

"Sometimes," Scarlett said.

"How about a very light coffee with milk?" Riley bargained.

She nodded her head happily. "That's how my mommy fixes it!"

Riley fixed a cup of very milky coffee for her and smiled with amusement as she slurped the coffee happily.

"You look a little rough this morning. Are you sure you're okay?" Riley asked of his brother.

"Yeah," Noah nodded. "Where's the doctor?"

"He left around three-thirty this morning to deliver a baby."

"Marty Lynn's having a baby," Scarlett informed them with little girl superiority of knowing something her companions didn't know.

"Speak of the devil," Riley said, looking through the window. Dr. Andrews was parking his van.

"Good morning," Dr. Andrews exclaimed as he entered his kitchen. "Ahh, the nectar of Gods," he exclaimed, heading for the coffee pot.

"Did Marty Lynn have a boy or a girl baby?" Scarlett asked.

"Little *who's it*, decided against making an appearance today, and neither Marty Lynn nor her husband wanted to know in advance," the doctor answered. He took a long drink of strong, black, caffeine-laden liquid. "I'll be going over there again in another couple of days. Noah, how are you feeling this morning?"

"A little sore but okay," Noah answered.

"Good, let me take a quick look at you. Then I'm going to try to catch a couple hours of sleep before Frank gets here." He kissed Scarlett on top of her head. "You behave yourself," he said. "Finish your breakfast, get dressed, and call Momma. If the oxygen tank comes in today, you get to go home."

Riley watched the easy way the doctor had with his young patient. The little girl obediently finished her breakfast and left the kitchen presumably to get dressed for the day. The doctor took Noah into his examining room.

He cleared the few dishes they had used and waited for his brother. Scarlett returned to the kitchen wearing a pair of pink overalls. She marched herself over in front of Riley and turned her back to him.

Riley grinned. He knew this routine well from having

younger sisters and nieces. He crisscrossed the two straps, spun her around, and buckled them in the front.

"Thank you," Scarlett said primly.

"You are very welcome."

Noah entered the kitchen a few minutes later with a frown on his face and holding a piece of cotton to his arm where he had been given an injection. Dr. Andrews followed him a few seconds later. Scarlett climbed into a chair, and he listened to her front and back with his stethoscope.

"You are doing fine, darling," Dr. Andrews said, turning to Riley. "So is Noah. He should take it easy for a few days, light-work duty. I'm going to catch a couple of hours of sleep. Keep an eye on things for me until Frank gets here."

For a seven-year-old, Scarlett was very good at gin rummy. Frank arrived twenty-seven games later. He delivered a package to Dr. Andrews, who opened and inspected the tank with great interest. While he was doing that, Riley asked the doctor what he thought of adding an oxygen tank to his emergency kit. The doctor was glad to know there was someone in the area with EMT training. He cautioned Riley about using his training unless he was certified in the state where he was living.

Marissa became Noah's champion at home, making sure he didn't attempt any tasks she thought were too strenuous. She had begun to trust the McKenna men.

Although they believed her story, Uncle Frank was still cautious. He would not endanger his nephews or his future program for disadvantaged children by harboring a criminal. Frank believed in offering a helping hand when needed. He just wanted to be sure his fingers weren't chewed off in the process.

Neither Riley nor Marissa told Frank she was in contact with her children. Comforted by knowing her children were safe, Marissa blossomed into a different person. She had a quick wit and was smiling more, but she was still skittish, and there was often a haunted look in her eyes.

Riley was sympathetic to her situation. He couldn't imagine the desperation it must have taken to force a mother to kidnap and hide her children. He did understand having children had very little to do with actually having the skills to raise them. The problem remained that they only had Marissa's side of the story. There was always more than one side in every situation.

Chapter 8

R iley had contacted his friend Shawn, and Frank had decided it was time to get John Henry involved. Marissa had been terrified at first, and John Henry hadn't been real happy about his friend keeping her a secret. Still, after hearing her story, he agreed to help and promised he would contact friends he could trust in law enforcement to follow-up on her claims.

Dry Rock Boy's Ranch was operated as a foster care center for reservation children, and when needed, for the County. It had, over the years, provided a safety net for many children. Frank and Katherine McKenna had given their time and lives to caring for children in need of a second chance. When Frank needed his friend's help, John Henry didn't hesitate.

Marissa began to take over tasks the male inhabitants of the house appreciated. One day she thoroughly cleaned the kitchen removing all traces of stacked and dirty dishes and cluttered countertops.

Riley poked his head inside the den. His uncle looked up.

"Have you seen Noah?"

"I think he went to the barn. He's getting testy about us

asking him if he's okay," Frank said. As his nephew turned to leave, he called him back. "Riley, do you know anything about computer programs."

Riley walked around his uncle's desk and looked over his shoulder. "That's a fairly standard finance and accounting program."

"It is, but for the life of me, I can't get the knack of it," Frank complained.

"I could do this in a couple of hours," Riley said. "Or, I can let Noah take a crack at it. He's got a good head for numbers and computers."

"Aren't you the genius in mathematics?" Frank questioned. "Your dad bragged about you boys finishing college like you promised. What did you get all those degrees in?"

"Music, business, mathematics, chemistry, and physics," Riley admitted. "The last three were interesting, but I knew I'd never make a lifetime pursuit of them. Noah can have this figured out in a couple of hours. He's on light duty for the rest of the week, and it will give him something to do."

"If he's willing, I'll get him to help me," Frank agreed.

"I'm going to find him now," Riley said. He left the house, making a leap from the porch and listening to the squeak and bang of the screen door behind him. They were comforting sounds the same as at his grandfather's farm when he'd been a kid. They'd lost Grandpa three years earlier.

There was a full moon in the sky. The large orange globe provided light on the desert landscape. There was a peacefulness to the desert, and it was growing on him.

The barn door was open, and Riley could hear someone talking in a low voice. He continued inside to investigate. He found Noah standing almost where he had been hurt. The gate had been reinforced with double planks.

His brother turned around slightly when he heard footsteps. He waved a large carrot in his hand. "I thought I'd try to make friends with him," he explained.

"Keep your fingers clear. John Henry said when a horse bites it's a one-way motion. It can't stop midway, so anything in its path is going to be chomped on."

The black horse snorted and shook its head back and forth.

Noah smiled. "He disagrees. I was talking real quietly like you do with him. He's been calm."

"How are you?" Riley asked.

"I'm okay," Noah shrugged.

"I don't think so," Riley countered. "You've barely spoken all day. Are you in pain?"

Noah shook his head.

"Sad? Tired?" Riley tossed out adjectives hoping he would get a reaction. "Depressed, Pissed off?"

Noah kept shaking his head.

"Homesick?" Riley guessed.

His brother looked away.

Bingo! Riley knew he had hit the bullseye.

"It's okay to be homesick, Noah," Riley said. "It's tough to be away from home. It takes a while to adjust, even as an adult and you move away from the family. I think this is the first time Mom and Dad have had a vacation by themselves since they started having kids, thirty-some years ago. I hope it's been good for them. They deserve it."

"I'll bet Dad doesn't miss me," Noah said.

"I would bet the opposite," Riley disagreed.

Noah shook his head and looked away.

"Well, little brother, you have been handed a 'Get out of Jail' card. It's your choice to use it or not."

Noah looked up at his brother with a puzzled look. "What are you talking about?"

Riley reached over slowly and scratched the stallion's ears.

"One call to Mom, and you would be on the next plane to meet them where ever their ship docks. If Mom finds out you were hurt, she might even cancel the vacation. You know she goes berserk if one of her kids is sick or injured."

Noah's eyebrows scrunched together as he considered the idea. "What about you? You made an agreement to let me stay with you for the summer."

Riley appraised his younger sibling. "That was a different kind of vacation planned, but circumstances change things. If you want to go home, it will be your decision. I'm not part of it."

"You could go anywhere and do anything you want. Why would you want to stay here?" Noah demanded.

"Because I made a commitment to Uncle Frank, and now I have promised to help Marissa. I also have an obligation to John Henry and Jefferson Ironheart to help them train this guy, even though I don't know what the hell I'm doing! Being here for the summer isn't what I planned originally. However, I'm not leaving until I'm not needed anymore. When a man gives his word, he has to live by it."

"I thought you came here so I wouldn't have to come alone," Noah said.

"Originally, I did, but now there is more to it," Riley admitted. "Dad went a little off the deep end with you getting into trouble, but he's the parent. They're allowed. We have to consider what he's been through for the last couple of years. Mom wasn't alone in her fight against cancer. Dad was with her every step of the way. He needed a break as much as Mom did."

"Mom came a lot closer to dying than they let on to us, didn't she?" Noah asked.

Riley shrugged, unwilling to admit to what he knew was true. "Maybe. I wasn't in on the discussions they had with the second-set because I don't live at home. They probably did keep the worst of it from the younger kids. Parents are weird that way. They don't want to scare their kids."

"Dad has backed off on letting me take gigs this last year. He said he didn't have the time, and it was more important for me to focus on school. It was more about him not having time because he needed to help mom."

Riley nodded. "A career is important, but family is more important. Don't ever forget it."

The two sat quietly for a few minutes, each of them considering what he'd said.

Riley broke the silence. "So, are you going to make the call?"

Noah shook his head. "No, it wouldn't be right. If I went home, you would be working off my punishment."

Riley threw his arm around his younger brother in a half hug. "Good choice, kiddo. Although..."

"What?" Noah demanded.

"I think you need to call Dad–transatlantic. I think you need to talk to him, and I think you need to continue talking to him until he is your *best bud* again. Look around at the fathers of your friends, Noah. We are fortunate. Our dad is a standup guy, and he's there when we need him. He's there when anyone needs him. You and Dad have always been tight. You've kind of been a replacement for us first-set guys as we grew up to be adults. Don't let this little rift mess up things between you."

"I'm still mad at him," Noah admitted.

"That's okay. Dad is probably still mad at you. There have been times when I have been scared, hurt, and angry, but Dad will listen if you keep talking. Talking, not arguing. Remember, in the long run, he believes he is doing what is best for you. His and Mom's goals have been to raise us to be good people. If they piss us off in the process, they're not going to worry too much about it. They know we have to go home to face them eventually. When they call for an *all-hands-on-deck meeting*, your ass better be there!"

Noah cracked a grin and laughed. "Okay, I'll make the call, but it's probably going to cost a fortune on Uncle Frank's landline." He turned, pulled a large carrot from his pocket, and handed it to his brother.

"Noah?" Riley said, and Noah nodded.

"I know, I'll keep my mouth shut about the horse," he said.

Riley nodded and laughed. "That too, I don't need Mom going off the deep end either. I wanted to remind you not to mention Marissa."

Noah nodded as he left the barn.

Riley turned back to the black horse and offered him the carrot.

"You're very good with kids, very patient," Marissa said as she stepped from the shadows of the barn's darkness.

Riley turned to face her. "Noah is usually a good kid. In some ways, he's too smart for his own good, and in other ways, he overcompensates because he wants to be *one of the guys*. It gets him in trouble."

Marissa took the carrot from his hand and approached the stall, but the stallion snorted and backed away.

"Be careful around him," Riley warned.

"I know. I've overheard Frank and John Henry warning both you and Noah about a thousand times. Is it true you don't know how to ride?"

"It was. I've been getting a crash course for the last couple of days. I'm walking bow-legged for a reason. How about you? Can you ride?"

"I haven't in a very long time. I used to love it. I had a pony when I was a little girl for a while," Marissa said. "We lived on what they called a ranchette. There was enough land to keep a pony or a horse. My parents' first separation was when I was ten. It broke my heart when my mother sold my pony. His name was Rowdy."

"This guy is rowdy," Riley said.

"According to what I keep hearing, he's dangerous."

"I've heard the same, but he likes me," Riley said, stepping to the gate and offering the carrot, which was taken from his hand. "This big guy needs a name."

"He has a name," Marissa said. "Kingston Destiny."

Riley looked at her. "For a woman who has been in hiding, you are full of information."

"I've been eavesdropping," she admitted. "I was scared you were going to turn me in."

"We gave our word. We wouldn't do that," Riley said.

"Men have given me their word before, and it wasn't worth the breath it took to lie," she said.

"That's a shame you've only known untrustworthy men," Riley said. "You can trust us."

"He trusts you," Marissa said, nodding toward the horse. "Experts say animals have built-in intuitiveness. Maybe he's your destiny."

Riley shook his head. "Music has been my destiny since I plucked the strings of my first guitar when I was a child."

"You want to be a singer or a musician?" Marissa asked.

Riley smiled at her words. She didn't recognize him, and it was a treat. "Something like that."

"Did you go to college?" she asked.

Riley gave her a startled look. "How old do you think I am?"

She shrugged. "I don't know, twenty-one, twenty-two?"

"Try twenty-seven," Riley growled. "And, yes, I have finished college."

"Sorry," Marissa said. "You look younger."

Riley frowned and shrugged. "How old are you?"

"That's a fair question since I brought it up," Marissa said. "I'm twenty-five, although there are times I feel a lot older."

"I know that feeling," Riley said. "By now, I should know what I want to do with the rest of my life, but I don't."

"Why not?"

"I don't know that either," Riley admitted. "I've succeeded at most things I've tried, but I've never been motivated enough to make them a life goal. Sometimes I feel my future is right in front of me, yet it's shrouded in fog, and I can't quite reach it."

Marissa nodded. "For me, the last years have been about survival. I know one thing that seems beyond you."

"What?"

"You don't clean your messes," she teased.

Riley gave her a wry smile. "Maybe, I'm a sexist. Cleaning and cooking is women's work."

"Ha!" Marissa exclaimed. "If that's true, go shoot something for dinner!"

"Well, I would," Riley said, agreeably with a grin. "Except, I've never been hunting, either! Whatever is in the freezer will have to do."

Noah, Riley, and Frank, one behind the other, came to a sudden and abrupt stop and jammed into one another as Noah made a sudden stop while entering the kitchen.

"Jeez, Noah!" Riley complained, rubbing his chin. He'd slammed into the back of his brother's head. He saw Noah sniff the air like an alert hound dog, and he inhaled the wonderful smell himself.

Noah looked over his shoulder to Riley with a look of surprise and delight, and Riley grinned.

Now Frank was sniffing the air, and he too looked intrigued.

"Apple Pie?" Noah guessed.

"Peach," Frank and Riley declared at the same time.

"Neither," Marissa said, standing by an open oven door. "Peach cobbler."

"Oh, wow," Noah exclaimed. He entered the kitchen and got a full view of dinner, ready to be set on the table. A platter of fried chicken, another of corn on the cob, a large bowl of mashed potatoes, and Marissa took hot biscuits from the oven, along with the peach cobbler.

"I hope you don't mind?" Marissa said to Frank. "I was tired of beef and beans."

"You are not the only one," Riley exclaimed. "I didn't even know that stuff was in the refrigerator."

"It was all there and in the freezer," Marissa said. "It was amazing what I found, although the refrigerator should have been declared a hazardous waste accident."

Frank laughed. "Boys, let's get washed for dinner. Marissa, you have my heartfelt thanks. Everything smells terrific."

"Except the lima beans," Noah exclaimed, peering into a pot still on the stove. "I can definitely live without lima beans."

"Today, you'll like them, and keep your trap shut," Riley growled, shoving his brother toward the hallway. "Thank you, Marissa."

"You are welcome," she said with a laugh and a blush. "Noah, you can skip the lima beans."

"You have my eternal gratitude," Noah exclaimed with a bowing gesture as Riley shoved him down the hall toward the bathroom.

Marissa had finished setting the food on the table when the McKennas trooped into the kitchen. The hats were gone, hair was combed, and hands were clean. Noah grabbed a chicken leg and took a bite before he heard his uncle clear his throat in disapproval.

"Sorry," Noah mumbled, and he laid the chicken leg on his plate.

"Someone's coming," Marissa exclaimed. She looked scared and ready to flee into the bedroom.

Riley stood and looked through the door window. "It's only John Henry," he said, laying a reassuring hand on the woman's shoulder. John Henry's uniform had terrified Marissa at her first meeting. She was still a bit suspicious of his offer of help. The Chief Deputy was quietly asking his friends in law enforcement to look into the records. He called it putting out *feelers*.

"He has a kid with him," Riley said.

John Henry entered the kitchen with a young boy of about twelve in tow. With a firm grip on the boy's shoulder, he propelled the boy ahead of him. Dark-skinned with eyes and hair as black as pitch, the boy had native Quechan features. He was short and stocky and had a fierce, angry scowl on his face.

John Henry removed his hat and yanked the baseball cap from the scowling boy's head, only to have the boy snatch it back and slap it on his head again.

"Sorry, I didn't mean to interrupt your dinner," John Henry said, looking longingly at the food.

Marissa took two more plates from the cabinet, added dinnerware, and motioned for them to have a seat. "Gentlemen, do not wear hats at the table," she said pointedly to the boy.

The boy glared at her as the chicken platter was passed around the table and passed over him. He removed his hat and stuffed it under his leg.

"Thank you," Marissa said. She caught the boy's eyes, and she slid several pieces of fried chicken on his plate.

The boy waited anxiously until it looked like everyone had a full plate. He grabbed a piece of chicken and bit into it, only to realize everyone was silent with bowed heads. He laid the chicken on his plate quietly and bowed his head too. He didn't shut his eyes. Instead, he looked around the table, and he saw the older kid at the table was watching him.

Marissa thought she had fried enough chicken to allow for leftovers for lunch the next day. She hadn't counted on three starving men and two boys who had bottomless pits for stomachs. Watching them devour the massive amounts of food was a pleasant experience. Even though she had fixed simple fare, they were loud in their praise and enjoyment.

She hadn't enjoyed cooking in the past. There were so many things she wanted to forget. No matter how hard she had tried to prepare the tedious gourmet meals her ex-husband preferred, he had never praised her efforts. He considered the complicated dishes his due and her stupid for not matching a professional chef's efforts.

"Earth to Marissa," Riley said with a teasing chuckle.

Marissa snapped her memories closed and smiled stiffly. "Sorry."

"No problem," Noah exclaimed. "Where did you hide the peach cobbler?"

"You can't possibly have room for dessert," Marissa exclaimed.

Noah laughed. "Sure, I do, right here," he pointed at his stomach. "I left enough space."

She shook her head and laughed. "I'll clean up the kitchen, and make fresh pot of coffee. We can have the cobbler in the living room," she suggested.

"Better yet," Frank said. "Marissa cooked, so why don't you guys do the cleanup? She deserves a break."

"Hey, kid, you can help too!" Noah exclaimed, talking to the smaller boy.

"Washing dishes is woman's work," the boy snorted.

"If you want peach cobbler, you better volunteer," John

Henry advised the boy with a stern warning. He looked at Riley. "Keep an eye on him so he doesn't escape. By the way, his name is Blue Eagle."

"Cool name," Noah said, tossing a dishtowel at the boy.

The boy glared at him.

Riley gave Marissa a gentle push toward the living room. "We can handle this. I'm not a sexist, and I'll make the coffee. We like it strong."

Marissa followed the men into the living room and listened to their conversation.

"Frank, if you don't take Blue, he'll be sent to the juvenile center over in Yuma. He has been in minor trouble before, but because it's been on the reservation, I've been able to smooth things over."

"And, now?" Frank questioned.

"He stole Joe Rickman's truck and went joyriding."

"What is he, ten or eleven?" Frank questioned.

"I know," John Henry chuckled. "He's twelve, but he's small for his age. Part of that might be a lack of good nutrition. I've calmed Joe down, but he wants the damages paid. He doesn't want to turn a claim into his insurance company. I've got enough discretionary funds to pay for the damages, but the kid is in a tough spot.

"Elaine Eagle returned to the reservation only nine months ago. I checked her into a rehab program for a reoccurring alcohol problem. His two sisters are with his aunt, but she claims she can't handle Blue. My choices are to find him a guardian on the reservation, which is unlikely, or I bring him here. I figure we can put his butt to work to pay back what he cost John, and we try to turn him around at the same time."

"Where's the father?" Frank asked.

"George Eagle has been in the federal system since Blue was seven, and he won't be up for parole for another twelve years. All Blue knows is his father went to prison, and everyone keeps telling him he is just like his father. We need to make him realize that's not true, and he doesn't have to end up in the system," John Henry said.

Frank nodded his head in understanding. "You know, my certification won't be renewed until the addition is finished. He can stay, but it has to be unofficial, as far as the state foster care system is concerned."

"More than half of what we do on the reservation defies regulations and rules," John Henry admitted with a rare grin. "Child welfare can't touch us unless they go through the Tribal Council, and they won't. I'll get his aunt's written permission for him to stay here. She'll agree. She wants to help Blue, but she's got her hands full. She has four children of her own and now his two little sisters, ages six and eight."

The two men shook hands, and the boy's temporary residence was a done deal.

Riley popped his head into the living room. "The coffee's done, and Noah sniffed out the missing peach cobbler. If you want some, you are going to have to move fast!"

The delicious dessert was appreciated and complimented, even more than the home-cooked meal Marissa had prepared. They spent an entertaining evening sitting around enjoying coffee, dessert, and good company.

When it was time for John Henry to leave, he cornered Marissa privately. "I have a few friends looking into your husband's dealings."

"Ex-husband," Marissa insisted.

"Ex," John Henry corrected himself. "My friends aren't finished, but they agree there appears to be shady things going on. Thing's people don't want to talk about. When I have concrete evidence, I'll tell you."

Marissa nodded her head. No one had ever caught onto Gregg's shady dealings. She had very little faith anyone would catch him now.

Chapter 9

Frank bedded Blue down in the living room on a mattress on the floor. He was sleeping on the couch to give Marissa the privacy a woman needed in a house full of men and boys. Frank could also keep an eye on the boy and make sure he didn't try to run away. After fifteen years of running a foster care house, he'd learned to be a light sleeper.

The next day, Frank had Riley and Noah stack their bunk beds and assemble another single bed. Frank had a dozen or more stackable bunks stored in the loft over the barn. He'd bought them at a surplus sale and was awaiting the addition to his house to be finished. Now he had even more reason to complete building the dormitory bedrooms. There would be eight new rooms when they were finished with the addition. Plus, the room the boys were sleeping in and his bedroom occupied by Marissa.

After a couple of days, Riley decided a grown man sharing a room with two boys wasn't ideal. He moved into a roughed-in room of the dormitory. The rooms weren't large, but they were big enough to house two single beds, two dressers, and two small desks. The proposed layout was similar to most college dorm rooms, not that he'd ever lived in one. He let Noah and Blue argue over the space in the room he'd left.

Riley had chosen the unfinished room deliberately. If he left the door open to the hallway, he wasn't far from Marissa's room. He was a light sleeper, and if she was having nightmares, he could talk her through the haunting memories. If it was a terrible night, he would sleep in the chair in her room.

Frank had thought there was hanky-panky going on at first until he realized his nephew was only offering her sanctuary from her demons.

Blue was a bad-tempered boy. He was puny for his age, resented it, and had a surly personality. Riley and Noah looked to their uncle to gauge his reactions to Blue's behavior.

Frank pretty much ignored the boy's inappropriate responses and simply acted as if the boy's sharp tongue didn't exist. They followed his lead, not allowing themselves to be drawn into arguments. Frank added Blue to the chore list. If you live on the ranch, you did chores.

Blue was influenced the most by Marissa. She didn't scold or snap at him when he misbehaved. She simply gave him *the look*. The boy would respond with temper and then with embarrassment. Blue was shamed from his swearing and misbehaving without a harsh word spoken. Riley and Noah were both amused. Having been raised by a loving but strict mother, they knew *the look*, and they didn't want it turned on them.

Blue had only been at the ranch a few days when Noah noticed the boy had a habit of stealing and hiding food. He found a stash of half-eaten sandwiches hidden in a dresser drawer in the bedroom. The meat was beginning to spoil and smell. Noah spoke to his uncle about it, and Frank wasn't surprised.

Frank explained underprivileged children often lived in fear of hunger. They didn't want Blue to get sick from eating old food. They also didn't want to attract bugs or mice into the house.

Marissa solved the problem. She asked John Henry to go by the convenience store and purchase individually wrapped snacks of cakes, crackers, and chips. She sat Blue down and explained she didn't want him to get sick eating spoiled food. She told him he could keep wrapped food that wasn't perishable.

One evening Marissa filled a basket with the individually wrapped snacks and set it on the table by the hallway. As the boys filed by the basket, she asked if they would like a snack to take with them. She also reminded the boys to remember to brush their teeth after eating.

Blue looked skeptical, but Noah helped himself to several of the packages. Once inside their room, Noah tossed them to Blue without comment.

As they thought he would, the boy hid them in his dresser drawer. Blue rarely ate the snacks, but he stored them religiously.

At the end of the week, Marissa casually offered him a plastic box with a lid. The boy looked shocked. "You ain't gonna take it back?" he demanded.

"Blue," Marissa said patiently. "When food is given to you, it's yours. We gave it to you, and you can eat it, save it or give it away. We won't take it away from you unless it is harmful. As I've explained before, we don't want bugs or mice to get into it, and that's why I'm giving you the plastic box. Maybe when you visit your sisters and cousins, you can take them a treat."

Blue didn't say anything, but he seemed less belligerent. He didn't stop stockpiling until the box was full.

Every morning Jefferson Ironheart came to work with Riley and the stallion. Marissa stayed in the bedroom until he left. She was getting used to John Henry being around in and out of uniform. She still doubted he would take her word over her ex-husband's. When anyone else came to the ranch, she hid in the bedroom.

Marissa climbed onto the corral fence's top rail and leaned over with her elbows on her knees to watch Riley.

He led Kingston around the corral with a rope loosely draped under his belly. As he walked the animal, he kept his head close to the horse's ear, speaking softly, gently encouraging the horse to accept the rope. Kingston pranced and shied, but he didn't rear.

Riley caught sight of Marissa, and he led the stallion over to the fence.

"Kingston, be nice to the lady," Riley said softly. "If he's in a good mood, he might let you pet him. Move slowly. He gets spooked easily."

Marissa looked skeptical. "What happens if he is in a bad mood?" she asked.

Riley smiled. "I've been told he bites."

Marissa chose to keep her hands to herself. "He's beautiful."

Riley looked at the woman. "So are you. The bruises are fading."

Marissa looked away for a second and jumped to the ground. "I think it's time for me to leave."

Riley was startled by her words, and with a quick release of the rope, he turned the horse loose and followed her. Marissa was heading to the house at a fast walk.

"Marissa, wait," Riley shouted as he ran to catch up. "I didn't mean to hurt your feelings."

She shook her head. "You didn't, honestly. I really do need

to move on. I'm taking advantage of everyone's generosity as it is, and my problems aren't your problems."

"You are not taking advantage of anyone, and we want to help with your problems," Riley disagreed. He looked over and saw Noah and Blue were watching them. He took her hand and redirected her to the barn. "You're doing more than your share around here. If you leave, we will be eating mystery meat and beans three times a day. You wouldn't want to make Noah, Blue, and me, suffer, would you?"

Marissa laughed. "You want to keep me here for my cooking skills?"

"Absolutely," Riley exclaimed. "You have no idea how bad it was before you arrived. You don't need to run, Marissa. You'll get an argument from all of us if you try to leave. We want you to stay. You should be relaxing and healing."

"I have," Marissa said wryly. "The bruises are fading. I should be able to travel without drawing too much attention to myself."

"And, what?" he asked. "Take your kids, and run again? That's no way to live."

"My kids are all I have," Marissa said.

"That's not true. You have good friends who are willing to help you. Whoever is taking care of your boys is a trusted friend, and so are we. Your boys deserve a decent life, not one of always looking over their shoulder.

"You have to wait until my friend Shawn or John Henry discover what is going on with your ex-husband. Shawn has already hinted that the more he digs, the more he's finding. His investigation has already warranted both the FBI and the DEA opening an investigation. I'm not sure exactly what that means, but those agencies don't get involved when a person is squeaky clean.

"On a personal basis, I would miss you like crazy."

Marissa looked at him with surprise. "Are you flirting with me?"

"Why wouldn't I?" Riley asked. "You are a beautiful woman, and you are as sexy as hell. You've kept me awake for a couple of nights thinking about you."

"You're kidding!" Marissa exclaimed.

"I never tease a beautiful woman," Riley said, and he lowered his head and kissed her. One kiss led to another. He pulled her against him and took in the taste and the scent of her. When he stepped away, she looked surprised.

"I never kid when I'm interested in a beautiful woman," Riley whispered in her ear again.

Marissa sat stiff, angry, and scared beside Riley in his truck. She was dressed in the best fitting of the thrift store jeans and a loose Boho style blouse. She was wearing flip-flops for shoes, and they were the reason why she was leaving the ranch. Her right foot was bruised, and her toes were purple because she'd been stepped on by a horse. She'd been taken to Dr. Anderson's clinic the previous day and x-rayed. There weren't any broken bones, but the injury had started a loud argument. One she had lost and it had cost her several hard whacks across her bottom.

Riley had insisted she could not keep walking around in flip-flops and sandals. She was living on a ranch. She was around animals, and there was always the danger of snakes, scorpions, and spiders in the desert. She needed boots, and Riley had laid down the law. Either she accept the offer of footwear, or she was restricted to the house.

She couldn't do that, and he knew it. She had to walk to higher ground to get better reception on the cell phone to stay in contact with her boys.

Her defeat in the argument was why she was wearing a pair of borrowed sunglasses as she sat beside Riley, and he drove to Yuma. It was a long trip, and Yuma wasn't a huge city. It did boast of three Walmarts. One of them was their destination.

Riley could see Marissa was terrified. He took her hand and squeezed it. "Take a deep breath," he said. "The chances of anyone recognizing you are probably several million to one. You can do this."

Marissa nodded as Riley grabbed a shopping cart and steered it toward the women's clothing section.

"We came for boots," she said.

"While we're here, we're going to get anything else you need," he said firmly. He pulled a piece of paper from his pocket. "Plus, we have a list we have to fill, and we'll get as much of it here as possible. Didn't you see the coolers in the truck? We'll stop at a grocery store on the way out of town."

"I can't pay you back!"

"I haven't asked you to," Riley said in her ear. "If you want another argument, I can give you one, loud and clear. I'm beginning to think a trip over my knee would be a quicker solution all the way around."

Marissa wheeled around to face him, but he only lifted an eyebrow. He was holding a coral-colored tee shirt in front of her.

"Do you like this?"

She took a deep breath. "Yes, I think it's cute."

"What size?"

"I think they might shrink, so get a medium."

"Good, check off shirts," Riley said as he proceeded to drop one of every color in the cart, except black and gray. That was how the shopping proceeded. Only when they got to the underwear department did he bail on her.

Surrounded by bras and panties, Riley pointed to the next

aisle over. "I'll be standing over there, in the men's department. Get whatever you want or need." He took two steps but turned around and pointed to a display. "Those look, umm... interesting."

Marissa smiled for the first time as she looked at the skimpy lace items. It was the first time she'd looked comfortable since they'd left the safety of his truck.

They cruised through the departments quickly, boots, sneakers, sandals, cosmetics, and toiletries, even the book department. The books were beside the music CDs, and Marissa stopped, turned, and gave Riley a look of astonishment.

"What?"

She snatched a CD from the rack. "Oh, my God!" she hissed.

"Crap!" Riley swore. "Put that back, and let's get checked out."

Marissa wasn't the only one to recognize Riley. The clerk looked at him in surprise, but he laid his finger to his lips in a motion for silence and shook his head.

"I know I look like him, but I'm not," Riley said firmly.

They checked out and filled the backseat of his truck with bags of merchandise.

"You're a celebrity, and you lied to her," Marissa said as they left the parking lot.

"Sometimes it works, sometimes it doesn't," Riley said.

"You're famous! How could I have missed it? You're Coyote McKenna! I remember you from when you were making music with your brothers."

"Coyote was a cute, talented kid," Riley said. "It's taken me several years to drop the nickname and the notoriety of being tagged as the wild child. I'm glad you didn't know. It's been nice not being a celebrity for a while."

"What's it like to be famous?"

"Like any other life, I guess. There are good parts to it and bad parts to it," Riley answered honestly. "My brothers and I were lucky. Our dad was already in the business. He was able to guide us around a lot of stuff that could have derailed us. Not that I think any of us were inclined toward those things because we weren't. Our parents are deeply religious and right and wrong was instilled in us at very young ages. They were and still are strict parents most of the time. We were the first-set, so I think they were a little tougher on us."

"First-set, second-set," Marissa said. "I've heard you and Noah calling yourselves that."

Riley shrugged. "First-set was Micah, Sully, and me. Three boys, all interested and talented in music. Our parents were vital to our success. We were still charting top-ten when the second-set arrived. The second-set is Allison and Macy, twins, and Noah and Lily. A distant cousin on my mother's side died, and their father was going to parcel them out among his family members. He wasn't exactly Father of the Year material. He was already an estranged parent, and he didn't want the responsibility. My parents stepped in to adopt and keep them together. After the adoption, their father disappeared. No one heard from him for about three years, and then we were notified that he died from an overdose of drugs.

"The second-set are great kids. Macy and my mom had some issues for a while, but those were finally straightened out. Macy is a First Position Ballerina in London, and I think that was her goal from her very first ballet lesson. Baby sister Lily is following in her footsteps.

"Noah has become a phenomenal drummer. He's been playing professionally since he was fifteen. He takes on gigs when a band needs a replacement or a back-up."

"And, Allison has problems," Marissa said. "I think I read something about her in one of those awful celebrity magazines while waiting for a dentist appointment.

Riley nodded. "Yeah, and we still haven't figured out why. She's always been jealous of her twin Macy, but she's been given every possible advantage and opportunity. She doesn't do anything with them, except drop out and blame everyone around her for the failures." He shook his head, thinking about his sister, and took a deep breath. "I know it's hard when your closest siblings are successful, but it doesn't mean you get to leach off their fame and fortune and pretend to be the neglected one. If anything, more attention was paid to her because of her complaints and issues.

"In Dry Rock, I'm simply one of Frank's nephews, sent to help him, and I like it." He pointed to a fast-food restaurant. "I'm hungry. Do you want to go through the drive-thru and get burgers?"

Marissa agreed. Several miles outside of the city, Riley pulled over to a picnic area. They sat at one of the covered picnic tables and ate.

Marissa didn't say much while they were eating. Their comfortable friendship had been swept away by the single word: celebrity.

He wadded up the wrappers and the cups and chucked them into the trashcan.

"Marissa, can you look at me and see me for me?" Riley asked. "Not the singer/musician, not the celebrity. I'm the same guy that's been sharing a house with you. I'm the guy who yelled at you for walking around in flip-flops and getting stepped on. I'm the guy who has smacked your bottom. Beyond the fame, I'm just a normal guy."

"Why didn't you tell me?" she demanded.

"Because you would have run," Riley said bluntly. "Or you wouldn't have believed we were worried about your safety. We care about you, Marissa. I don't know why you can't accept the idea that we are trying to help."

"You have helped," Marissa said. "You took me in, and

you believed me. It has meant the world to me. No one believed me before, not social services, not the judges, not the courts. You gave me a phone. Letting me hear my sons' voices has meant everything to me! But, Riley, if you get caught in my nightmare, my ex-husband will destroy you!"

"He can try," Riley said, sounding unconcerned. "I believe you, Marissa, and I'll fight for you! I believe Frank and John Henry will do the same. There's an old saying, *Hell hath no fury.* It usually pertains to a scorned woman. However, messing with a McKenna and those under the umbrella of our friendship and family has the same response. We may seem mild-tempered, but there can be serious consequences if someone tries to screw with our friends and loved ones."

"You can't mean that!" she exclaimed.

Riley growled. "I do. Loyalty was bred into my family from strong pioneer stock. Sometimes I think one of the worst parts of being a celebrity is that people believe you are different. I'm not different! What I do for a living doesn't make me less of a caring human being. I still want the same things most people want. I want the people around me to love and care about me as much as I care about them. You should want that too!

"The reality is, it takes a hell of a lot of hard work and luck to be successful, and it never ends. The entertainment industry is probably one of the most cutthroat businesses out there. Everyone wants a piece of you.

"As a performer, you have to stay on top of every detail and make sure everything gets done the way you want it done. I've recently finished a seven-month tour, and believe me, it's no picnic. I love performing, that's the fun part, but the rest is exhausting. After a while, you have no concept of time or distance, even night and day. Everyone expects us to be on top of our game when all we want is a little time to stop pretending and be ourselves. Working on Frank's ranch has been an oasis of calm, and I needed it."

"It doesn't sound like much fun," Marissa exclaimed.

"It isn't all bad, and I've given it one last shot, and I'm done with it. I'm at a crossroads, again," Riley admitted.

"What do you mean?"

Riley leaned forward on his elbows on the picnic table. "What it means is I've denied who I am and what I want for a long time."

"You're gay?" she asked.

Riley shook his head. "I kissed you! Didn't it feel like I was enjoying it?"

"Yes, but you could be bi-sexual," she said.

Riley shook his head. "People really need to stop obsessing over other people's sexuality. I'm not gay or bi-. My preference is a one hundred percent straight woman.

"What I mean is I've denied what I want to do with my life. You asked me if I finished college. I've been going to college since I was fourteen. I have bachelor degrees in music, business, and mathematics. I have a Ph.D. in Physics."

Marissa blinked in surprise. "Are you a genius?"

"Technically, by IQ, I am, although most of the time I walk around feeling like a dumb shit," Riley said. "In reality, the music and business degrees are valid. I use those every day. The rest were simply marking time while trying to decide what I wanted to do with my life. I thought I was heading in the right direction, but then I chickened out and hit the road as a single."

"I don't understand," she said.

"Neither do I," Riley admitted, and he sounded frustrated. "I have one more degree. It's the only one with any true meaning, but I've been too much of a coward to admit it."

Marissa simply waited for him to continue.

"I have a Masters in Theology."

"You're a minister?"

Riley shook his head. "I have the degrees to apply to be one. What I want to do is help people."

"Would you abandon your music?"

"Not necessary," he said. "I've always considered myself more of a writer and composer than a performer. I've been playing and performing music since I was a child. I've also never felt it was the right path, and the last couple of years have proven that I should have trusted my instincts.

"Becoming a minister isn't necessarily the end-all of a theology degree. I don't think I could be a person who preaches to others. Who am I, to be the broker of right and wrong? I've considered missionary work and other organizations and foundations dedicated to helping people. I feel the need to help, but I haven't been able to commit to how. I am committed to helping you in whatever way you need."

"Riley, I really do like you," Marissa exclaimed. "If my problems were different, we might have had a chance to develop a relationship, but I don't dare. You don't know what Gregg Novak is capable of doing. I know of at least three men serving life sentences, and my ex-husband knew they weren't guilty. I've heard him bragging about charging innocent people and taking them to trial because it would look good on his record if they were convicted. I have tapes of his bragging. I thought I would be able to expose his wrongdoings, but I was stupid and naïve. When I tried to fight him, Gregg took my boys away from me. It took me a while, but I finally realized he had the entire arsenal of corrupt people in his back pocket.

"If he thought I was involved with you or your family. He would destroy you, Frank, and everyone related to you. You don't know what he is capable of doing!"

"Marissa, we took a vote, and we decided to stand by you. I called my parents to make sure they didn't want to yank

Noah out. My dad told me to do what I thought was right. He trusts I'll do what is right, and you need to show a little faith.

"Your ex-husband isn't the only person who wields power. He has used his position and connections to victimize you. We have connections, who have connections, and we don't deal with men who are crooks. We're in a holding pattern right now until all the facts can be pulled together."

"If Gregg finds me, he'll drag everyone through the mud."

"We're not going to let him," Riley promised. "Gregg Novak has no idea who and what is about to fall on him. Not all people use their influence to control and hurt people. There really are people out there that still wear the white hats." He reached across the table and touched one of the fading scars. "For this alone, if it takes every cent I have, I will take him down!"

"We are in a different state from Gregg Novak. He's not going to get a heads-up on the investigations until it's too late. We also have the added protection of living on a native reservation. The state police can't interfere with reservation law unless the Governor of Arizona intervenes. We know the Governor. Marissa, you are safe with us, and I'm falling in love with you. The only question I have is will you consider a guy like me?"

"Yes," Marissa said. "If we ever get through this mess, yes, I would."

Chapter 10

Marissa stood by the kitchen door and gave a wave as Riley jogged by, drenched in sweat and leading the black stallion.

Frank McKenna stepped behind her, squinted, and shook his head. "What's he doing?"

Marissa turned amused eyes to her friend. "Riley is running, and he thinks the stallion needs more exercise. Kingston has been restricted to the barn and paddock. Since Kingston can't be ridden yet, he's running with him."

Frank chuckled and took a cup of coffee from her. "He's such a damn greenhorn."

Marissa joined his laughter. "He would admit it too."

Frank shook his head again. "Kingston could probably run ten miles before breaking a sweat."

"He's made a connection with the stallion, and that's what Jefferson Ironheart wanted. The stallion isn't fighting him. In fact, they both seem to be enjoying themselves," Marissa stepped away from the door and inside the kitchen. "I made cinnamon rolls. Would you like one?"

"Two," Frank said with a smile. "I sure do appreciate you

taking over the cooking. I'll just take these with me and get to work on the addition."

"I'm curious," Marissa said. "Does anyone ever call Jefferson Ironheart by his first or last name only?"

Frank shook his head. "I've never given it any thought, but no. He's a respected elder. Thanks for the coffee." He started to walk away but turned around. "Have you ever iced a cake?"

"Of course," Marissa said. "Do you want me to bake a cake?"

"No, well yeah, any time you want to make one. I'd never turn down a cake," the older man said. "But, I want to show you how to skim-coat plaster on drywall. It's sort of the same thing as icing a cake, but on a larger scale. All the bending and twisting is killing my ribs."

"Let me change," Marissa agreed. "I've never done it, but I'm willing to learn."

"But you, my dead, my flesh, my treasures, those whom I have completely and totally loved, all of you with me in the grave now—without eyes or flesh to warm me—you are with me!"

Frank listened to an excerpt from what sounded like a horror story. "Are you trying to terrify yourself or Kingston?" he asked, leaning over the stall gate.

Riley looked up from the book with a grin. "It's Anne Rice's book: *"Violin"*. I borrowed it from your bookshelf. I don't think Kingston cares as long as he hears my voice, and it is scaring the crap out of me. I think I'll look for another book to read."

"One of the kids gave it to me as a Christmas gift a while back," Frank said. "I haven't read it either."

Frank watched as his nephew tossed the book carelessly into the straw beside the horse's front hooves. He slid from the horse's back where he'd been sitting casually and reading aloud.

A few weeks earlier, either action would have caused the horse to react violently. Riley ran his hand along the horse's neck, petting him and scratching his ears. He retrieved his book and joined his uncle.

"How long have you been riding Kingston?" Frank asked.

"I'm not," Riley denied. "He lets me sit on him. We don't go anywhere."

"It's still amazing progress," Frank commended. "What does Jefferson Ironheart say?"

Riley grimaced. "He doesn't know because I haven't told him. Jefferson Ironheart says the next step in breaking Kingston is to tie a bale of hay on his back to get him used to the weight."

"I've seen that method used before. It's slower, but it works." Frank admitted.

"It seems cruel," Riley said.

Frank grinned at his nephew. "Kingston is a thousand pounds of pure rage with most men. A sixty-to-hundred-pound bale of straw on his back is not going to hurt him. A horse his size can carry a two hundred and fifty-pound man easily. The other alternative is to break him."

"Like the rodeo riders?"

"Breaking a horse is the real thing here. It's not entertainment. Ranchers need horses, and horses have to be broken. Ranch and working animals aren't pets," Frank said.

"Do you think I'm making Kingston a pet?" Riley asked.

"I'm wondering what's going on in that old man's head," Frank said. "If you're the only one who can get near him, who does he plan on using as a rider in the races?"

Riley raised an eyebrow.

Frank shook his head. "No way. You're not what I'd call an experienced rider by any stretch of the imagination, and river races can get rough and dangerous. I have to return you in one piece, preferably with no broken parts."

"That option has my vote," Riley agreed with a laugh.

Marissa, Riley, and the boys sat in the kitchen the next day while a loud discussion was taking place outside.

They could hear the tone of the argument but not the actual words. Jefferson Ironheart stomped off to his truck, and Frank stormed toward the barns.

Riley watched the retreating figures with concern. "Maybe I could ride Kingston, at least in the first race," he suggested.

"No, you can't," Noah exclaimed. "I asked John Henry, and he said the riders have to be members of the tribes they are representing."

"Maybe they could make me an honorary member."

"You have to have proof of lineage and bloodlines," Blue said. "Even if they wanted to cheat and fake it, you don't look like us. Last year at the Deer Creek race, a rider broke both of his legs!" The boy regaled the story with gleeful enthusiasm as he described the gory accident.

"Boys! There's work to be done!"

At Frank's shout, Marissa was left alone in the kitchen. She went to the door and watched as one of two trucks loaded with fence posts and wire was driven away. Riley would work with Kingston for an hour or so, and he would take the second truck to the site.

Taking advantage of privacy, Marissa changed her footwear from sandals to cowboy boots. She walked to a rise in the desert, where she had discovered the reception on the cell phone was the best. She spoke to Jenna Harrison and each of her boys.

Marissa knew Frank would return when Riley joined them. An adult always worked with the younger boys. He or John Henry usually went to the fence site to direct the initial work effort. Frank would return to work on the house addition if his ribs weren't bothering him. At most, she had thirty minutes to an hour of solitude.

She was overheated by the time she returned to the house, and she removed the boots. She looked around, didn't see either of Frank's trucks, and decided to take a swim in the reservoir tank. Raising the lid, she climbed the ladder and enjoyed an invigorating swim in the cool water. Climbing out of the tank, she lowered the top and stripped off her tee shirt. She squeezed the water from it and pulled it on, and did the same with her shorts. Slipping her feet into flip-flops, she walked through the barn and was startled when Riley stepped out of the tack room.

"Oh!" Marissa exclaimed. "I didn't know you were still here."

"I was about to leave," Riley said, frowning. "You're not supposed to be in the barns without your boots on," he scolded. "What are you...? Jesus, have you been swimming in the reservoir tank?"

"Yes, I was cooling off," Marissa said.

"Cooling off," Riley repeated. "Are you out of your mind? You've been reminded a dozen times along with the boys! No one swims alone! That tank is eight feet deep, and anything could go wrong. You could have a cramp, or the hydraulics could fail and drop the top! There are rules not only for the children but for the adults. They're posted on the walls everywhere around this place."

"I'm an adult, Riley," Marissa exclaimed. "And, I don't appreciate you yelling at me."

"And, I don't appreciate you taking chances with your life," Riley said firmly, taking her hand and pulling her into the tack room. He slammed the door shut. "The next time you decide the rules don't apply to you, you'll think twice about it."

He sat on a bench, and with a jerk, she was over his lap.

Riley spanked Marissa hard, with stinging blows across her bottom that had her crying from the first whack. His hand seared an imprint all over her wet bottom.

Marissa was shocked and angry. Her bottom was stinging, and she was sobbing because it hurt! Riley continued whacking her bottom with stinging spanks. She thought his hand would never stop when suddenly he did.

He stood her on her feet. "Don't you ever put your life in danger again! Never!" Riley exclaimed furiously. He stood, frowning at the tears on Marissa's face. He pulled her into his arms, kissed her long and hard, and then pushed her away.

"Damn it! I don't know if I want to spank you again or make love to you!"

He turned on his heel and stalked out.

Marissa wiped her tears away, sat down, jumped from the bench, and rubbed her stinging bottom. She ran from the barn to the house and locked herself in the bedroom to cry out her frustrations.

Frank returned with the older work truck and brought Blue back to the house. Blue wasn't expected to work a full day. His job was primarily to fetch staples, nails, and tools needed in rebuilding the fences. Frank believed the more time Blue spent under his guidance, the sooner he would respond positively. Sometimes Blue helped in what was left of the construction of the new dormitory rooms. Several hours a day, he was parked at Frank's desk with fifth- and sixth-grade books in front of him, and he was expected to study because he would be quizzed.

Marissa was sure she had disguised her swollen eyes from crying. She wished she could have done the same for her still stinging bottom.

She saw Frank return with Blue, and they went into the barn. She gave a swipe here and there to an already clean kitchen. She stood for a moment, reading the posted rules. Riley was right. The rules were posted in every room as a reminder to the foster children when they were in residence. They also applied to adults.

She went into the living room and began to dust the bookshelves flanking the fireplace on both sides. Like most people who lived a distance from a town or city, Frank had an extensive collection of books, music, and DVDs.

She tidied books into placement along the shelves. On one shelf, she discovered a stack of CDs and DVDs and started to match them with their corresponding plastic cases. Finding the correct casing, Marissa looked closely at the picture. There in the small photo was a very young Riley holding a guitar almost as long as he was tall.

When Riley was launching a career, she'd been in grade school, listening to her parents argue every time they were in the same room together. Her parents had fought an unending battle for three years before they'd divorced when she'd been thirteen. Her mother had moved to San Diego, and Marissa had been trying to fit into a new school environment. Riley had been touring the world with his brothers and family.

She found a DVD, plugged it in, and watched Riley's brother Sully portray a Navy sailor who had been taunted for being gay when he wasn't. The hero of the story had taken on those who were trying to intimidate and destroy him. She cried through the latter part of the film. She was still crying when Frank entered the living room. A few of her tears were for the movie. Most of them were because she needed a good cry, and her sore bottom was a reminder of how she had messed up her life.

"What's wrong?" Frank demanded.

Marissa turned around, wiping her cheeks of tears. "I'm

sorry. I had every intention of dusting and working on the drywall again. I stopped to watch this movie. I've only known for a couple of days that Riley is Coyote McKenna of the I-35 band."

Frank grinned. "It still amazes me. My nephews are famous. Sully earned an Oscar for that movie. Riley has been performing on stage since he was about eight or nine with the I-35 band. My brother's first-set of kids are a talented bunch. The second-set is pretty darn talented too. Noah is a drummer, and the girls are into ballet."

"Why didn't you tell me?" Marissa asked.

Frank shrugged. "One of the best things I can say for my brother's kids is they have grown into good men and women, and they don't have big heads. The second-set, most of them, are hard workers and successful too."

"I wish I'd known," Marissa exclaimed. "I've tried to talk to Riley, but he refuses to listen. You don't know what my ex-husband is capable of doing. I'm afraid if Gregg finds me here, he will destroy their careers and your efforts and plans to take on more foster kids."

"Riley told me. We'll face it head-on if it comes to that," Frank promised. "I've told you before, technically, this land belongs to John Henry and the reservation. I'm only a temporary holder. The tribe accepted Katherine and me as surrogate parents to John Henry and later for more kids. County and State departments have to go through a lot of legalese to interfere with Tribal decisions.

Frank put his arm around her shoulders. "Stop worrying and go about doing what you need to do."

"Do you have children, Frank?" Marissa asked.

He shook his head. "No, my Katherine couldn't get pregnant. In those days, we didn't have the treatments available today. John Henry's father was a friend of mine when I was in the service. He didn't make it out, and Katherine and I got involved in helping to raise him. His momma had reoccurring problems. We used to take him every summer, sometimes during the school year too."

"John Henry's mother died when he was seventeen. He came to live with us while he went to college, but his ties were always strong to his people. We had to respect it. It was his idea for us to move here and open the foster home. He's the closest thing to a son I've ever had, and I've never had a day that I haven't been proud of him. He's involved with the kids who are placed here." Frank took a picture from a desk drawer and handed it to her. "This was my Katherine."

Marissa looked at the photograph, and she saw far more than the pretty, non-descript woman in the picture. She saw the woman Frank had loved so profoundly that he couldn't bear to have her photograph displayed, even after so many years had passed. She handed it to him. Frank looked at it, rubbed his rough fingers over the face of the picture gently, and stored it in the drawer.

"I knew your connection with John Henry was strong. Now I know why. Thank you. I'd better get something done," Marissa said. "I promised Blue I would bake an apple pie today."

Frank smiled. "With this bunch, you'd better make several. You're good for Blue. I don't think he's had much TLC in his life."

"I heard what John Henry said about his mother being in a rehab facility. It's a shame he's being separated from his sisters."

Frank's head snapped around. "You're right, and I should have realized it. Blue needs to visit his sisters and his family."

Riley and Noah, returned to the ranch house for lunch. Usually, they packed a lunch, but it was Saturday, and they only worked half-days on Saturdays.

"So what are you going to do this afternoon?" Marissa asked of them.

"What is there to do?" Noah asked. "Entertainment on a Saturday night around here is going to the convenience store, drinking beer, and sitting on the hood counting the cars as they go by."

Frank chuckled and nodded. "That's true. There's a lot of getting drunk on Saturday nights and going to church Sunday morning to repent."

"There's a drive-in theatre in Murdock," Blue said.

Riley looked interested. "A real drive-in?"

"Yes, there is, but the movies are probably playing on Netflix," Frank said.

"Which you don't have," Riley said. "I'm not much of a movie fan unless it's one of Sully's, so I probably haven't seen what's playing." He turned to Marissa. "Would you like to go to the movies tonight?"

"Drive-in," Frank corrected. "It's one of a dying breed."

"Yeah, we'll all go," Noah interrupted.

"I have a better idea for you guys," Frank suggested, turning to the two younger boys. "Blue, would you like to go visit with your sisters."

The boy closed his eyes and stared down at his plate.

"Blue, you do want to visit your sisters, don't you?" Frank repeated softly.

The boy nodded his head, and Frank exchanged a glance with Marissa. The boy was close to tears.

Marissa gave Blue a quick hug, and the boy slid from the table and ran outside.

"What's wrong with him?" Noah demanded.

"Why don't you use your head more and your mouth less?" Riley asked his brother. "Blue misses his family."

"Well, why can't I go to the movies?"

"You weren't invited," Riley said. "I was inviting Marissa."

He looked at her and asked the question. "Would you like to go with me to the drive-in?"

"I would," she admitted. "I've never been to one. I've only seen them in the movies."

"I'll go see if they have an online site and get the information," Riley said.

Noah made a move to follow him, but his Uncle stopped him. "Let him be, and go find Blue. Tell him he's going to visit his family."

"Why do I have to go with Blue?" Noah demanded. "I'm sick of being stuck here, and you won't let me online!"

"Those were your father's instructions, not Riley's, and you'll survive," Frank said sternly. "Go tell Blue to come in and get showered and changed, and make peace with your brother."

"Man," Noah grumbled, but he went outside.

"Teenagers," Frank said to Marissa. "I prefer the younger kids. They're not so self-absorbed."

Riley went into the bathroom still under construction. It wasn't complete but had the basics working.

Noah flopped on the single bunk in the unfinished room his brother had moved into. After twenty minutes, his brother emerged from the bathroom. He was wearing jeans but was barefoot and had a towel loosely hanging around his neck. Riley ignored him.

"I was only messing with you," Noah said.

Riley continued to ignore him.

Noah gave an exaggerated sigh and rolled his eyes dramatically. "Okay, I'm sorry for butting in," he exclaimed.

Riley turned around and surveyed his brother critically and snapped the towel from around his neck, and let it fly with a resounding whack as it struck his brother in the arm.

Noah yipped and retreated to the door. "I said I was sorry!" he repeated.

"You had better be very careful," Riley warned ominously.

Noah ignored the implied threat. "How was I supposed to know you've got the hots for Marissa?" he asked.

Riley eyed his younger brother again. "Keep it up, and I'll make sure you're shoveling shit with a teaspoon for the rest of your time here!"

There was a light knock on the door, and Riley opened it.

"I'm sorry to interrupt," Marissa said. "Frank's on the phone, and he asked me to get you, so it must be your parents."

"I'll take it first," Noah exclaimed with a grin. "It will give you more time to *get pretty* for your date," he smirked, and he ducked as the wet towel was thrown at him forcibly.

When Marissa turned, Riley caught her arm. "Are we okay?" he asked.

She nodded. "I was wrong."

"So was I," Riley said. "You're not my girlfriend, at least not yet, and we don't have an understanding. Not that I don't want both. Still, I had no right to spank you."

"Maybe not, but you got your point across," Marissa said. "I'll follow the rules."

The phone call, typical of the McKenna parents, lasted a while. Their mother was feeling fine, and their father sounded like the vacation was doing both of them good.

"Noah," Frank said, raising his voice. He tossed the keys to his older truck at his nephew. "After you get cleaned up, can you drive Blue to the reservation to visit with his sisters?"

Noah looked at the keys in his hand with total surprise. "I can't drive," he protested.

"You don't know how to drive?" Frank questioned.

"Well, yeah, I know how," Noah said. "My brothers let me

drive their cars and trucks when we're out at the lake property. I haven't had Drivers Ed yet, and I don't have a learner's permit."

"That's good enough," Frank said. He walked across the room and laid his hand on his nephew's shoulder. "This is Arizona. Every farm and ranch kid over thirteen knows how to drive ranch equipment.

"I want you to take Blue over to the reservation to see his family. There's a back road from here to the reservation housing developments. Blue will show you the way. Take your time and no goofing off. Being behind the wheel of anything moving means you have to be responsible. I want you home before dark. I expect you to drive carefully," Frank said sternly.

"I will," Noah said, astonished his uncle was entrusting him to drive at all.

"Go get the truck and take it for a couple of turns around the house and barns, so I can be sure you can handle it," Frank suggested.

"Okay," Noah exclaimed as he dashed through the door with excitement.

Marissa looked at Frank with concern. "Is that wise?"

Frank shrugged. "Kids have to grow up, and it helps if you force responsibility on them once in a while. Besides, he's taking my old truck, and it won't go over thirty miles an hour. Chances are they won't run across another vehicle. Hardly anyone uses that old road anymore. If he does run off the road, he'll go into the desert.

"Let's go see if he can handle the truck." Frank led the way outside. Blue was already sitting in the passenger seat of the truck cab.

Noah climbed into the truck cab, smiling broadly, and he proceeded to drive the truck around the dirt lanes running from the house to the barns and other ranch buildings. He stopped and parked outside the porch. Both boys bailed, heading for the bathrooms to shower and change.

Blue was the first one back in the truck. Marissa carried Blue's plastic box of snacks and set them in the truck bed. "I thought you might want to share these with your sisters and cousins," she said to the boy.

Noah leaped from the porch to jump into the driver's seat.

"Don't forget to use the signals," Frank yelled.

"They're broken!" Noah shouted.

"Hand signals," Frank shouted. "Remember?"

Noah nodded, grinned, and demonstrated the hand signals for right, left, and stop. Hand signals were no longer on most of the urban driving tests. In the backcountry, though, ranch vehicles were not traded in because of slight dents and paint chips. They were used until they couldn't be fixed again. Vehicles were often missing essential features. They wouldn't pass state inspections, but they got the jobs done on farms and ranches.

Frank waved Noah and Blue away, and he smiled. "They'll be okay, and it will be good for Noah to see another side of life. You two have a good time tonight. I think I'm going over to Moonbeam's place. He has a friendly poker game every Saturday night."

Riley drove, and he and Marissa talked about movies and music. Once they were on the highway, he noticed the billboards for the Yellow Horse Trading Post. They were hard to miss. The billboards began at several mile increments, but the distance between signs became shorter and shorter until they were a couple hundred yards apart. Every billboard was different, but they all had the same message, *Stop at the Yellow Horse Trading Post*.

Riley drove by a small single-story structure. It looked to be little more than an extended shack, and suddenly the billboards were stating warnings. *You passed the Yellow Horse Trading*

Post! Turn around! You missed the Yellow Horse Trading Post! Stop! Turn Around, Now, Don't Miss the Yellow Horse Trading Post! He stepped on the brake and made a U-turn in the road.

"Where are you going?" Marissa asked.

"We missed the Trading Post," Riley explained. "Any place investing in so many billboards deserves a look."

Marissa laughed. "It will be a tourist trap."

"I can be a tourist," Riley admitted with a smile.

Marissa laughed, and she followed him into the old building, painted a shocking color of bright yellow, and trimmed in fire engine red.

The interior of the Trading Post was typical of older souvenir shops in the southwestern states. It was unpainted, and the flooring was uneven and unfinished. Old glass-topped jewelry cases held genuine handcrafted original and expensive jewelry behind locked doors. The look-a-like replicated jewelry was in large cases with hundreds of rings, necklaces, and bracelets. If you looked close, you could spot a *Made in China* tag missed when they were set out for display. Huge bins and barrels were filled with amateur-looking hatchets, bows and arrows, and a whole assortment of fake *Native American Artifacts*. There were unusual features to the Trading Post too. A real cougar was stuffed, mounted, and perched in the rafters. It looked like it was ready to pounce on customers. Expensive hand-woven rugs and blankets were displayed beside cheaper imported versions. The authentic rugs and woven pieces were priced in the high hundreds while their cheaper-made counterparts were less than twenty-five dollars. There was an entire section of printed tee shirts.

"This place is amazing," Riley exclaimed, examining a display of Kachina figures. He was shocked when he looked at the price tags.

A young man around Riley's age was conducting business at the front counter. He was a Native American. He handled the customers with practiced ease, answering questions, and accepting the credit cards on a piece of equipment Riley didn't recognize.

When there was a lull in the incoming customers, the young man approached Riley, held out his hand, and let out a coyote howl. "Coyote McKenna! I am a fan!"

"Thanks," Riley said. "Old or new music?"

"Both, and by the look on your face, I'll bet you're tired of the nickname."

"That, I am," Riley agreed. "We're playing tourist, and your signs drew us in."

"Christian Hawkins," the young man said. "The signs came with the place. They've been alongside the highway before it was paved! The trading post has been here for sixty-eight years."

"Are you related to Yellow Horse?" Marissa asked.

"No, we think he might have been a myth," Christian said. "The original place was built in 1953. It's changed hands a dozen times since and been added-on. It's always had the same name. It would be too much trouble to repaint the signs."

"You have a wide variety of stuff in here," Riley said.

Christian Hawkins smiled. "Look around. Everything is for sale. If it doesn't have a price tag, make me an offer."

Riley smiled, and they did look around. He wasn't interested in the tourist stuff, but he liked the jewelry. Against the store's back wall, he found several boxes filled with an assortment of sporting equipment. The boxes were labeled with names on the sides. A pair of name-brand skis caught his attention, as did a box of expensive climbing equipment.

"Have you found something you're interested in?" Christian asked.

"Yes," Riley said. "There's some good stuff in these boxes."

"College students on vacation usually bring that stuff in and want to sell or hock it for quick cash. I'm a soft touch for a kid who wants to go home and has blown his budget. I've got everything from bowling balls to ice skates."

"Are these for sale?" Riley asked.

"You point to it, and I'll sell it," Christian said. "I write their names on the boxes, and they promise to return, but they rarely do. After sixty days, it's mine to sell."

"I'll buy the skis and the box of climbing gear," Riley said. Then he haggled with Christian until he'd negotiated a price he thought was a steal. "Can you hold it for me? I don't have a cover on my truck. I'm looking for a used toolbox if you hear of one for sale. I'll come back for this stuff."

"Riley, if we're going to make it to the drive-in before dark, we need to go," Marissa suggested.

"Okay, but I want to buy this necklace," Riley said, motioning towards a silver-plated arrowhead on a string of rawhide he was carrying.

"Don't buy that junk," Christian protested.

"It's your merchandise!" Riley protested.

"That's why I know its junk," Christian said. "When you come to get your equipment, I'll show you the good stuff, and at reasonable prices. You're heading to Murdock, right? Look for an adobe building with a green tiled roof right after you pass the town sign. If you have time, stop in there. They have authentic *native* goods too! My cousin runs the place."

"Okay," Riley said. Do you want me to pay for that stuff now or later?"

"Later," Christian said. "I've already shut down the power booster needed to reach the on-line credit-card services."

"Hold it for me," Riley promised. "I'll be back."

"You're big, but not as big as Schwarzenegger!" Christian yelled with a grin and another coyote howl.

Marissa pointed to a sign indicating Murdock was three

miles ahead. They still had plenty of daylight, so Riley pulled into a parking lot with a lettered sign for the Fort Yuma Indian Museum.

They entered the building, and it was half museum and half gift shop. They walked through the exhibits stopping to view and read the displays. When they finished, they went to the gift shop, and this time every item was authentic and expensive. There were several cubicles with native weaving art hung on the walls. Riley didn't think they were as good as Glenda Two-Trees' pieces.

"Mrs. Two-Trees should have her pieces displayed here," Riley said.

"This shop and museum may not be connected to the reservation," Marissa said. "Notice the sign doesn't have the word *Reservation* on it."

"With these prices, it can't be a scam," Riley said.

"It's probably legitimate. Anyone can open a museum," Marissa said. "A lot of these items come from tribes all over the southwest."

Riley frowned, but he held his tongue. He was still sure he'd seen Glenda Two-Trees work in a gallery in Los Angeles. He wasn't an art expert by any means, but he'd been dragged into museums and art galleries since he was a little kid. The only paintings he'd had in his home had been painted by his older brother Micah. They'd been destroyed in the fire, but Micah had promised to replace them.

If he'd seen Glenda Two-Trees' work and liked it, he would have remembered it, and he was pretty sure he had. Tomorrow he was going to call Micah to find out for sure.

Chapter 11

R iley drove along the isolated road, and he was enjoying being alone with Marissa. They hadn't made it to the Drive-In. The movie playing was different from the one he'd been told on the phone recording. The movie playing was a comedy, and neither of them was interested in seeing it. They'd found a small restaurant, enjoyed a good meal, and shared a bottle of wine tucked away in a corner.

His date with Marissa was low-key, and they were enjoying the privacy to really get to know one another. No one recognized him, and it was nice not to be bothered. On the return trip, he pulled into a roadside picnic area, and they'd talked more and kissed. They started sharing stories and telling past secrets.

"First boyfriend?" Riley asked.

"That goes back a while," Marissa laughed. "Brian Price, I was fourteen, and I wasn't allowed to date, so he was an *in-school only* boyfriend. We walked together from class to class."

"What broke you up?"

"I was sick three days from a stomach virus, and when I

returned, he was walking Shirley Parkinson from class to class. I was so mad at them until Wayne Wilkerson asked if he could walk with me and carry my books! What about you?"

"I was anti-girl for longer than most boys," Riley admitted. "We were home-schooled, so there weren't many girls around, only the neighborhood kids, and then we were traveling. When we were on our first tour, there were thousands of screaming female fans of all ages, and I didn't know how to handle them. To me, they were silly girls who wouldn't shut up, so the audience could hear us. I think I was just shy of sixteen before I had the nerve to ask a girl on a date. It turned out she was a fan of Sully's and wanted an introduction."

"That's rotten!" Marissa exclaimed. "She was using you to get to your brother!"

"Sad, but true," Riley admitted with a grin.

"What about more recently?" she asked.

"I dated, but I had to be careful. Those were our top-of-the-chart days, and I never knew if a girl wanted to date a famous guy or me. It was dicey. Most of the time, I hung around the same guys I'd grown up with from the neighborhood.

"I was involved with a woman for two years," Riley said. "Leigh Ann is a couple years older than me, and we met in theology classes. She's a minister of a small church in Luling. That's a few miles outside of San Antonio. We kept our relationship on the quiet, and I'm glad we did."

"Would I be too nosey if I ask what happened?" Marissa asked.

Riley was quiet, and he took her hand and squeezed it. "Have you heard of domestic discipline?"

Marissa nodded. "I felt it this morning. Was she into it?"

"Yes, and I'm a believer in it," Riley admitted. "Domestic discipline is a lifestyle. My grandparents practiced it, my parents, aunts, uncles, and brothers. We were raised in a church that sanctioned it as a way of life. When you're surrounded by it, it becomes second nature.

"D/D is two consenting life partners in which the head of the household takes the necessary measures to achieve a healthy on-going relationship. That's a quote verbatim from a website I looked up once. I was doing research to make sure I wasn't a deviant of some kind. I discovered it's a widespread doctrine.

"The husband is usually the dominant figure. It can go the other way too, but I guess being a macho guy, I find that a bit kinky. The whole idea harkens back through history until about the early 1960s. Until then, a man spanking his wife wasn't uncommon. There are no hard and fast rules, but my family are traditionalists. They believe marriage is forever. Most people nowadays have one major fight or disagreement, and they go running to a divorce lawyer. The rules of the relationship are between the husband and wife. It usually involves spanking, but it's not in any way connected to the BDSM community.

"I thought Leigh Ann and I were in a relationship heading toward marriage. We had a few arguments, and I spanked her several times. I also spanked her during sex because I enjoy it, and so did she." Riley looked directly into Marissa's eyes. "Am I scaring the crap out of you?"

"No," Marissa said, shaking her head. "Go on."

"We'd taken our time, been careful with each other before we started sleeping together, which I have to admit is frowned upon by our teachings. Parishioners don't want to believe their minister wants or needs a sexual relationship. We kept our relationship under the covers, so to speak. We were a couple, but after a while, I started getting suspicious. Leigh Ann was doing things, saying disrespectful things. An argument would lead to my spanking her.

"She was getting off on the spanking, more than just discipline or fun. She asked me to take it further. She wanted me to whip her with a belt. She asked and pleaded with me, but I wasn't going there.

"I walked in one day unexpectedly and caught Leigh Ann with another woman. They were dressed in BDSM leather outfits, and her friend was beating her with a leather strap. I walked out. Leigh Ann swore she wouldn't do it again, swore it was her first time to try it, but I didn't believe her. I'd been there long enough to hear what she was saying to the other woman. She knew what she was doing, and I couldn't be a part of it.

"The strange part of this whole scenario is that Leigh Ann is involved with a network supporting women trying to get out of abusive relationships. I support her work, and I will continue to support it, but I can't be an abuser. I can spank a woman for misbehaving, but I can't beat her because she has a psychological need to be beaten. Mentally I can separate what Leigh Ann does in her work from what she wants or needs in her private life. I have to admire her for what she does to help people, especially women in trouble. But, I couldn't accept what she apparently needed to fulfill her sexual life. Does this make any sense to you?"

Riley took a deep breath. "Well, you know the down and dirty on me. One word from you and any career I want or had will be destroyed. Couples who practice D/D are very much maligned by those who don't understand."

"I wouldn't do that to you," Marissa promised. "I was raised in a domestic discipline environment. It didn't work between my parents. They divorced when I was thirteen. My mother was the one who changed. She was the sweetest woman in the world until I was about nine-years-old. At least that's how I remember her. I don't know what happened between them. Suddenly she turned into a person who was critical of everything. My father couldn't do anything to please her, and neither could I. Any agreement they had made on the rules of marriage was tossed out.

"My mother never remarried, and she became a *Karen* long before there was a name for her obnoxious behavior. She was a very unhappy woman, and when I left home for college, she started drinking heavily. I lost her in my freshman first. She died of alcohol poisoning.

"My father moved away and remarried. After the divorce, I wasn't allowed to see him for years. We stayed in touch, but we're not close. He lives in New Hampshire, so we rarely see each other. I do know he's happy in his second marriage.

"My marriage wasn't in any way an agreement," Marissa said. "We never discussed anything ahead of time, and I know that was a mistake. It was a whirlwind romance based on a lot of lies. Within the first few weeks, Gregg became overtly controlling, and it got increasingly worse. I left him after only ten months. When he discovered I was pregnant, he became a monster.

"I researched narcissism, and it describes him perfectly. He has a sense of entitlement, a total disregard for others, and can't handle criticism. Nothing matters except what he wants and demands."

"He's your ex, and he's not unbeatable," Riley promised. "When we get past this, I would very much like to consider a relationship with you."

"Me, too," Marissa whispered as he leaned over and kissed her.

"I know you've been hurt," Riley said. "Where I might be ready to take our relationship further, you might not be ready. I don't want to push or scare you, so I'm letting you take the reins."

As Riley drove closer to the ranch house, he suddenly became alert. It was after midnight, and the front part of the house was ablaze with lights. The lights were usually out by eleven. Even though he and Noah were accustomed to later hours, they had adjusted to Frank's early to rise, early to bed habits. Being bone-tired from physical labor had a lot to do with their compliance.

Riley took note of John Henry's Deputy vehicle parked beside the porch, and he took Marissa's hand in his. All eyes turned to them as they walked in.

"What's wrong?" Riley demanded.

"He's going to arrest Marissa!" Blue snarled, pointing to John Henry in accusation.

John Henry cast a stern look toward the boy. "I am not going to arrest Marissa. I'm going to wait until we get the reports from Shawn Williamson at the FBI." The Deputy settled his hat on his head. "I'm sorry, Marissa, but that's the best I can promise. If we don't shed light on this situation soon, I won't have a choice. I have to ask you not to leave the ranch."

"I understand," Marissa said, trying to release Riley's hand, but he wouldn't let go.

John Henry tipped his hat and took his leave politely.

"What happened?" Riley demanded again.

Frank turned to Noah and Blue and suggested it was time for them to turn in for the night. Blue hesitated, but he left the living room without an argument.

The three adults waited until they heard the bedroom door close.

Frank faced them. "John Henry has received feedback from the people he knows in law enforcement. People who can snoop around undercover. Not only is Marissa wanted for non-custodial kidnapping, but there is a warrant issued because she's under suspicion for the disappearance of her ex-husband."

"How is she responsible for his disappearance?" Riley asked.

Frank shrugged. "Apparently, he was reported missing about the same time we found Marissa. Novak hasn't shown up at his office, and no one has seen or heard from him. His secretary said his last words to her as he was leaving the office, was he was going to try to talk sense into his ex-wife.

"Novak and Marissa didn't have a friendly divorce. He accused her of all kinds of awful things in court, from stealing money from his business accounts to taking drugs. The charges were unproven, but he cast doubts in Child Protective Services and the Judge's mind about her character. Novak got custody of the kids, and he bad-mouthed Marissa to anyone who would listen. According to his secretary, everything was Marissa's fault. When he didn't show up for work, his secretary reported him missing. Marissa is wanted for questioning."

"Novak beat Marissa up and tried to kill her," Riley protested.

"They don't know that," Frank said, turning to Marissa. "We have the proof you were assaulted. We don't have proof your ex-husband did it. Dr. Andrews took photographs when you were unconscious. He also completed an assault exam when he first treated you.

"John Henry has the clothing you were wearing when we found you and has logged them as evidence. He says there is probably DNA proof it was your ex-husband."

"Why did he do that without my permission?" Marissa asked.

"He was doing his job. Dr. Andrews is the only expert we have in this part of the county," Frank said. "It was his duty, and you would have needed the evidence if you'd wanted to press charges for assault. You were out cold, and we didn't know what had been done to you. All the Las Vegas police know is Marissa has kidnapped her kids, and now Gregg Novak is missing. It does make her the most likely suspect in his disappearance."

"Is John Henry going to arrest her?" Riley demanded.

Frank shook his head. "Not yet, but Marissa being here isn't a secret anymore. Many people know, and it wouldn't take much for it to slip to the outside. John Henry says he's waiting for the FBI's report from your friend. If her husband was as rotten as she claims, he's liable to be guilty of a lot of illegal stuff."

"I know he was. I even have proof if he hasn't found and destroyed it," Marissa said. "He would never explain where all the money came from, and he was living way beyond what he made in the District Attorney's office."

"We've talked this through as much as we can tonight," Frank suggested. "We need to turn in,"

"I'm calling Shawn," Riley said.

"Light a fuse under him," Frank suggested grimly.

"Don't worry," had been Shawn's advice when he talked to Riley. "I've got this covered."

"That doesn't tell me anything," Riley complained.

"I don't want you involved," Shawn said. "Give me the number of the deputy you've been dealing with. I might get an accommodation or a promotion from this case!"

Marissa left her room and checked to make sure the doors were locked. Then she compulsively rechecked them again and again. She locked herself in the bedroom, but she couldn't take her eyes off the doorknob, expecting any second for it to be smashed in. She looked to the chair where Riley had sat watching her many a night, so he could wake her from the nightmares.

Riley was lying awake in his bed when the door opened, and Marissa came in.

"I can't sleep," Marissa whispered. "I'm so scared. Can you hold me?"

He opened his arms. "You're shaking," he said, wrapping his arms around her. "Shawn said not to worry."

"How can I not?" Marissa whispered.

"I wish there was something I could do, but they are not telling us anything. All we can do is wait and pray."

"I've almost quit believing in prayer," Marissa said. "In the last five years, all I've known is fear and evil."

"I'm not going to let anyone hurt you again," Riley promised.

"I don't want promises. Please just hold me while you can," Marissa whispered. The security of his arms was the only safety she'd had for years."

Frank McKenna was an intuitive man. The door to Marissa's room wasn't closed, and she wasn't in the bathroom opposite her room. She wasn't in the kitchen preparing breakfast. The door to Riley's room was locked when he tried to turn the knob.

He woke up the boys and hustled them from the house to do the morning chores early. Once the boys were out of the house, he knocked on Riley's door. He heard a gruff "Ugh!" from inside as a response.

"I've got the boys doing the morning chores."

Riley opened his eyes, and he smiled. He was still holding Marissa as he had all night, and he wished he could continue doing so.

"I'm awake," Marissa whispered. "Is Frank going to be mad?"

"It's none of his business," Riley said, but then he thought—maybe it was. "He's from another generation, so he might disapprove. I'll deal with it if I have to."

Marissa turned in his arms and kissed him lightly. "Thank you." She slipped from the bed and was gone.

Riley, his forehead against Kingston's neck, was involved in a one-sided conversation while he brushed the horse's mane. He heard the barn door slide open, and he looked up, expecting it to be Frank, but it was Noah. His brother appeared at the stall door, looking tired and angry. The previous day had been one of worry, but they hadn't heard from Shawn or John Henry.

"What's bugging you?" Riley asked.

"The same as you," Noah growled. "How come bastards get away with being bastards and innocent people get screwed over?"

Riley gave Kingston one last stroke and walked out of the stall. "I personally haven't known very many people I would classify as bastards. If you have, you need better friends." He handed Noah a pitchfork while he took the handles of the wheelbarrow.

"Why can't they tell us what is going on?" Noah demanded as he followed, and they worked together side-by-side, mucking out the barn stalls.

"I wonder where Marissa's ex-husband is hiding. If he left the country, there would be records, airline tickets, port of entry... all kinds of travel-related records," Riley mused. He leaned against the stall gate while his brother used a pitchfork. "A man who Marissa says values his status and wealth above all else doesn't just vanish. He'd be too concerned about the money he'd lose or the clients he might alienate."

"He could be on a beach somewhere with a bikini chick getting a tan while Marissa gets accused of doing something bad to him," Noah complained.

"Marissa needs an alibi," Riley suggested. "Or, at least an account of her whereabouts when he disappeared."

"She's been here ever since he hurt her," Noah supplied.

"Yes, but she has no proof except what Dr. Anderson

collected when he examined her. The blood samples would have to be compared to Novak's DNA. She only has her word, and he's not going to crawl out of the woodwork to help her," Riley said.

"She was staggering around in the desert barely alive," Noah snorted. "Dr. Anderson took pictures. He said it was a miracle she survived."

"We believe Marissa because we saw her, and we know and trust her," Riley said solemnly. "But, I don't think the police would take into account what we think or believe. They need concrete proof. I think we need to talk to Marissa again."

Once it was decided, Riley and Noah went to work with a little more vigor because they wanted to get finished quickly.

Marissa was setting the table for breakfast when Noah returned to the kitchen, fresh from the shower. Both of the McKenna brothers had agreed they could not live with the worst of the barn odors all day. They were in the habit of showering after the bulk of nasty chores were done in the morning. After breakfast, they would go to work again, but they could tolerate the smell of sweat better than manure.

"Marissa, would you answer a few questions for me?" Riley asked after the breakfast platters were passed around.

"Sure," she responded.

"Questions about the last night with your ex-husband," Riley elaborated.

Marissa looked uncomfortable.

"Riley, I don't think it's any of your business," Frank interrupted.

"The more we know, the more likely we will be able to help," Riley suggested. "What Marissa might remember as a minor detail may be the difference between proving what she says happened is the truth and getting arrested."

"I don't think that's for you to determine," Frank said. "That's John Henry's business."

Riley sighed. "John Henry thinks like a cop. He's automatically suspicious even if he believes Marissa, and I believe he does. His first loyalty has to be to follow the law."

"That's true," Marissa admitted softly. "What do you want to know?"

"Tell us the details of the last night. How Novak was acting. What he said. Try to remember the details of where he drove."

Marissa set her fork on her plate and looked pointedly at Blue, who was sitting in the chair next to hers.

"I want to hear too," the boy exclaimed loudly. 'Don't try to get rid of me!"

"Calm down," Frank admonished firmly, but he gave the boy a rub on his head.

Marissa smiled, and she gave Blue a reassuring hug. She closed her eyes for a moment. "I left the office building where I worked after six o'clock. I'd worked overtime. My company has flex hours, and I usually worked from seven to three. The overtime helped make ends meet."

"Wait," Noah jumped up from the table and returned a few seconds later with a notebook and a pen. He shoved it over to his brother to take notes.

"Where were you working?" Riley asked.

"I worked at the Mahoney Insurance Agency," Marissa answered. "I don't know how Gregg found me. I was working under an alias. I had a social security number supplied to me by the network helping me. I was careful to look around and check for anyone watching me. I didn't see anyone looking suspicious, and I walked across the street to the parking lot to get my car. I wonder what happened to my car. It wasn't worth much, but it was all I had."

"We'll figure that out later," Riley said.

She nodded. "I stopped because a car was coming toward me. I recognized it as a Porsche because Gregg has one almost like it but in metallic red, not dark gray. I didn't suspect anything because he drove flashy cars, always red or gold. He pointed a gun at me and told me to get in the car. He said I didn't want to *make* him use it. I didn't have a choice, and I got in the car.

"Gregg said he only wanted to talk, and he kept referring to me as his wife. When I said I wasn't, he slapped me. He threatened to call the police and turn me in for kidnapping. He said if I cooperated, things could return to normal. I should have let him make the call or jumped out at the first stoplight!"

Marissa stopped speaking and rose from her chair, crossing her arms over her torso. She was obviously upset reliving her kidnapping and those moments of terror. "What choice did I have? He was threatening me with a gun. I knew I had to agree to everything he said, or he'd go crazy. All Gregg has ever been interested in was getting his way.

"He talked about us living together again. He said he missed having a family. I told him I wasn't interested, but he wasn't listening. In his head, he had this twisted idea, this fairytale that everything was perfect while we were married. He talked about the good times, the parties we hosted, and the fun times.

"There were no fun times! All I could remember were the threats, him throwing things at me, but it was my fault if I was hit by them. We argued, and I guess he finally realized I wasn't going to go along with his plan to return to what he called *normal*. When he made contact with reality, he flipped out. He could do that as fast as flipping a light switch. He could turn from his version of reasonable to horrible. He pulled a knife from beside his seat and said if I didn't come back to him, he'd kill himself. When the threat didn't work, he turned it on me."

"Where were you when he was doing all this talking?" Riley asked.

"In his car," Marissa said.

"No, I mean, where was he driving?" Riley asked.

"We left Irvine on Interstate 86 South. He switched to Interstate 15, and I don't know after that. After it got dark, I couldn't see much of anything. There were very few cars on the highway. I remember seeing a sign stating we were in Yuma County. He took an exit, and then he started making turns onto other roads. It was pitch black, and the roads were getting worse, and then he was driving on a gravel road, not asphalt.

I was scared, and he kept talking and jabbing the knife against my face and throat. I screamed once, and that's when he sliced my arm. It was my fault, of course. I made him do it."

"Then what?"

"He yelled and threatened and became more violent," Marissa stopped. "I can't..."

"Riley," Frank said softly with a warning tone to his voice.

"I'm not interested in the violence," Riley said gently. He rose and went to her and pulled her into the shelter of his arms. "I saw what he did to you. I don't need a blow-by-blow description. What I need to know is where he took you. Where were you when you jumped from the car? What did you have with you?"

"Why?" Marissa cried.

"Because you must have been at least semi-aware of where he was going. He dumped you out there in the desert. If you were carrying a purse, maybe you have a receipt or something in it to prove your whereabouts before Gregg forced you into the car. We need a timeline and a path to follow. We need every detail you can remember. Every road sign, gas station, the smallest detail could make a difference."

"Okay," Marissa whispered, and she laid her head on his shoulder. "I went to an ATM in the lobby of the building when I left work," Marissa said. "The receipt would be in my purse, and the bank would have a record of my withdrawal. When I left the building, I had to punch in my employee number on a keypad to open the door. It was recorded for security reasons, and there are cameras in the lobby. I said goodnight to Ray, the security guard. I'm pretty sure there are cameras in the parking lot.

"I left my purse in his car when I jumped. I also left a shopping bag from Braxton's because I'd gone there during my lunch hour to buy Star Wars sheets for my boys. Again, I used my bankcard, so there will be a record. I had a small backpack with me in the desert. I carry it instead of a lunch bag. When I jumped and tumbled down an embankment, I remember being surprised that I had it. My arm was caught in one of the straps."

"What embankment?" Noah asked, sliding the notebook over in front of him and picking up the pen.

Marissa closed her eyes.

"We'd been off good roads for a while. As soon as he left the interstate, he opened his window and threw out the wig and glasses I'd been wearing. Gregg was on a gravel road for a long time, and then he was on dirt roads. He drove over several bridges. I noticed those yellow signs warning of skidding on ice. I remember because they look so out-of-place in the desert. He turned onto another rough dirt road. He was driving fast, swerving around rocks, and bouncing in potholes. I thought a tire was going to blow out. We went over another bridge, but that sign was an alert for flooding.

"He was swearing, angry about the road conditions, and driving too fast. I think he was lost or had taken the wrong road. He kept squinting through the windshield and mumbling about finding Ricardo's cabin.

"Suddenly, he slammed on the brakes because there were javelinas all over the road. He hit several of them, grabbed the steering wheel with both hands, and the car nearly went airborne over railroad tracks. We were thrown forward, and I opened the door and jumped. I rolled down an embankment of sand and brush."

"Go on," Riley said.

"I heard a loud crunch like he'd hit something. The head-lights went out, and I think he was trying to turn around because I could hear the engine being gunned and the wheels spinning. I ran into the dark, stumbling, and falling, but I kept running. There was just the tiniest sliver of the moon in the sky that night.

"He was swearing and shouting. The gun was fired several times. It was quiet for a few minutes, and I kept running. Then he started screaming my name over and over again. He kept screaming *Marissa come back! Marissa help me!*

"Gregg couldn't stand for his plans to be thwarted. I kept running. I don't know when I stopped hearing him. Finally, I realized I was hurting myself crashing around in the dark. I tripped over a fence post, and I leaned against it and waited for daylight. When daylight came, I started walking again, following the fence. I didn't know what direction to go in, so I headed toward the sun because at least I knew the sun rose from the east. I didn't see a highway or a dirt road or anything. I kept walking until I saw the roof of the barn. When I got here, I saw the old-fashioned water pump. I don't remember anything beyond that until I awakened and saw Riley sitting in the chair."

"When we found you, you didn't have a book bag," Riley said.

"I must have dropped it, my jacket too," Marissa admitted.

"Jacket?" Noah asked. "What jacket?"

"A blazer, burgundy with leather patches on the elbows,"

Marissa described. "The office tends to be cold with the air-conditioning. I lost the scrunchie in my hair."

"Scrunchie?" Frank asked.

"It's one of those things girls wear around a ponytail," Noah explained. "My sisters wear them all the time."

Marissa went silent.

"Anything else?" Riley asked.

She shook her head. "I don't remember much of anything after the first day in the desert. I guess I wasn't very smart. It's a miracle I managed to get here."

"It was, but you were smart," Frank said. "By using your tee-shirt to cover your face, you avoided sunburn, maybe sunstroke. Our deserts are not kind to people who aren't prepared to survive them."

"I didn't exactly plan on being there," Marissa said.

"What was in the book bag?" Riley asked.

"A bottle of water, I tried to ration it. A pear and an orange that I also rationed," Marissa detailed from memory. "A mystery novel, a daily planner, and a hairbrush."

"Keys?" he asked.

"No, my keys were in my purse. Gregg threw it into the backseat."

Noah was busy writing the details.

"Okay, so we know Marissa was out in the desert for at least three days, and we found her on the fourth day," Frank said. "We knew that before."

"True," Riley admitted. "But now we know she came from the west because she was walking towards the east. We also know she was off the main road, and there was a bridge and railroad tracks. Gregg Novak was a son-of-a-bitch. Sorry, Uncle Frank, but it's true. He hurt and dumped Marissa in the desert. He wouldn't want to get caught carrying her stuff around in his car, so he probably dumped it too. All we have to do is trace backward and hope Mr. Stupid was so angry with Marissa that he tossed her stuff in the desert."

"He didn't dump me. I jumped," Marissa corrected, "And, I don't think it was his car. There was a rental agreement contract on the dashboard.

"That's more information that can be traced," Riley exclaimed. "What company?"

Marissa closed her eyes and tried to remember. "Fantasy Exotic Rentals," she said. "I remember thinking it was a pretentious name. It suited Gregg with all his grandiose ideas and his ego. He owned two Porsches of the same model, to the cost of over a hundred thousand dollars, each. The one he was driving was a dark gray one."

Riley scribbled down the name and model. "That shouldn't be hard to trace. He left you, knowing you were somewhere out in the desert. I don't imagine he's hoping you'll reappear."

"So, the plan is to find the stuff Marissa left behind in the desert?" Noah asked.

"Yes, it helps to create a timeline which is equal to an alibi. If Marissa was wandering around half out of her mind in the desert, she couldn't have been in Las Vegas kidnapping her ex-husband."

"If he ran off the road and got his car stuck, he would have had to call for a tow service," Noah said.

"It makes sense," Frank admitted. "I'll have John Henry call all the auto shops and gas stations to see if he got a tow."

"Meanwhile, we'll be looking out in the desert for her stuff," Riley said.

"It will be like looking for a needle in a haystack. Marissa may think she was heading east, but that's not a sure thing," Frank warned. "Exposure to the sun can scramble your brain, and she might have been delusional. She also remembers railroad tracks, and that can't be right. The nearest railroad tracks are in Kerns, and that's sixty miles north."

"Well, maybe it wasn't railroad tracks. It could have sounded like one," Noah said.

"It could have been a cattle grate," Blue said.

Frank looked over at the boy. "That's using your noggin, kiddo. In the dark, a cattle grate might have sounded and felt like a railroad track. Driving over them at high speed will put you in a ditch!"

"So, are we going to investigate?" Riley asked. The younger boys were nodding in agreement.

Frank was slower to make a commitment. "If we get the chores done earlier, we can search for a couple hours at daybreak, and we can search a couple of hours in the evening," Frank agreed. "But, remember, boys, the ranch work still has to be a priority."

Everyone at the table nodded in agreement.

Chapter 12

Riley adjusted his baseball hat's bill and his sunglasses to shield his eyes. He squinted in the almost blinding sunlight. He scanned the desert landscape with binoculars carefully and gave a sigh, as again, he'd found nothing. He waved his arms over his head and got the same signal from Noah and Blue, who were riding parallel to his path but with a separation of two hundred yards between them. They moved another two hundred feet slowly and repeated the process of search again.

Marissa's clues were vague at best. A dirt road, railroad tracks or a cattle grate, a bridge. Almost all the roads were packed dirt this far inland. Almost all ranch roads had cattle grates at one place or another to keep cattle from crossing ungated roads in fenced areas. The bridge clue was more challenging. Marissa didn't remember hearing water. They had concluded she must have mistaken a dry wash bridge for a real bridge. Dry riverbeds did flood, especially during the monsoon season. Flash floods were known to overrun their banks and form huge washout areas where water would spread greedily over the flat areas and disappear into the desert. On county or state roads known for flooding, the elevation was raised above flood levels. Those raised roads gave the impression of a bridge. However, there was no water underneath it.

Every morning and evening, Riley and the boys continued their search. They were determined but disappointed each day. They'd been performing their search for three days and hadn't found any trace to make them believe Marissa had taken this path. Frank experienced the same lack of progress driving around the property in his old truck when he had time.

Riley looked at his watch. "Blue!" he shouted. "Mark the trail! It's time to head home."

Blue nodded, dismounted, and removed a red and white flag tacked to a wooden dowel and stuck it deep into the sand. After he remounted both boys, rode a parallel path to where they had been searching, and positioned themselves for the return search. With this method, they could cover twice the area in one trip. Suddenly Blue gave a whoop and waved his arms frantically. Noah rode over to him, and the boy was pointing to an empty water bottle.

"She was here," Blue exclaimed, using a plastic bag to drop the plastic bottle into a zip-lock bag. "I found the first clue."

"Maybe," Riley said. "Or it could be a bottle left by a rider. The fingerprints will have to be checked."

Blue rolled his eyes. "Only city folks and tourists drink water from plastic bottles. Let's go further west."

Riley looked across the desert and at his watch. "Okay, but only for few more minutes. We have to head back. We have work to do."

Fifteen minutes later, Noah was the one who spotted a dark blue canvas backpack. Riley picked up the item with rubber gloves from his medical kit. He opened it and looked through the contents, seeing a book and a hairbrush. He enclosed the pack in a large plastic bag.

"This is Marissa's! Blue, mark this spot! We are on the right track," Riley concluded. "At least we have evidence to show for our efforts this time."

Noah and Blue rode back to the ranch with enthusiasm. From their excitement, Frank and Marissa knew they had found something.

"We found the backpack!" Blue blurted out. "Can we go back out and search again!"

Frank examined the pack through the clear plastic. "You may be on the right track, but remember she may have been traveling in circles. She was hurt and probably confused."

"We found the water bottle and the backpack," Noah insisted. "That's proof she was there."

"But not proof of when," Riley said. "We need to find her purse or jacket if possible. She could have receipts dated with time-stamps, and even if it's not proof, it would be helpful."

"Can we go back?" Blue demanded.

Frank shook his head. "Jefferson Ironheart is going to be here any minute to work with Riley and the stallion. We'll have to wait until after he leaves. We have chores to complete and work to finish before we can ride this evening. Right now, you need to take care of your horses. You pushed them pretty hard on the ride home."

Blue subsided, but he looked stubbornly resentful toward Riley and the stallion. He and Noah led their horses into the barn to care for them.

Blue didn't have a patent on stubbornness. Jefferson Ironheart refused to listen when Frank and Riley tried to talk to him about who would ride Kingston in the races. The old man simply changed the subject and ignored them.

Kingston would allow Riley to talk to him, stroke, and brush him. The horse would tolerate Riley throwing a blanket across his back. Riley could climb on his back and sit as long as he didn't move around too much. This new development encouraged Jefferson Ironheart to believe it was time for the horse to be broken to the saddle.

With Jefferson Ironheart's urging, Riley was trying to get a saddle on the stallion's back. The horse shied, bucked, and reared every time Riley came close to swinging the saddle on its back. After almost an hour of trying, Kingston reared and clipped Riley on his forehead with his sharp hoof. It wasn't a nasty blow, but it broke the skin and produced a goose egg. He was going to have a headache for a couple of hours for sure.

Frank called a halt to the day's exercise and sent Riley into the house, advising him to apply an ice pack to his head.

Blue was unhappy about the delay in continuing the search, and he was very verbal in his complaints. He was grumbling and griping and taking potshots at Frank for not letting him and Noah go out on their own. Loud and nasty, he deliberately crossed the line to rudeness that got him in trouble. When Frank threatened to make him stay behind altogether, the boy changed his tactics.

Marissa was quiet over lunch. She doctored Riley's injury and even smiled when he teased her. She was worried and scared. Instinct was telling her to run. Her sense of honor told her she couldn't. Frank, Riley, the boys, and John Henry had done a lot for her in the past couple of weeks. She owed it to them to stay. She owed it to them not to bolt and leave them unwilling accessories. Gregg Novak's high-placed legal friends could do them untold damage. Marissa was so busy with her thoughts the discussion at the table barely registered.

"What's more important?" Blue demanded. "Some stupid old fence or Marissa?"

Riley looked at the young boy, and he had to admire his loyalty. He looked over to his uncle.

Frank nodded. "Marissa is more important," he admitted. "Okay, how about this? I'll pull John Henry into the dormitory this afternoon, and we'll work on the last of the drywall.

The three of you can continue the search. Will that be acceptable, Blue?"

The boy blinked. He wasn't used to any adult giving him a choice. He nodded his head slowly, and a rare smile appeared for a bare second before disappearing again.

Riley, Noah, and Blue rode quickly across the desert until they reached the spot where Blue and Noah had found Marissa's belongings. They split apart and followed the same search path spreading over a wider area. After several hours of fruitless results, Riley signaled Noah and Blue to meet him.

"What's up?" Noah asked.

Riley waited until Blue joined them. "Blue, are there any roads near here?"

The boy looked over the horizon and pointed. "Old Buckboard Road is over in that direction. It's not used much except by locals if the new road floods. It's been pretty much forgotten since the county road was graveled."

"What about a railroad track?" Riley asked.

The boy shook his head. "We don't have any trains. I've never seen a train except on TV."

"We have a dirt road but no railroad tracks," Riley said. "How about a cattle grate on the road."

Blue looked up. "Yeah, there are cattle grates, but there are also railroad tracks but no trains running on them. A long time ago, there were lots of freight trains moving cattle. When they stopped using the trains, they left the tracks behind. They haven't been used for a long time. My teacher told us about them in school."

"Where are the tracks?" Riley asked.

Blue pointed in a direction opposite of the way they were headed.

Riley was disappointed. "How about side roads, dirt roads extending off Old Buckboard Road going to ranches?"

Blue's eyebrows formed a straight line in concentration. "There are ranch roads..." he said, and then he stopped and looked excited. "I know! It fits Marissa's description."

"What?" Noah demanded.

Blue pointed in a southwestern direction. "My uncle took me there once rabbit hunting. There's an old dirt road leading to a mine."

"Mine?" Noah questioned. "What is there to mine out here except sand?"

The boy shook his head. "I don't remember, but the mine shaft is still there, although the entrance has been boarded over. There are a couple of old buildings, and..." the boy paused.

"What?" Noah and Riley both demanded.

"There are railroad tracks," Blue continued, his eyes flashing with excitement. "The miners used pushcarts, and there are tracks from the mine entrance to one of the buildings."

"Two out of three," Riley said. "A dirt road and railroad tracks. Now, all we need is a bridge and an embankment.

"Marissa didn't say anything about buildings," Noah said.

"Maybe she couldn't see them in the dark," Riley suggested. "Blue, can you take us there?"

The boy nodded and kicked in his heels.

It was a long ride in the hot afternoon sun. They rode at a steady pace being careful not to overheat the horses.

When they saw the buildings in the distance, Riley thought it looked encouraging. The dirt road was on a raised gravel incline. It could explain the embankment Marissa remembered falling down.

Noah pointed ahead, and with a shout, dismounted. He carefully pulled a dark red jacket from the sand.

Riley grinned, but his attention was focused on something else. The boys looked in the same direction. There was a sand-covered car crashed into one of the crumbling buildings. Both front doors were open, and the wheels were sunk deep into the sand.

Riley's mind was racing. This wasn't what he'd anticipated. Marissa's ex-husband was missing, and apparently, the car he had been driving was abandoned here. The same place where she had jumped from his car to keep him from attacking her.

"You guys stay here for a minute," he ordered. He rode over to the car, dismounted, and looked inside the vehicle. There was a long-bladed knife lying on the dashboard with a dark stain on the blade. A woman's handbag was on top of a department store bag in the backseat. The interior was covered with sand. Thinking of his list, Riley was mentally checking off items. Riley motioned for the boys to come closer. "It looks like it's been here for weeks. Look at the dust and sand inside. Don't touch anything, inside or out," he warned.

Noah looked through the open door and shuddered at the sight of the knife. He remembered the long slash on Marissa's arm.

"Look around, but be careful and don't touch anything," Riley repeated.

Almost by unspoken command, they split up. Noah and Blue began to follow the narrow set of railroad tracks toward the mine opening. The boys tried to peer past the boards and into the dark hole disappearing into the earth. Riley looked in the largest of the buildings only to find it completely empty and caving in. He walked around the building and followed posts buried deep into the desert to a second building, caved-in worse than the first. Whatever this had been, it was returning to its natural state of wild grasses and sagebrush. He scanned the desert floor and spotted something unnaturally dark against the natural beiges. He half-walked, half slid down a slope and stumbled backward as the shifting sands gave him a sickening feeling of being sucked into the sand. He scrambled and rolled to his knees and crawled around a clump of sagebrush and gagged.

"Hey, Riley!"

Riley jerked his head up. "Don't come any closer! Don't come over here!" he shouted.

Noah stopped and stared, as his brother was bent over and vomiting in the brush.

Riley raised his head and deliberately kept his eyes averted. He made a wide swing around what he'd found and joined Noah and Blue.

Noah's expression was one of worry. "You okay?"

Riley nodded. "I think we've found Gregg Novak."

Noah tried to turn around, but his brother wouldn't let him.

"Don't," Riley warned. "It's worse than you can imagine!"

Blue turned around and faced the brothers. "What's *he* doing here? Did Marissa kill him?"

"Of course not," Riley stated emphatically. "It means he never left here, and he's very much dead. I want you two to sit in the shade of that building. Drink some water, and I'm going to ride over to that hill and see if I can get a signal through to John Henry. Don't move, and don't touch anything!" He rinsed out his mouth from a canteen of water, mounted his horse, and rode the short distance to a higher elevation. He dialed John Henry's number and was surprised to get through. He left a message. A few minutes later, his cell phone rang, and he answered. Riley gave the deputy the news of their discovery, and he disconnected the call. Noah and Blue were both watching him, obeying and anticipating a plan of action.

"John Henry says to stay here and not to touch anything," Riley advised as he dismounted.

"We've sorta got the 'don't touch anything' order," Noah grumbled.

"We have to wait until the police get here," Riley said, joining them.

All three of them sat with their backs against the building, anxious and silent. Each of them was afraid of how Gregg Novak had died. Almost an hour later, John Henry, followed by Uncle Frank, an ambulance, a rescue squad vehicle, and several County and State police cars, drove slowly into the area. Riley stopped them from coming closer, pointing out sunken areas.

The boys were joined by Frank, who had brought a large thermos of water with him.

Riley retraced his original path, pointing John Henry and the various policemen toward the dark patch in the sinkhole, and warned them about the shifting sands.

"It's really gross," Riley warned John Henry. "He's buried in the sand to mid-chest level, but animals or birds have gotten to him."

The deputy went to his vehicle, removed a rope, gave one end to Riley and the rescue workers, and fought his way through the shifting sands to get as close to the body as he could. He yelled, and they pulled him back.

"Do you know if that's Gregg Novak?" John Henry asked.

Riley shook his head. "I've never met the man, although I did research him online, so I've seen a photograph of him. I don't think his mother would recognize that."

John Henry nodded in agreement. "It's been what, seven or eight weeks? The body has gone through decomposition and started to mummify in this dry heat. Add the damage from birds, insects, and animals, and that's what's left."

"I saw it, and I wish I hadn't," Riley said. "I don't watch horror movies for a reason."

They heard a siren in the distance.

"That should be the State Medical Examiner and probably more state police," John Henry explained. "This is going to require a full investigation. It's going to be difficult to get what's left of the body out of the sinkhole."

"How is this going to affect Marissa?" Riley asked.

John Henry shook his head. "I have no idea, and I don't want to guess. This substantiates her story. But he never left here, so it also makes her a prime suspect if he was murdered."

"Marissa didn't kill him!" Blue exploded as the boys joined them.

"I didn't say she did," the deputy said calmly but firmly. "I told you, boys, to stay put, and I meant it. Get back over there and stay there until I give you permission to do otherwise. Before we jump to any conclusions, this whole scene has to be documented by experts."

The state police cordoned off the mine area with police tape. Getting near the body was an impossible quest, as the disturbed sand kept sucking the body in further. The state police forensic team decided to remove the body before needing to bring in excavation equipment to get it out.

Watching through binoculars, John Henry turned to Frank. "He's got a gun tucked into the front of his pants."

"He was holding a gun on her. She said she heard shots after she escaped," Frank said.

Riley and the boys were questioned individually and told taped and written reports would have to follow. The police wanted to escort them to Murdock to document everything at the sheriff's office. Frank volunteered to return to the ranch with the horses. Riley drove the boys to Murdock in Frank's truck, escorted there with a State Trooper vehicle in front and behind him.

It was after two in the morning when Riley and the boys were released to go home. Frank had joined them at the police station, as Noah and Blue's temporary guardian, along with John Henry.

They drove home in their vehicles in almost total silence. Later, they were sitting around the kitchen table drinking coffee and looking quite shell-shocked. No one felt any urge to retire for the night. Sheriff Steven Bevens had arrived a few minutes later and had taken Marissa into custody.

"I'll be right behind you," Riley promised.

They heard a vehicle outside and a light rap on the door before John Henry came inside.

"I saw the lights still on," the deputy said, speaking more to Frank than to the boys.

"You bastard!" Blue snarled. "You had Marissa arrested!"

John Henry looked into three sets of unfriendly eyes, and Frank's, although not hostile, were angry.

"Listen, guys, I didn't have a choice on this. There is a man dead, and by her own admission Marissa was probably the last person to see him alive."

"Marissa didn't kill him! You saw what he did to her," Riley exclaimed angrily, coming down the hall with only a towel wrapped around him.

"I don't believe she did either, that's why I had Sheriff Bevens take her in. He's a friend of mine, and he can hold her in his jail for 48 hours. He'll treat her well, and it will give me time to pull together the facts. I didn't want the State Police to take her in because then I wouldn't control that situation."

"I've already called Shawn," Riley said. "Shawn said you'll get a hand-delivered package from a team of FBI and DEA agents in the morning. It's already morning. He wouldn't tell me what he'd discovered because he said it was a law enforcement issue, but he did say, *Gregg Novak, is in for one hell of a fall!*"

John Henry raised his eyebrows. "He's already taken the fall, but I'll take anything I can get that will help Marissa. I promise you guys. I'll do the best I can."

Chapter 13

Riley left for Murdock, and Sheriff Bevens, although surprised, was cooperative. He opened the unlocked cell and told Riley he could keep Marissa company. It was a long day with no news. The day seemed to stretch on endlessly. It ended the way it began, and as they were the only occupants in the single jail cell, Riley and Marissa slept in the single bunk, wrapped in each other's arms.

Frank kept Noah and Blue busy doing chores and working back at the ranch, but they were all anxiously awaiting a phone call. John Henry called twice, but each time it was with the same disappointment of no news yet. Riley had repeatedly called from the jail, and the boys talked to Marissa to keep her spirits up.

The following day at the ranch was a repeat of the day before, except for the telephone ringing every five minutes. Rumors had spread among the locals. Friends of Frank's were calling and wanting to know what was going on. The discovery of a dead man was news and startling to the peaceful community. Many people were asking questions for which there were no answers yet.

On the third day, John Henry woke everyone up before dawn by pounding on the front door.

"What is it?" Frank demanded.

"I'm taking Marissa to Las Vegas this morning," John Henry said. "I've already talked to Sheriff Bevens, and I'm on my way to pick up Marissa and Riley. Both of them want some clean clothing."

"Are they going to arrest her?" Noah demanded.

John Henry shook his head, and he almost smiled. "Marissa is only going in for questioning. I don't have all the answers yet, and I can't tell you what's going on, but it's good. It looks really good for Marissa."

Frank and the boys watched John Henry drive off, hoping for the best when they had no idea what could be the worst.

They completed the daily chores, and Frank set the boys to work painting since the drywall was complete. They made sure both Frank's cell phone and the house phone were close by. Except for the neighboring friends, the phones were silent.

Frank was frying grill-cheese sandwiches for supper when Blue saw the cloud of dust.

"Someone's coming, two vehicles," Blue shouted.

Sliding the pan from the stove burner, they stood on the front porch waiting. John Henry pulled his vehicle to a stop, and Riley parked beside him.

Noah and Blue shouted at the same time. "Marissa's home!"

Riley's truck had barely come to a stop when the door was flung open, and Marissa leaped out, hugging everyone.

"Are you free?"

"What happened?"

Riley deflected the questions. "Let's go inside. I could use a cold drink."

Marissa took a seat on the couch with Blue and Noah. Riley perched on the couch arm, and Frank leaned against a doorjamb. John Henry disappeared for a minute, and they heard him banging around in the kitchen.

"What's he doing?" Frank demanded.

Riley only shrugged and held Marissa's hand.

When John Henry rejoined them, it was with a cake pan full of mugs and glasses, a bottle of soda, and a wine bottle. He filled the glasses and mugs.

"It's not champagne, but it will have to do," John Henry said, as he poured the wine while Riley poured the soda into two glasses for the younger boys. He lifted his glass in a toast. "To Marissa's freedom!"

Everyone clinked the glasses and mugs together.

"So, somebody better start talking," Noah exclaimed.

Riley looked to John Henry to deliver the news.

"Marissa has been cleared of all charges. With a little more legal work to be completed, she will be exonerated of all existing charges. Any records on file will be expunged. As soon as we get a Judge's signature, she will be in the clear and a free woman."

"What does exonerated and expunged mean?" Blue asked.

"It means the files and records accusing her of things she didn't do will be destroyed, and her record will be clean," Riley explained. "Every trial Novak was involved with will be reviewed. If there's a shred of evidence indicating there might be doubt, those cases will be retried, and the innocent will go free. Marissa had proof of Novak bragging about sending innocent people to jail. Now the federal agencies are digging deep to find out who is legitimate and who is crooked.

"Gregg Novak died of natural causes," John Henry explained. "The coroner's report stated he died of exposure. He had a high concentration of cocaine in his system. When a body has been exposed to the elements in temperatures over a hundred degrees for forty-six days, it's difficult to pinpoint the actual cause. There were no wounds on his body.

"The drugs could explain some of his erratic behavior. After Marissa jumped from the car, Novak apparently tried to follow her. Those mineshafts running underground have been collapsing for years. The whole area needs to be fenced off with warnings. We'll get that done as soon as the Fed's release the area. We have to guess what happened. When Novak slammed on the brakes because of the javelinas in the road, he swerved and crashed into the building. The car wheels sank into the sand. He couldn't get the car out, and he couldn't see where he was going in the dark. He walked or fell into a hazardous area. Either the sinkhole already existed, or his weight caused the mineshaft to collapse. Either way, he was trapped. The more he fought to get free, the more he sank into it. There was no escape."

"So how does that clear Marissa?" Noah asked.

"The facts fit her statements exactly. So does the timeline, the fingerprints, and the DNA collected by Dr. Andrews," Riley explained. "The knife he threatened and cut Marissa with was in the car. His fingerprints were all over it, but the blood belonged to Marissa. Her purse, the ATM receipts, and the timestamp when she left her workplace corroborate her timeline and testimony. The car he was driving was a rental. The gun was recovered, and it only had his fingerprints on it.

"So we were right trying to track where she was while she was wandering around in the desert," Noah said.

"We also discovered a briefcase in his trunk with twelve kilos of cocaine and three hundred thousand dollars in cash," John Henry said. "All the fingerprints on the evidence belonged to Novak, and a kingpin drug dealer, who has inconveniently disappeared. All other fingerprints were traced to the rental company employees who detailed the car before it was rented.

"The briefcase, the drugs, the money, and weapons were full of fingerprints, all Novak's, and the dealer. The cash and drugs fit into the evidence Shawn Williamson uncovered of a drug-smuggling syndicate.

"Novak started taking large payoffs from upper-level drug kingpins to keep their middlemen out of jail, around the same time Marissa divorced him. He had a very profitable business going for a long time. Novak's flaws were greed, and he was corrupt. The more involved he got with the drug dealers, the more he wanted. He wanted a more significant piece of the action. He was willing to blackmail anyone and everyone who got in the way of what he wanted.

"He was blackmailing bailiffs, judges, and other lawyers. When he tried his methods on a reputable District Attorney, it was his downfall. The D.A. went to the FBI and was cooperating with a sting operation to nail Novak. The D.A.'s office was already involved in a full-scale investigation. So far, there are thirty-two people in law enforcement and court-related positions being charged with various crimes. There are also investigations taking place in the Department of Child Protective Services."

"So, where does Marissa fit into this?" Frank asked.

John Henry shook his head. "She didn't, except as a pawn in Novak's personal plans. When Marissa divorced him, he used his contacts to hurt her. He paid off a county social worker and a judge to get custody of the kids. Why idiots pay by check, I'll never know.

"He tried to force her back into his life by using her sons as bait. About the time Marissa snatched the twins, Novak was already in trouble. His deals were falling apart. People he thought he had control over suddenly turned the tables on him and were making deals with prosecuting attorneys, the FBI and DEA agencies."

"This next part is supposition." He turned to Blue. "That means we can only make an educated guess of what happened. We think Novak went over the edge. He was losing control of everything he'd spent years building. He needed someone to blame, and he made Marissa the scapegoat. Men like him are all ego. They have to be able to blame someone else for their failures. They can't accept responsibility themselves.

"Luckily, Marissa got away. Luckily for the investigation teams, Marissa knew her ex-husband's habits. Novak was a methodical person who kept records–detailed records. One of the FBI experts told me that's another symptom of a narcissistic personality. They are so sure of themselves; they believe they will never be caught.

"With Marissa's help, a search warrant, and the combined efforts of the FBI and DEA organizations, they were able to find records of most of his illegal transactions. The evidence trail may go back as far as five years. That's five years of criminal extortion, bribery, and a dozen more charges for illegal behaviors.

"It will be a very long and involved investigation, and a lot of the legal eagles in Las Vegas are involved on the wrong side of the law. Novak thought he was a big man in a large syndicate. In reality, he wasn't. The records Novak kept are more important to the case than the man himself. My guess is, if he hadn't killed himself by falling in the sinkhole, someone from the syndicate would have taken him out. You can't get involved with those kinds of people and expect to win. He won't be missed."

"Except by my children," Marissa said softly.

"Sorry," John Henry said.

"Your children deserve better, and so do you," Riley said softly, wrapping an arm around her. Everyone in the room agreed.

Riley watched from the front room window, and when he saw the dust cloud, he signaled to Noah and Blue. The boys paused the movie they were watching and descended on the kitchen.

"I'm hungry!" Blue exclaimed, sitting at the kitchen table. "Something smells good!"

Marissa looked from the newspaper she was reading and gestured towards the oven. "I have brownies baking. They'll be done in about eight minutes."

"Great," Noah exclaimed, leaning over Marissa's shoulder. "What are you reading?"

"John Henry dropped off these newspapers. It's the current District Attorney's version of the investigation on Gregg's alleged criminal activities," Marissa said. "I love how they say *alleged* when everyone knows he was guilty. The new Las Vegas District Attorney is sharing credit with the FBI and DEA people. Do I hear a car coming?"

Blue glared at Noah, but he only shook his head slightly. "That's Riley leaving," he said. "He said he needed razor blades."

"Well, I guess it's only us for dinner," Marissa said, setting the paper aside. "Are burgers okay?"

Both Noah and Blue agreed as they watched Marissa begin to assemble ingredients from the refrigerator.

They heard the front door slam, and Frank's voice called out, "Marissa!"

Marissa looked at the boys, startled. Frank had left earlier in the day with John Henry on what he called *business* without a hint of when they would return.

Marissa stepped into the living room, and she burst into tears as two little boys ran across the room, crying, "Mommy! Mommy!" She gathered them into her arms and smothered them in hugs and kisses. "Jake! Jackson! My babies!" Marissa cried, clutching her boys to her.

Everyone else looked on with smiles of satisfaction.

Marissa wiped her eyes. "How did you do this?" she asked.

"I know you said you wouldn't get the kids until a judge reversed the court order of custody, so we decided to fast-track the process," John Henry explained. "Frank knows a Family Advocate Counselor, and I know the Judge."

"Just like that," Marissa cried. "After all this time, and it was that simple?"

"They are your children, and what Novak and his friends did to you has been front-page news for a week now," Frank said. "We explained the circumstances, and my friend was more than willing to review the case. By the way, the judge who signed the original custody papers has been charged with felony tampering. He *retired* yesterday, although I don't think that's going to prevent him from being indicted. It made the reversal decision easy. Several judges in Nevada are going to have many of their decisions going under review."

"I didn't tell you where the boys were staying," Marissa exclaimed.

"That was me," Riley admitted. "I swiped your phone, and I hit redial. I talked to your friend, Jenna Harrison, and I explained everything to her. She already knew from the newspapers what was going on. She said if we showed her proof of the custody order being reversed, she'd let us bring the kids home."

"I didn't betray you, Marissa," a woman said from the doorway. 'I only agreed when they showed me the signed legal papers and when they agreed to let me follow them here with the twins."

"Jenna!" Marissa rose to her feet and hugged her friend.

"Honey, I am so glad this nightmare is over at last," Jenna exclaimed.

"It is, isn't it?" Marissa sobbed, swiping at her tears. "It's finally over."

Riley's concentration was broken when Noah and Frank, each with a twin perched on their shoulders, moved to the side of the corral to watch.

Kingston reared on his hind legs, and suddenly the saddle shifted to the side. It had taken him the better part of an hour to get the saddle on the stallion's back.

"Pay attention!" Jefferson Ironheart barked.

Riley tightened his grip on the lead rope, and the horse calmed, but it was still trying to dislodge the saddle.

"Careful!" Jefferson Ironheart ordered. "Try to get close enough to tighten the cinch."

"Easy for you to say," Riley mumbled, straightening his posture and taking a firm stance with the horse.

"Bring him this way," the old man commanded, and Riley pulled the reins, but the stallion resisted his efforts.

"Pull on the bit! You are in charge!" Jefferson Ironheart ordered. "Make him understand he must obey you."

Riley did as he was instructed but with more gentleness and coaxing than the old man would have preferred. He repeated the same exercise a dozen times. Each time Kingston shied away and fought him. Each time Jefferson Ironheart didn't look pleased.

After several hours, Jefferson Ironheart threw up his hands in disgust.

"You don't listen," he complained.

Riley uncinched the saddle and removed it. Kingston reared and bucked wildly for a few seconds. He pulled the reins tight, tossed the blanket on the stallion's back, and tried to re-saddle him. Once again, Kingston bucked and went wild. He pulled free of Riley's hold, pranced, and pawed the air in total freedom.

Jefferson Ironheart opened the gate and glared at Riley.

"I won't treat him rough," Riley complained. "That's what has made him this way!"

Jefferson Ironheart grunted with disapproval and took the saddle from him. On the way to the tack room, he was joined by three other tribesmen who had come with him this morning. It wasn't unusual for other men to watch the stallion's progress. Still, they usually kept to themselves and at a distance. Sometimes they didn't even talk among themselves. They only watched. It was okay with Riley. Dealing with Jefferson Ironheart was tough enough. They had been trying to saddle Kingston for weeks.

Kingston would let Riley get on his back, but he wouldn't tolerate the saddle. Jefferson Ironheart had brought several tribal members to the ranch earlier in the week. Kingston had proved he was still extremely dangerous to anyone daring to try to tame him. The men had failed miserably and limped off from their attempts.

Riley could almost feel the animosity from the tribal riders. They didn't say anything directly to him, but he recognized the anger in their eyes. They didn't understand why an outsider could handle the stallion. Riley didn't understand it either, but he was beginning to realize how big a problem he'd created.

Jefferson Ironheart came out of the barn and gave a slight wave of his arm. It was as much of a signal as he ever received from the elder when the session was over.

Riley walked over to his uncle and the boys.

"Tough going?" Frank asked.

Riley nodded his head towards Jefferson Ironheart's departing truck. "I have an idea, but I need to talk to you about it. In fact, I need to talk to you... period. In private."

Frank lifted Jackson from his shoulder and handed him to Noah. "Take the boys to their mother, and go with John Henry. Riley will join you later."

"What's on your mind?" Frank asked, stepping over beside the barn and into the shade.

"This place," Riley said. "What you and Aunt Katherine have built and, more importantly, what you've been doing here all these years for homeless boys."

"What about it?"

"It's what I want to do," Riley said. "I've been floundering for years trying to decide what I wanted to devote my life to doing."

"Hell, Riley, you've got a stack of degrees and a career," Frank said.

"I do," Riley agreed. "But, all I've been doing is killing time and rejecting what I know in my heart is my true path."

When Riley was finished talking, Frank pushed his hat to the back of his head. "Son, it's hard to believe, but I reckon that's been part of the problem. I knew you were never as wild as those entertainment shows claimed. I think all that acting up was a cover, but I never suspected why. Serving others is a calling from a higher power."

"One I've been fighting for a while," Riley said. "I have plenty of time to learn, and for the first time in a very long time, this decision feels right."

Uncle Frank looked straight into his nephew's eyes. "I believe you. I'm a little stunned, but I believe you. Have you talked to your folks about this?"

"No, but I will when the time is right."

"Does this have anything to do with Marissa?" Frank asked.

"Yes, but I have to move very carefully there. Marissa has been hurt and needs time to recover," Riley said. "I know you think we've been sleeping together, and we have slept in the same bed, but it hasn't been about sex. I have held her in my arms all night, many nights trying to banish her fears as she trembled for hours with nightmares. I have never felt so close to a woman before. I wanted to relieve her fears and nothing more, but I have fallen in love with her."

Frank nodded. "That's a good thing because while she hasn't admitted it to herself, and she wouldn't because she was afraid of dragging you into her problems, I think she's in love with you. I've seen that look in a woman's eyes before. It was my Katherine's, and there is no mistaking it. Have you told her you love her yet?"

Riley looked toward the house. "That's something else I have to get off my chest."

"Ain't no time like the present," Frank grumbled, and he headed for the barns.

Riley looked to the house, but he knew it wasn't the right time yet. Marissa wasn't ready yet.

"Car coming," Blue announced, slamming into the house. "It's a fancy car, with Nevada plates," he warned.

Frank looked, squinted, and grimaced. "Lordy boy, you can see the tag from that far? Let's go see who's driving that fancy car. I still don't trust those government people."

"I thought Marissa was clear of everything," Noah said.

"She is," Riley said, but he was moving purposefully through the house to intercept the stranger at the front porch.

The man who emerged from the black Lexus was GQ style, from his haircut to his Italian loafers. He was quick to take note of the men and boys blocking him.

"I'm looking for Marissa Novak?" the man said as a way of introduction.

"It's Marissa Miller, and what do you want?" Riley demanded.

"David Corrigan of Corrigan, Corrigan, Lewis, and Novak," the stranger said, offering a business card.

"Although, the Novak part of the name is being dissolved as we speak."

Marissa opened the screen door. "David," she greeted him with a smile. "What brings you here?"

David Corrigan looked a little uncomfortable at the four imposing males.

"Down, boys!" Marissa commanded with a laugh. "David is a friend. Please treat him like one. David, ignore them. They're a little overprotective." She opened the door and led the man into the living room, followed by Riley.

Frank corralled the boys and pointed them outside.

The twins obviously knew David. He set his briefcase on the floor and put a twin on each knee.

"How is the office holding up?" Marissa asked.

David looked up, smiled at the boys, and grimaced. "My father has heartburn every time he opens a newspaper and sees his company mentioned in an article about *you know who*. The partnership will survive, but public relations are a nightmare right now. We have cooperated fully with the agencies and the state police. There was no connection between the illegal activities of *you know who* and the firm. Whatever he did, he did on his own."

"Why are you here?" Riley asked.

"Would you go get me a soda or a glass of water?" David asked of the twins. The little boys jumped from his lap and ran to the kitchen. When they left the room, he opened his briefcase. "Gregg's last will."

Marissa looked confused. "We've been divorced for years, and he told me when I divorced him that I would never get a penny from him, and I didn't."

The twins ran into the room with a bottle of water. Riley squatted to their level and whispered something to them, and took the bottle of water as they raced each other to Marissa's room. He handed the water to the attorney. "I told them it was nap-time."

"They never obey me so quickly," Marissa complained.

"I have little boy instincts," Riley said with a grin.

David removed a legal document from the briefcase. "As I was saying, this is about Gregg's will. Regardless of what he told you, he didn't change his will. The house, the joint bank account, the cars, the furniture, it's all yours."

"I thought the DEA confiscated everything when drugs were involved," Riley said.

"They have confiscated a great deal," David admitted. "Gregg was a successful attorney for years before he started dipping into illegal activities. There were separate accounts and assets in his name only. Those have been confiscated to the tune of several million dollars so far."

David Corrigan returned his attention to Marissa. "I don't know if you knew about it, but there were assets in your name solely. DEA can't touch anything in your name unless they can prove a direct connection to illegal activities. Gregg was putting assets in your name as late as this past February. The DEA doesn't want to be unfair to family members who aren't involved with the crimes. There is absolutely no evidence that you were involved with his deals. There was also a large insurance policy, and it's going to pay double indemnity. Regardless of what he was doing at the time, falling into a sinkhole in the desert qualifies as an accident."

"I was only married to Gregg for ten months. I'll admit I was naive at first, and I signed anything he told me to sign, but I don't want anything from him," Marissa said.

David Corrigan ignored her outburst. "Marissa, please don't reject this windfall based on anger. You can sell the house, sell everything, and start a new life. You can use the insurance money for the boys' college funds or invest it in trust funds. After the way Novak treated you, it's a fair settlement.

"I also want to apologize. I knew Gregg was changing, but I didn't know what was going on. I swear I didn't. I had to turn all his office paperwork over to the DEA and the FBI. There were copies of your divorce settlement among the files. I couldn't believe what he did to you, claiming you had a gambling problem. He was acting like a rabid dog. He screwed you out of everything, including your children."

Marissa was shaking her head. "I didn't want anything from him, only my babies and my freedom." She reached for Riley's hand and felt somewhat assured when he gave it a squeeze.

"Mr. Corrigan is right," Riley said gently. "You shouldn't think of it as taking something from him. As long as the money came from legitimate sources, it's a legacy for the twins. If you don't want to use it, invest it for the boys. Alternatively, you could use it for good causes. While he's frying in Hell, his money could do a lot of good."

Marissa smiled at his suggestion. "David, please stay for dinner. It will give me a couple of hours to think about what I want to do."

David Corrigan left five hours later with the signatures he needed to file the legal paperwork. The insurance money she would invest in trust funds for the twins. The rest of the assets would be sold, and she could decide later what to do with the proceeds. Even if she only kept half of it, she would never have to worry about working again. David had asked Marissa to return and go through the house for personal items, but she shook her head.

"There's nothing there I want, and I never want to step foot in that house again. I've finally stopped having nightmares, and I don't want to start having them again. If you feel it's necessary, you can go through his things or hire someone to do it. Otherwise, send it all to an auction house or to charity thrift stores."

Standing side-by-side, Riley and Marissa waved as David Corrigan drove away. "I doubt David's BMW has ever been that dirty," she said with a smile.

Riley looked over to his truck, covered with the same sand and dust. "It takes a while to get used to it."

Marissa leaned against Riley's chest. "Do you think I'm crazy?" she asked.

Riley shook his head. "Not at all. I can understand why you didn't want any part of it, but excess money is never a problem. You can always find a way to spend it doing a lot of good."

Marissa turned in his arms to face him. "Are you really going to stay here and work with Frank and his foster kids?"

"I'd like to, but he hasn't given me a definitive answer," Riley said. "He needs help, and with a few required classes, that help can be me. I'm more than qualified. Frank realizes he's getting older. He needs someone ready and willing to take over. Some people will think I'm nuts, but I really don't care. What do you think?"

"I think it should be your decision. You've been looking for something to fill an empty space, and I believe this foster ranch could be it. You have a need to help, and so do I. Others may doubt and not understand, but I do," Marissa said. "If it makes you happy, go for it."

"I think Frank is skeptical," Riley said. "You told him you wanted to stick around and help in any way you could when he reopens and is ready for the kids. A day later, I tell him the same thing. I'm not sure he believes we weren't aware of what the other was doing."

"He knows we've grown closer," Marissa said.

"Yeah," Riley said. "He knows you have been coming into my room. I don't think he believes we *weren't* having sex."

"You've been a gentleman," Marissa said. "Patient and understanding."

"I have, but your spending nights in my arms has been a strain on my self-control. I need a rain-check," Riley teased.

"You won't need self-control the next time," she promised with a kiss.

Riley pulled her in for another kiss, and he raised his head, looking around the weather-beaten ranch. "Money doesn't buy happiness. It doesn't buy integrity or satisfaction. I want to continue the legacy Frank and Katherine started. I want the children who pass through this place to leave, knowing happiness comes from knowing you are the best person you can be. Frank has kept it going by himself for a while, but imagine how much good we could do as a team. Blue has changed so much since he was brought here. His self-esteem has grown by leaps and bounds."

"Blue only needed a little TLC and someone to believe in him," Marissa exclaimed. "I think you must have a degree in tender loving care."

"So do you," Riley agreed, pulling her into a kiss that promised so much more.

The next morning Marissa called her landlady in Irvine, where she had rented a small apartment over a garage. Mrs. Porter was a woman who was in the secret network and had helped her disappear. Mrs. Porter hadn't known her married name, and she was thrilled to know Marissa was alive and safe. She promised to store Marissa's belongings until she could retrieve them.

Marissa's next call was to her former employer. The FBI had already informed the company of her dual identifies. Although her position had been filled, her co-workers were glad to know she was safe. The payroll department promised to forward her final paycheck in her real name to the ranch. She could also expect a box of personal items cleared from her desk after she left.

Chapter 14

"I need to open a bank account, any suggestions?" Riley said, sticking his head into Frank's office the next morning.

"Local or in Yuma?" Frank asked.

"What do you consider local?" Riley asked with a grin.

"Murdock is the closest with a national affiliate. There's a credit union in Wolf Springs and one on the reservation."

"Forty miles, or ninety miles," Riley mused. "I feel like I'm back in college, splitting my classes between the San Antonio and Austin campuses. I was cruising up on five hundred thousand miles on my jeep before it went up in flames. At least I could stop at the lake on my way."

"Your dad sent me photographs of what you boys built on that lake property. Do you miss it?" Frank asked.

"Not really," Riley said, smiling. "The best part of commuting between the two campuses was spending time with Micah and Katie. I love Tess and Karina, but marriage changed both of my big brothers. It was for the better, and it's all part of growing up. I guess I'll go to Murdock. Make sure Marissa gets a list of what you need from town."

Riley assumed Marissa would want to go with him, and he was right. Where she went, though, so did her boys. She wasn't willing to let them out of her sight yet. Noah and Blue weren't about to be left behind, either.

The first stop was the bank, and the second was at a grocery store. While the boys were playing video games, Marissa filled two carts with food supplies. It took a while to store the cold and frozen foods in the coolers they carried in the truck bed and covered with a heat reflective tarpaulin.

When they parked outside the Yellow Horse Trading Post, Noah and Blue hurried inside, Riley sneaked a few kisses, and he and Marissa followed at a more sedate pace with the twins.

Christian waved and smiled, but he was busy with customers. Noah asked to borrow Riley's phone, and he was taking pictures as he wandered around.

Marissa was keeping track of the twins, as they wanted every toy in the store. Riley waited for Christian to finish with his customer.

"Aaah-ooooh!" Christian howled, walking over and shaking Riley's hand. "My man, Coyote. Good to see you again! Have you brought your family with you?"

Riley got it that Christian wasn't going to let go of the nickname he'd carried most of his life. He shook his head, smiling and wished he could claim Marissa and the twins as his.

"The taller boy is my youngest brother. The other boy is Blue Eagle. Deputy Walker has him living at the ranch. I'm pretty sure you heard about Marissa and her problems."

"Oh, yeah, I've heard about all the stuff going on at your place. We don't get much excitement around here."

"Believe me when I say we didn't want it either," Riley said. "Did those college kids return and claim their stuff?"

Christian shook his head. "No, I moved it into the storeroom so no one would make me an offer I couldn't refuse. I would have hated to disappoint you. My motto is everything in the store is for sale."

"You sold the equipment to me!" Riley protested.

Christian grinned. "I know. That's why I moved it to the storeroom. I didn't want to be tempted." He yelled at a young woman sitting in a small office behind the counter. "Jean, watch the store. I need to show Coyote something!"

Riley was led into a large storage room. He scrutinized the skis and the box of climbing gear again. "It's all in good shape," he said, pleased with his purchases.

"I have something else you might be interested in," Christian exclaimed. He walked over to another area behind a table and pulled a tarp off a motor cross bike. "What do you think of this?"

The motor cross bike was strapped to a small trailer and looked to be in perfect condition.

"Very nice!" Riley exclaimed, walking around it.

"A college kid stopped in here a couple of weeks ago with a bunch of other kids," Christian explained. "Said he was sick of the desert and wanted to trade the bike for enough cash for beer and gas money to get them back to Los Angeles. He had the title, so we made a deal, and it's all legal and tidy. His old man may kick his ass when he gets back, but that's not my problem! I can make you a heck of a deal on it. I had Lenny Holcomb over at the garage check out the engine before I forked over the cash. He said it was cherry."

"How much?" Riley asked, checking out the motor amps."

Christian quoted him a more than reasonable price.

Riley whistled. "Look, Christian, it's a great deal, but I..."

"Shoot, Coyote, I was counting on you," Christian interrupted. "You said to keep my eyes open for good equipment, and when we were talking, you mentioned motor cross."

"I did, but I also said I was a spectator. My brother is the motor cross rider, my *younger* brother," Riley explained. "Noah just turned seventeen. I have to clear it with our folks first. Noah's a great rider, but he tends to be fearless. This bike might be more power than my folks want under him."

Christian was nodding his head in agreement. "I see your point. Okay, I'll hold it for a week and keep it under wraps so no one makes me an offer I can't refuse. Oh, and you need to stop over at Holcomb's garage. He's got a toolbox over there for sale that might fit your truck. You said to keep my eyes open for a good used one, and he's got one."

"I'll stop on my way," Riley said. He hoisted the box of climbing gear, and Christian carried the skis. They took them out to the truck, and Riley stowed them in the back. He followed Christian inside and sacrificed his Visa card.

"Bro, this place is so cool," Noah exclaimed, dumping a handful of tourist toys on the counter. At his brother's raised eyebrows, he reddened. "It's for the twins," he exclaimed.

"Better leave off the guns and holsters," Riley suggested. "Marissa hates guns, and with good reason. I overheard her talking to Uncle Frank about it. Even playing Cowboys and Indians isn't okay with her."

"What?" Noah exclaimed in protest.

"Think," Riley said to his brother as a reminder.

Noah did, and then he nodded. "Okay, I get it." He shoved the two sets of toy guns aside, and Christian moved them under the counter.

The bell over the door jangled, and a new family of tourists entered the shop. Noah pushed a twenty-dollar bill at his brother and took off through the back door.

"I want to see the canyon," Noah said over his shoulder.

Riley paid for the toys and pocketed the change in his shirt pocket to keep it separate from his money. The tourists gave him the once-over, and he knew from experience it was the dawning of recognition.

Christian leaned over and handed him a plastic bag. "I see what she has for her boys. I'll put it on your tab. You can pay me later when you come back for the motorbike."

"Maybe," Riley said with a grin. "If they ask, tell them no, it's not me. I hope you're as good a liar as you are a salesman! I have a feeling you can stonewall them." He bagged the toys and snagged a twin while hustling Marissa and the other twin outside.

The canyon advertised on the Yellow Horse Trading Post billboard signs was only five hundred yards behind the trading post. It was posted to walk at your own risk. *Watch Your Footing* signs were posted every couple of hundred feet along the path. There were signs stating *Parents are Responsible for Children's Safety, Establishment Not Responsible for Accidents, Safety Is Your Concern*, and *Don't Walk Off Posted Path* signs. The Yellow Horse Trading Post placed significant importance on signs.

Marissa held twin Jack's hand to make sure he didn't run ahead, and Riley did the same with Jake. Blue and Noah were ahead on the path. When they caught up with them, Noah wasn't impressed.

"I don't get it," he complained, gesturing at the large expanse of the canyon. It stretched across a space of a quarter mile and was probably a thousand feet in depth. "What's the big deal? It's another canyon, like a thousand other canyons around here."

"I told you so," Blue taunted softly.

"That's true," Marissa commented. "It is a canyon, like many others. However, if you were a tourist from New York or Wisconsin and didn't know canyons were everywhere, this canyon would be impressive. A lot of tourists never see anything beyond the main highways or interstates."

"Okay, I've seen it, and I'm done," Noah exclaimed. "Can we head home now?"

Riley cocked an eyebrow at his brother's almost petulant tone.

"I'm going back to the truck," Noah mumbled.

A half-hour later, back on the highway and almost to Holcomb's Garage, Noah questioned Riley about the Trading Post. "I wonder how many times that place has been robbed?" Noah said.

"Why would you think it has been robbed?" Riley asked.

"Because there's only Mickey Mouse locks on the front and back doors. I know because I looked. The windows have bars on them, but they wouldn't stop anyone determined to break in. He doesn't even have a security system."

"Who would hear an alarm if he did?" Marissa asked. "The Trading Post is thirty miles from everything in every direction. It's literally in the middle of the desert."

"In L.A. or back home in San Antonio, it would have been looted in less than twelve hours," Noah said ominously.

"We're not living in those cities," Riley said over his shoulder. "I, for one, am glad there are places where people can trust their neighbors and not seize the first opportunity to take advantage of others."

Marissa squeezed Riley's hand and whispered. "I don't ever want to live in fear again."

He raised her hand to his lips. "If I have anything to say about it, you won't."

Blue was sitting quietly in the backseat reading. He was a little squashed between the two car seats, but it kept the twins from pestering each other. The boy was reading voluntarily. Small paperback books, mostly adventure tales, appeared almost magically in the mail. He read slowly, keeping one finger somewhere on the page as if to keep him anchored to the words. Blue's private library of books was growing, and he kept them in a small stack on top of his dresser. Personal possessions were important to the boy. He took nothing for granted and took great care of the things he'd been given since coming to Frank's ranch. As if he could feel someone watching him, the boy looked up with a fierce frown.

Noah smiled and pulled a paperback from his pocket, and soon there was nothing but quiet from the backseat as the twins had fallen asleep.

Riley pulled into the Holcomb Garage, looked at the toolbox for sale, bought it, and had it bolted into his truck bed in a matter of minutes. He checked off one more thing from his mental list of replacements.

Every day for four straight days, Jefferson Ironheart drove to the ranch with a new unknown rider to try his skill at riding Kingston. Every day Kingston bucked, and the rider landed in the dirt, hard. Every day Riley climbed onto Kingston without a saddle successfully. When he tried to saddle the horse, he fought the same battle.

In clandestine meetings with Blue, Riley was introducing the boy to the stallion in the gentlest of ways. Riley held the boy firmly in front of him, so he couldn't get away. He retrieved the dropped carrot from the straw and closed Blue's fingers around the carrot.

"Gently, Blue. You can't let Kingston know you're afraid of him."

The boy shook his head and tried to back away. "I am! He'll bite me."

"He won't bite you. It's a very long carrot," Riley promised and sent a quick prayer to whatever angel kept an eye on young boys. "Kingston responds to gentleness. Talk to him, try to be his friend."

"This horse is crazy, and so are you!" Blue protested.

"I'm not crazy," Riley corrected the boy. "Look at him. Kingston is a magnificent horse, but inside he's scared. He's been bullied and mistreated. Everyone talks about him behind his back, and they say he's bad, but he isn't. You wouldn't like to be treated like that, would you?"

The boy shook his head and eyed the horse suspiciously but with a little bit of understanding.

Riley was making a connection with Blue because he knew that's exactly how the boy had been treated.

"Wouldn't you like to be a special friend? Kingston likes me. He likes Noah as long as he keeps his distance. If you continue to work with Kingston, he'll like you too."

Blue shook his head stubbornly.

"You know how we told you roughhousing with the twins was okay, but you have to be careful because they're smaller and can get hurt more easily?"

Blue nodded.

"Kingston is the same. He may be bigger, but he gets scared because someone has hurt him. He needs another friend, someone who won't hurt him, and someone who is from the Quechan Tribe."

Blue looked at Riley suspiciously. "Do you really think he likes me?"

"He will if we ease him into liking you."

The boy tentatively offered the carrot while Riley coaxed the stallion forward. After two full minutes, Kingston took the carrot in one swift motion, and Blue snatched his hand back.

Riley stroked the horse's head and turned to the boy. "We'll try again this afternoon."

Blue looked at his fingers and wiggled them as if he were taking a full count. "I heard a man tell Wayne Crow the only reason Kingston responds to you is that you're too dumb to be scared of him."

Riley laughed and ruffled the boy's hair. "There may be truth in that statement. God knows I don't know much about horses. However, remember, dumb or not, at least I am able to work with him. No one else has been able to accomplish the same, except maybe you."

By the end of the week, Blue was able to feed and pet the horse without the stallion threatening him. Blue was losing his fear of being close to the stallion. He usually spoke to him in the native tongue of his people. This was something Blue was beginning to take great pride in, and he gloated his new skill over Noah with an adolescent zeal.

After an incredibly discouraging session with Kingston, Riley asked Frank for an old saddle that would be no loss if it were destroyed. Frank didn't have one, but he made a few phone calls and found a rancher friend who had an old saddle fitting Riley's description of *a piece of junk no one wants*. Frank went to get the saddle, and a few hours later, he delivered it to his nephew. To his surprise, Riley took it into the tack room and proceeded to rub it with saddle oil.

Frank scratched his head. "Riley, what are you doing now? That saddle won't last five minutes on Kingston."

"I've been researching on the internet, and I found this method of introducing horses to the saddle. I'm going to nail this old saddle to the wall of his stall. Some horses have stronger sensitivity to smells than others. If we can get him used to the smell, maybe it won't be such a threat to him."

Frank nodded. "You're a rookie, but I have heard of this method."

The saddle lost several inches of leather, but gradually Kingston began to ignore it. For the second phase of the saddling process, Riley took an old saddle blanket, oiled it with saddle oil, and attached half of a belt to each side. When he tossed the blanket on Kingston's back, there was no reaction at all. After the first hour, the belt was hooked together under the horse's belly. It was loose, at first, and every hour, Riley tightened it until it was snug. He left it on Kingston all day. The next day Riley repeated the exercise in half the time. By the third day, Kingston wasn't fighting him when he tightened the belt. On the fourth day, he saddled Kingston without a struggle. His patience had paid off.

Frank teased him that Kingston was the only horse he'd ever heard of that was being broken over internet advice.

Saturday was the day Riley planned to spring his surprise on Jefferson Ironheart. He was keeping his fingers crossed the elder would listen.

They were finishing breakfast when they heard a vehicle pull in.

Noah looked up and lifted his head slightly, listening. "That's not Jefferson Ironheart's truck. It sounds more like…"

There was a light rap on the screen door, and John Henry walked in dressed in full uniform, as he did when he wasn't planning on working on the ranch.

Marissa looked frightened. "Is there a problem?" she demanded.

"No, no," John Henry assured her gently. "Marissa, you're going to have to stop this. I am an officer of the law, but it doesn't mean I'm going to arrest you. Your problems have been straightened out. In fact, you should get a letter of apology from the District Attorney's Office in Las Vegas for their past mistreatment of you." The deputy grinned. "It's not likely to happen, but you should. It would happen faster if you filed suit against the city government of Las Vegas. After what they did to you, they deserve a wake-up call."

Marissa gave John Henry a smile. "Sorry. It's a habit I need to break, and no, I don't want to sue anyone. They cleared my name and my record, and I'm thankful it's over. Would you like a cup of coffee?"

"Any time," John Henry said, accepting the offered cup but not the chair. He leaned against the kitchen counter. "I am here on official business, and I need to speak with Riley."

"Me?" Riley said, surprised.

Noah looked amused. "Are you going to arrest my brother?"

Frank was looking interested. John Henry looked over to his friend, and he gave him a wink.

"Let's go talk outside," the Deputy suggested.

Riley followed him outside. "What's this about?"

"I had an e-mail come into the office last night from your brother, the one named Micah." He pulled a sheath of papers from the front seat.

"I gave him your e-mail because Uncle Frank's computer and printer are ancient. The matter concerned you more than him," Riley said, looking over the papers. "I knew it!"

"You could have given me a heads up," John Henry said. "It doesn't take a genius to figure out what this is about." He pointed to the printed pictures with the gallery names and phone numbers printed on the bottom. "You want to clue me in so I don't go off half-cocked."

"Can I finish my breakfast?" Riley asked.

"Lead on," John Henry exclaimed, and they returned to the kitchen.

Frank looked at both of them questioningly.

"Anything said from this point on is police business," John Henry warned. "No one talks until I have a chance to take care of my business." The deputy had everyone's attention. He poured himself another mug of coffee.

Riley spread the packet of papers on the table. "Micah has been snooping for me. When I saw Glenda Two-Trees' woven and macramé pieces, I thought I recognized her style. Micah is the artist in the family. He'll drag anyone with him into art galleries."

"Been there, done that," Noah complained.

"The point is," Riley continued. "I recognized her artwork and her name. Rainey told me her mother's agent, Mr. Duquette, was only getting a couple hundred dollars for her pieces. What I remembered was we were in a gallery in Los Angeles. There was nothing priced under a couple thousand dollars in that place.

"I'm not an artist, but I do have good people instincts, and I didn't like Mr. Duquette from the get-go. I asked Micah to do the snooping for me. He has a lot of contacts in the art world, and this is the result. Glenda Two-Trees' weavings and macramé pieces are being exhibited in some very swanky galleries on both coasts. Her biography describes her as a reclusive person who keeps her private life a secret."

"In other words, don't try to contact her," Marissa interpreted.

"Exactly," Riley said. "The perfect ruse for an agent who is buying art on the cheap and selling it for maximum profit."

"We are so isolated, it only made it easier," John Henry said. "I've known Glenda most of my life. She is a bit of a recluse because she spends most of her time making her pieces to support her family."

"Are you going to arrest Mr. Duquette?" Blue asked.

"I'm not sure what he's done is illegal," John Henry admitted. "It may be unethical, but I'm not sure it's illegal."

"Really?" Riley asked.

John Henry nodded. "Hey, give me a break. There are thousands of laws on the books, and I'm not an expert in all of them. I'll launch an investigation but making a profit, regardless of how large, may not be against the law. Mr. Duquette has never forced anyone to sell to him. Even if I can't arrest him, we can warn everyone on the reservation.

He's an authorized buyer with the Quechan Co-op. Do you want to come with me, Riley? Glenda is going to be very surprised to discover she is famous."

"I'd like to, but Jefferson Ironheart should be here any minute," Riley said with regret.

"He'll want to know about this. The Tribal Council approved Stanley Duquette as a buyer," John Henry explained. "I can't wait on my uncle, so would you explain what's going on to him?"

Riley agreed, and John Henry drove off. Twenty minutes later, the phone rang, and Frank answered it.

"John Henry said he met Jefferson Ironheart on the road, and his uncle is following him over to Glenda Two-Trees' place. Let's get to work. John Henry will update us later," Frank said.

"How come every time anything remotely exciting happens around here, all we do is wait?" Noah complained.

"Do you honestly think Blue could become a tribal rider?" Noah asked, standing back and watching his brother work with the boy. "He's only a little kid."

"I am not!" Blue snarled over his shoulder.

Kingston shifted at the change in the boy's voice.

"Quiet," Riley ordered softly. "Yes, I do. Not this year, not for a couple of years, but anything is possible if you try hard enough and put your best efforts into it."

"I don't think anyone is going to like this idea," Noah warned.

"That's why I'm going to let Blue and Kingston become friends first," Riley said, closing the stall gate.

"I think you're asking for trouble," Noah exclaimed. "But, hey, if Blue is willing..."

Riley and Noah both looked to the boy, glaring up at them with unreadable black eyes.

"I said okay. Okay!" Blue growled, and he stomped from the barn.

"He said okay. Okay!" Riley repeated to Noah.

"It's no sweat off me," Noah said, following his younger friend. "It's not my butt that's going to get kicked this time!"

Chapter 15

F ive days passed, and they heard nothing from John Henry or Jefferson Ironheart. They were sitting around the living room drinking coffee and watching a video when the phone rang.

Marissa answered and handed the phone over to Riley. It was Rainey Two-Trees. She was so excited she could hardly speak. She asked Riley if she could come over, and he agreed.

"Rainey is coming over," Riley explained. "She sounds excited."

When the teenager arrived, she looked over at Marissa. "I know he's yours, but shut your eyes for a second." She presented Riley with a kiss and a huge hug.

"So, tell us what's going on?" Riley asked. "John Henry and Jefferson Ironheart have gone AWOL, and someone named Owen is answering the phone at the station."

"That's Owen Chandler, sometimes John Henry hires him as an acting deputy. Because of what you found out, I'll be able to go to college next fall, and I won't have to go into debt with student loans. I'll get a scholarship from the tribe, but we didn't know how we were going to manage the other expenses."

Riley's forehead furrowed. "That's great, but what happened?"

Rainey smiled. "Mr. Duquette was brought before Judge Glassmeade yesterday morning. I'm not sure of all the details because it was a closed meeting. The Tribal Council members tend to be close-mouthed, but Mr. Duquette is in jail. John Henry found this nifty little law that says when negotiating with a client, the buyer has to give the seller a *known and reasonable,* fair price. Mr. Duquette knew what my mother's pieces were selling for, but he didn't inform her of the actual selling prices. He was keeping seventy to eighty percent of the profit. Stanley Duquette has been ripping off artists and craftspeople for years. John Henry and Jefferson Ironheart got the Tribal Court to issue search warrants to review Mr. Duquette's office records in Phoenix. There are lots of people across the southwest who have been cheated by him.

"Jefferson Ironheart told my mother, Mr. Duquette is a wealthy man now, but when he gets through with him, he's going to be a very poor man. They're trying to contact all the people in his files. Mr. Duquette's lawyers are following them around, offering cash deals not to press charges.

"Wouldn't it be better to sue Mr. Duquette?" Frank asked.

Rainey shrugged. "Mom said she'd take what she can get; otherwise, the case could be tied up in the court system for years, and the only people who would make money would be the lawyers. A lot of the stuff he bought and resold had a *reasonable profit margin,* so part of his business was legitimate. There are a few people like Mom who he has been making a lot of money on."

"Shouldn't you get a lawyer to figure all this out?" Riley asked.

Rainey and Frank spoke at the same time. "Jefferson Iron-heart is a lawyer."

"What?" Riley exclaimed, surprised. "Why didn't anyone tell me?"

"Sorry," Frank apologized. "It's common knowledge around here. That's one of the reasons he's a leader of the Tribal Council. He wears a lot of hats. He'll make sure the compensation is handled fairly."

After explaining what was going on at the reservation, Rainey excused herself to return home. Riley and Marissa walked with her to her mother's car.

"Riley, I can't thank you enough for what you have done for my family," Rainey exclaimed. "My mom has already called four galleries, and two of them said they would like to display her pieces. Jefferson Ironheart advised my Mom to get an art agent before dealing with the gallery owners. This is so unbelievable. My mom is a famous artist, and we didn't know it!"

"I told you I'd seen her work before," Riley said. "There can't be many artists named Glenda Two-Trees. A name like Two-Trees isn't exactly like Jones or Smith."

"Maybe not where you live, but around here, it's a regular name," Rainey exclaimed, laughing.

Riley grinned and nodded. "So when and where is your mom going to have a show?"

"It's too soon to know, but as soon as I know, I'll tell you," Rainey promised. "Oh, and Christian said to stop by his place. You have a deal to finish."

"If you see him again, tell him I've been busy, but yes, it's a deal. I'll get over there as soon as possible."

Riley took two steps backward and held his breath, and he was holding tight to Kingston's reins. Blue was sitting on the stallion's back, and so far, Kingston was calm.

"Keep talking to him," Riley said softly. "Let him know it's you."

Blue leaned forward and talked to the horse softly while running his hands along the stallion's neck. In reality, he was pleading with the horse, in his native tongue, not to hurt him. He'd already learned the words didn't matter. The tone of voice was important.

Riley and Blue were concentrating so much on the accomplishment they didn't notice a figure stepping from the barn's dark shadows.

He cleared his throat, getting Riley's attention. In turn, Riley remained calm, lifted Blue from the stallion, and set him on his feet. Blue stepped outside the stall, took one look at Frank McKenna, and tried to make a run for it. Frank caught him by the back of his jeans and held the boy in place. He motioned Riley out of the stall and with a silent thrust of his thumb. He pointed to the tack room.

Blue was squirming underneath Frank's hold. He looked scared and belligerent.

"Let him go," Riley said. "Your beef is with me, not him."

Frank let go of Blue, and he ran.

"Are you out of your mind?" Frank demanded as soon as the tack room door closed. "Putting a twelve-year-old kid on an unbroken horse?"

"He's not exactly unbroken at this point. And no, I think it's a good idea," Riley said. "I've been working with Blue, and Kingston is beginning to trust and bond with him. He doesn't shy away or threaten Blue."

"Blue is a child," Frank repeated.

"I didn't put him in any danger," Riley said. "I've been

with him every second. The idea is to get Kingston weaned from me and onto Blue. Blue is not afraid of him anymore."

"Of all the hair-brained ideas," Frank exploded. "I'm responsible for Blue's safety."

Riley removed his baseball hat and slapped it against his leg in aggravation. "Uncle Frank, this whole situation has been hair-brained from the beginning!

"It didn't start with me. I didn't ask to become Kingston's trainer. It was forced on me. I said from the beginning I don't know anything about horses. Maybe it worked to my advantage because I was too dumb to be afraid of him, but I'm learning! Kingston has responded to me and my methods. I don't want all the time and effort I've put into him to be for nothing. The tribe owns him, not me. I may be a greenhorn, and I've been getting my methods from the internet, but it's working.

"If Jefferson Ironheart tries to force a rough rider on Kingston, he'll go nuts, and someone is going to be injured, if not killed. Blue may be too young to race for years, but if he keeps working with Kingston and becomes the primary trainer; he will be able to race him in the future. Unless Blue gets a significant growth spurt, he's probably not going to be a large man, and most jockeys are small.

"I think working with Kingston has helped Blue's self-esteem," Riley added. "Handling the stallion makes him feel important."

"Blue doesn't belong to us," Frank commented. "He's not officially a foster child, and if he gets hurt..."

"He hasn't been hurt," Riley interrupted. "I would never endanger a child. I've been with him every second. I never take my eyes off of him. Uncle Frank, this makes sense. Stop seeing Blue as a little boy and see the potential this offers for his future. Think of what it will do for him.

"Blue told me he was a *throwaway kid*," Riley said. "He said his mother wants booze and drugs more than she does her kids. He said no one wants him. Dear God, what has this world come to, that a twelve-year-old can say something like that matter-of-factly without any feeling?

"Being Kingston's rider will give him a purpose and pride in what he does and who he is as a person. He will be respected for doing what the other so-called experts can't do. I don't think Blue has ever felt like he was worth anything. Isn't building his self-esteem what you want? You built this place to take throwaway kids and convince them of their self-worth, so they could tackle real life."

Frank exhaled, and his anger faded. "You're right, but you can't do this kind of thing on the sly."

"Jefferson Ironheart isn't listening to me. I know he's the respected elder and Chief of the Indian Council and all that, but he is also one stubborn old coot. He's got the idea in his head that I am the only one who can tame Kingston, and he won't let go of it.

"Then, when I started making progress, he brings all those yahoo riders here to break him. All that's accomplished is it makes it harder for me to control him. Kingston is only going to be tamed on his terms. I thought if I could get Blue used to him and him to Blue, at least someone from the Quechan Tribe will have control over him. The kid's not afraid of horses, and he loves to ride fast and wild. They're a good match. It may take a while for Blue to become Kingston's trainer and rider, but I believe he can do it. Jefferson Ironheart won't listen. That's why I took matters into my hands. Maybe you and John Henry can make him listen!"

"All right," Frank said. "Sometimes, these things have a way of working for the best."

The next day, Riley stormed from the barn, exasperated. He'd been working with Jefferson Ironheart for hours, and regardless of what ideas he suggested, the old man stubbornly rejected them. Riley pumped several times on an old-fashioned iron pump handle and stuck his head under it when he heard a gurgle of water rising. After dousing himself, he sat on a wooden platform to cool off.

Jefferson Ironheart followed him and stood with his hands on his hips, glaring. "Are you going to sit there all day?" the old man demanded.

Riley looked up. "Yes, I am, damn-it!" he snapped. "If you think you can do any better, go for it. He's not going to be ready this year, and miracles don't happen overnight. If you want Kingston to be a viable contender in your river races in the future, you'd better start changing your mind about some things, and one of those is Blue!"

"Blue is too young," Jefferson Ironheart grunted as he had been doing all morning.

"He will grow older. We all do!' Riley exclaimed. "If you keep trying to break him by using strangers, you're asking for trouble. It will be a case of *when* someone is killed or crippled, not *if*!" Riley raked his fingers in his hair. "You've known from the beginning I can't race him! Blue can't do it either this year, probably not for another five years. That's not his fault, and he will do it later if that's what he wants to do! If he keeps working and gaining the horse's trust, they could make an unbeatable team."

"Huh!" the old man grunted, and he walked away with a purposeful stride toward his truck.

"That's all he said?" Frank asked later in the evening when Riley related the gist of the argument he'd had with Jefferson Ironheart.

Riley nodded. "What can I tell you? Jefferson Ironheart is the definition of inscrutable.

"Blue, what do you think about replacing Riley as Kingston's trainer?" Frank asked.

"I'm okay with it," Blue said softly. "He's not as scary as he used to be. I can do it."

"He's dangerous," Marissa interrupted. "Blue is too young."

"Marissa, it's more up to the stallion than us," Riley explained. "I'm not going to plop him into a saddle anytime soon. If Kingston didn't trust Blue, he'd have shown it by now. The surprising thing is Kingston has accepted Blue, like he has me. The hard part is over."

"What if Kingston can't be tamed?" Marissa demanded. "Blue could be hurt. I think it's too dangerous, and he's too small and too young."

"Like Riley said, it's not going to happen overnight, and I think it's too late to worry about Blue's age, now," Frank said. "If he's willing and if Jefferson Ironheart agrees, I think it might be a long-term goal. We'll have to get his mother and his aunt's permission."

"I'm gonna go watch TV," Blue said, bored with the conversation.

"Me, too," Noah said, deciding to bail and let the adults fight it out.

Marissa smiled at the boys but turned a frown toward Riley and Frank. Clearly, she wasn't convinced, and her maternal instincts were on full alert to protect.

"Marissa," Frank said with a calm voice. "This could be great for Blue. If the Tribal Council goes along with us, they'll have to give him time to grow up. Being a rider is a position of importance within the tribe. Blue will get a lot of attention and respect.

"Jefferson Ironheart won't do anything to endanger the boy. He may not be happy about missing several racing seasons. Still, he's not going to abandon the idea of Kingston racing. If he wanted to give up on the horse, he would have sold him by now and moved on."

"If I continue to work with Blue every day, I think it will work," Riley said. "It's kind of weird because I did think the old man was crazy at first. Now, I really care about Blue and the horse."

Riley hugged Marissa. "You know I wouldn't do anything to hurt a child. We've got lots of time. Both of us have decided we're not going anywhere."

"I know," she said, taking a deep breath. "Blue is so small, though, and Kingston is so big!"

Frank nodded, listening to Riley's words. He hadn't given much thought to his nephew's investment in time and care in taming the stallion. He'd also had his doubts since Riley had told him he wanted to join his efforts in running Dry Rock Boy's Ranch. Those doubts were vanishing.

The Friday mail, dropped off by John Henry, bought a large envelope in Riley's name. He opened it at the kitchen table to find several business letters from his home and vehicle insurance companies.

"Is this private?" Marissa asked, nodding at the envelopes he hadn't opened.

"No," Riley said. "Nothing is private from you." He opened the envelopes and laid the checks on the table. "These are the insurance payments for the cars, boats, and everything destroyed in the fire. This is the insurance payoff for the house and the boathouse."

Marissa blinked at the number on one of the checks. "Are you going to rebuild?"

"At the lake?" Riley asked. "Why would I? The boathouse will have to be rebuilt and the boats replaced, but we can discuss that with my brothers. My older brothers and I own the lake property between us. Still, it's open to all of our family, immediate and extended. As far as me building there again, it wouldn't make sense unless it was a small cabin for vacations or visiting, and we could always stay at the lodge.

My parents rarely use it. Are you set on staying here at the Boy's Ranch?"

"I am," Marissa responded. "I accepted the offer on the house. The realtor wanted to hold out for more, but I just want to be rid of it. I won't have to worry about working for a long time, and I'll be able to stay home with the boys." She looked around the kitchen. "Frank has been generous sharing his home, but I think we need a home of our own."

"I agree," Riley said with a smile. Marissa was coming around slowly, and he wasn't going to push her for a commitment she wasn't ready to make yet. "There will be plenty left over from these reimbursement checks to build it."

"Tribal Council meetings are going on over at the reservation this weekend," Frank told Riley and Marissa later that evening. "I need to be present in a few of those meetings, so I'm taking Noah and Blue with me. I'll get a room at the casino for us tonight and tomorrow night. Blue can spend some time with his family, and the boys can have a day of movies, bowling, arcade games, and fast food. As long as they stay out of the gambling area, they'll be okay."

After the chores, showers, and packing, Noah and Blue piled into Frank's truck, with a suitcase between them, and drove off.

"Alone at last," Marissa said.

"Not entirely," Riley laughed as the twins came tearing into the room at a run.

"Close enough," Marissa said, kissing him. "What are we doing this evening?"

"I think you know what we're going to be doing. How soon can the boys go to bed?" he asked, kissing her long and hard.

"If we turn the clock in the living room up an hour, they'll never know the difference," Marissa suggested in a whisper. "Jack has figured out how to tell time."

"You keep them busy. I'll take care of the clocks," Riley said, helping himself to another taste of her lips.

It took another hour and ten minutes for the twins to be tucked into Blue's bed. Tonight was an adventure for them to sleep in a *'big boy'* room. They'd been sleeping in their mother's room, in Frank's old room, which had become Marissa's room since she'd come. Frank, like Riley, had moved into one of the finished dormitory rooms.

Marissa checked on the boy's three times before she kissed Riley, took his hand, and led him into her room.

They stripped out of their clothing, and Riley stood looking at Marissa. He stepped across the hall, turned on the shower, and together they stepped under the flow of water. His hands roamed free over her slick and smooth body, and she did the same with his. His hand went between her legs. She reached for him, and he grew hard and stiff under the play of her fingers. His mouth latched onto one of her breasts, his tongue making circles around her nipples while his fingers pumped into her, making her tremble with need.

Marissa had been a little apprehensive about their first time, but she wanted to be with Riley. She wanted him inside her, as much as he wanted to be there. Riley must have had the same idea because he turned her around and bent her over for better access. Suddenly he was in her, filling her. He was thrusting so hard she was lifted to her toes. He had one hand on her hip, and she gasped as his other hand spanked her buttocks between strokes.

Marissa hadn't had this in her first marriage, but she had wanted it. She hadn't dared suggest it with Gregg after she discovered he was a control freak. *'Big ego, little dick,'* floated through her mind.

She hadn't enjoyed sex before, but wow, she was enjoying every second of Riley being inside her. She wanted him to keep pumping into her. She wanted to be taken, and he was fulfilling a lot of her secret fantasies without realizing it.

She loved the feel of Riley inside her. She arched her back and spread her legs further apart. "Oh!" Marissa moaned.

He froze. "Am I hurting you?"

"No!" she cried. "Don't you dare stop!

"Yes, ma'am," Riley murmured, and he took her harder and deeper.

Their moans and cries of pleasure were masked by the shower water beating on them. Marissa turned in his arms, and he held her until she stopped trembling. He turned off the shower and dried her from head to toe, and did the same for himself.

Giving a quick glance outside the bathroom door, Riley lifted her in his arms. He carried her into the bedroom and laid her on the bed.

"I can't ever remember wanting a woman as badly as I want you. I don't want us to be apart any longer. I need to be with you all the time."

"I can't imagine anything more wonderful," Marissa whispered, and they wrapped their arms around each other.

They were quiet for a while, and Riley began to stroke her body again. "We talked before about my believing in domestic discipline and my spanking during sex. Did you mind it?"

Marissa shifted in his arms until she was facing him. "Not at all, I was surprised, but I liked it."

Riley smiled. "Great, we're going to get along perfectly. There isn't any part of a woman I don't like, but there's something about a woman's bottom that really turns me on," he admitted, stroking hers.

Marissa awakened, tired, and very satisfied as she stretched and felt the aftermath of hours of making love with Riley multiple times over the night. The little twinges in various parts of her were so worth it. She had barely opened her eyes when Jake and Jackson burst into the bedroom, full of four-year-old energy. They climbed on the bed and tried to tuck themselves under the sheet, but Riley was a little quicker.

"Hey, guys, we're going on a trip this morning, so why don't you get your clothes and go to Blue's room and get dressed," he suggested. "Be good boys, and wait for us quietly on the couch!"

The boys rushed to the bottom drawer of the dresser. Marissa organized their clothing by complete sets. They each grabbed one and ran from the room.

Marissa watched as Riley stepped from the bed naked and closed the door. He was a big man, thick and long. He might be an ass man, but she realized she liked a broad chest with muscles, and his package was impressive. "That was quick thinking, but it's not going to last long."

"Long enough for me to dispense with a morning hard-on," Riley teased and proceeded while making her surrender to yet another orgasm.

Running back and forth between the bathroom and the bedroom, Riley and Marissa got dressed. They made the bed together, and he pulled her into his lap. Riley decided when the time came to build a house; there would be a master bedroom with an en-suite bathroom.

"Thank you!" he said, kissing her. "Are you okay?"

"I'm feeling euphoric," Marissa admitted. "Except for one very bad relationship, I haven't had much experience with men. Last night was wonderful. I'll be sitting gently today, but it was worth it."

"We know we are compatible in bed," Riley said. "Not that lovemaking is restricted to a bed. Have I asked you to marry me?"

"No," Marissa said. "We have sort of talked around the subject."

"Actually, every time I mention it, you change the subject,"

Riley said sternly. "This is for real, Marissa. I love you, and I already love those boys. I'll give you time, and I'll let you decide when it's the right time for you. I'm not going to hide our relationship. I'm going to swap where I sleep with the twins. I'll share every part of my life with you and the twins, but I also need to share your bed. Are you agreeable?"

"I am," she said, kissing him. "Now, we'd better go check on the twins. They've been awfully quiet, and that usually means they've gotten into mischief."

The twins were sitting quietly on the couch as they'd been asked to do. Jackson was pressing a remote and trying to turn on the old television, but the remote was to an equally old VCR/DVD player.

"Does anyone want McDonald's for breakfast?" Riley asked, knowing the answer he was going to get loud and clear from the twins. "We're going to drive for a little while, so if you want McDonald's, you have to be good boys," he warned.

"That's bribery," Marissa said as they hooked the boys into safety seats.

"It always worked when I was a kid. After breakfast, I have a few stops to make, and I need to deposit those checks," Riley admitted. "I didn't have any doubts, but after last night, I want to be with you forever. I love you."

"I'm not sure I'm ready for the big leap, but I love you too," Marissa agreed.

"Good," Riley grinned, capturing her in his arms and kissing her soundly. "We have to buy a ring, and it's going to be a big one!"

"I don't want or need a big diamond," Marissa said, shaking her head. "Those kinds of things don't mean much to me. What I want is to be loved."

"Cherished," Riley added. "Loved and cherished. That's my job!"

Chapter 16

Marissa stood watching from the window. Frank and Riley studied a large piece of paper in Frank's hand and pointed to somewhere beyond the house. Noah left the group, walking towards the house, and he seemed to be pacing or measuring a distance. Curiosity got the better of her. With a glance into the other room to make sure the twins were napping, she went to join them.

When Frank saw her coming, he collared the two younger boys and headed for the barns.

"What are you up to?" Marissa asked.

Riley showed her a blueprint. "Frank had plans for a new house drawn years ago, but he and Aunt Katherine never got around to building it."

Marissa looked at the house she now considered home and at the blueprints. "I thought the idea was to be with the foster kids."

"It is, but it doesn't mean we have to devote all our time, privacy, or our family life to them. It will be a while before we get the certifications to be foster parents. We're both going to have to take the required classes. I shouldn't have to take the first aid and CPR classes if I get my Arizona EMT accreditation first. The junior college in Yuma offers the classes. While we're taking the classes, Frank can be supervising house construction for us."

"Are you sure?" she asked.

"Why would you think I'm not?" Riley asked.

"More than a decade of earning degrees, but not deciding what you wanted to do," she said.

He nodded. "That's fair, I guess. Are the twins napping?"

She nodded.

He rolled the blueprints and offered her his hand to walk toward the house. "I started playing with my brothers in a band almost before I knew what being in a band meant. I did it because I was precociously talented at a very young age. That's not bragging. It's stating a fact. I wanted to be like my big brothers, who are incredibly gifted. Being part of my brothers' band came with the nickname of Coyote and my being labeled wild and fearless.

"Truthfully, I was one hell of a guitar player for my age, but I was also shy. I covered the shyness by being wild and crazy. I knew how far I could go before my parents would crack down on my antics.

"I was about eleven when my parents noticed I was not only a straight-A student, but I was on par with my older brothers' studies. That was about a year before we went mainstream. When I was supposed to be doing fifth-grade work, I was at a tenth-, and twelfth-grade level or beyond. We were on the road making a name for the band.

"Homeschooling led to tutors, and on-line classes, summer classes, private classes. I've been taking college courses since I was fourteen. Sully and Micah branched off into other venues, acting, and musical scores because they were adults growing up. Their interests were changing. They didn't have much time for the band anymore, and I kept studying. I enjoyed the challenges, and it kept me busy. I'll always be a musician who writes songs and music. It's what I do. It doesn't mean it has to be my top priority."

"When did your interests turn to theology?" Marissa asked.

"I think it was always there," Riley said. "I started focusing on it about six years ago. It's the only secret I've ever kept from my family. I'm meant to serve at something. I thought I'd found the right person and right cause, but when my relationship with Leigh Ann imploded, I took it hard, and I began to doubt myself again. I dove back into music again because that's what I'm familiar with. I knew within a couple of months it wasn't what I wanted anymore, but I'd signed contracts, and they're a devil to try to break, so I fulfilled them."

Riley stopped and kissed Marissa. "A friend of mine told me that sometimes, a guy has to be hit by a bolt of lightning to make him pay attention. Luckily, the first lightning bolt didn't strike me directly. Still, it destroyed nearly everything I owned, so it was definitely a wake-up call. The boathouse/tower project took me six months to finalize the blueprints and another six months to build, but I was only filling time. Still, it was a shock when it was destroyed. I didn't realize, at first, that I didn't have the initiative to start rebuilding.

"When my dad called because Noah got in trouble, I came here. While it might not have been the best thing to ever happen to you, it was for me. This place, and you, are my second bolt of lightning, and this time it was a direct hit. I found you, and I've found my true calling. I'm going to work with Uncle Frank, and I want to help children. If you are willing to take this journey with me, it would be the topping on a beautiful plan. I haven't said it very often because you weren't ready to hear it, but I'm madly in love with you."

"I am with you too," Marissa said. "Let me see those blueprints."

Riley drove on the lonely highway through the desert, lulled into a quiet peace. He could have turned on the radio, but he knew neither of the two available stations was a favorite, and he didn't want to wake Marissa. She'd been living in fear for the last five years. It was nice to see her relax and be able to rest.

They'd left the ranch after taking a three-way call from his brothers on Frank's landline. He needed to transfer a portion of the insurance money into Micah's bank account. His brother would start the rebuilding of the boathouse. He'd tried several times to make the transfers on his phone app, but it wasn't connecting, so he'd driven to the bank in Murdock. One of the first things he was going to look into was boosting the cell tower coverage. There were too many blind spots between the ranch and the nearby towns, but the casino and Murdock had full coverage.

He was twenty miles from Dry Rock when he heard more than felt the tires leave the paved road surface and go over into the soft shoulder. He jerked awake and blinked his eyes several times. Looking into the rearview mirror, he saw no one coming in the far distance, in front or behind him. At night, he would be able to see headlights for a good five miles. He stopped his truck in the middle of the road, got out, and leaned against the front hood, looking at the great expanse of moon and stars.

The lack of motion awakened Marissa, and she joined him. "Is there something wrong?"

Riley never took his eyes from the sky. "No, I needed a

break to wake up. You don't see this very often, especially when you live in a city."

"And, we forget how beautiful it is," Marissa said. "I'm getting used to how distant everything is, and I don't mind it." She leaned into him, looking upward at the sky.

They stood side-by-side, appreciating the twinkling stars.

After a long silence, Riley turned her to face him. "Is something bothering you?"

"There's a lot to think about and a lot of changes coming," Marissa said.

"Very true, and the McKennas will descend on us, in full force in a couple of weeks," he said. "Minus three sisters."

"Are you worried about Allison?" Marissa asked.

"I've been worried about Allison since she became a teenager," he said. "She was about fifteen when she started acting out. By the time she was twenty, she had escalated into real trouble. We haven't heard from her in six months. That's not unusual. However, our dad usually puts a private detective on her trail when they start worrying that she needs help again. He hasn't this time."

"I'll get to meet most of your family," Marissa said.

"And, they'll love you," Riley promised.

She smiled. "This place has grown on me, and so have the people here."

"It's become home," Riley said.

"Will your parents try to talk you into returning to Texas?"

Riley shook his head. "No, it takes a while for them to realize their children are adults, but once we get past those hurdles, they don't interfere. Dad still has a tendency to give advice, but that's just him pulling out the Dad card. He knows we will make our own decisions. We'd better get moving. Tomorrow is another day, but our days don't end until I make love to you!"

Riley stood inside the corral and watched as Blue led Kingston around in a circle. Uncle Frank stood barely visible behind the gate, ready and prepared to intercede should the boy need help.

"He's doing it," Noah whispered from behind the fence.

"Quiet," Riley hissed."

"Has Jefferson Ironheart agreed?" Noah whispered.

Riley shook his head. "No, so far, he hasn't agreed to anything. John Henry says he's been busy with the Tribal Council business, but..." Riley leaned towards his brother. "Personally, I think he's sulking. He is one stubborn old man."

Noah pretended shock. "That's disrespectful!" he whispered, and he shared a grin with his brother.

Not for a second would either of them have shown disrespect for Jefferson Ironheart because they did respect him. The Tribal Leader was the kind of man who made you want to pull back your shoulders and stand straighter. Everyone felt it. Although the old man rarely spoke, when he did, it was usually a command. He was used to being obeyed.

"Blue, I think that's enough for now," Riley said softly and nodded as the boy brought him the lead rope and stepped from the corral. Riley tipped the boy's baseball hat back and smiled. "You did a real good job today."

Blue didn't say anything. His mouth sort of tilted on one side, and he looked pleased.

Noah backed away, keeping his distance as his brother led Kingston toward the barn and into his stall.

The addition to the house was finished, the rooms painted, furnished, and ready. Riley and Marissa were registered for the classes required to become foster parents. Frank was taking refresher courses in first aid, CPR, and a new required class in adolescent development. Riley was signed-up for a paramedic refresher course to get his EMT certification in Arizona.

The McKenna family was scheduled to arrive in two weeks in a convoy of rented recreation vehicles. Uncle Frank had told Noah at breakfast that he could consider himself jobless until his parents came beyond the regular chores.

"So, what are we going to do for the next two weeks?" Noah asked.

"I thought I was going to get some climbing in this summer," Riley said, looking off into the distance.

"Tell Micah to bring his gear when he comes," Noah said.

Riley opened his mouth to explain he did have some gear, but he clamped it shut. Climbing was his and Micah's sport, not Noah's. They had given him an introductory course, but Noah hadn't shown any interest after the class. Riley took a long look at his brother. "I've got an idea. Go get cleaned up, and grab Blue. Toss him into the shower too!"

Noah extended his long gait to match his brothers. "Where are we going?"

Riley said over his shoulder. "I'll tell you later."

Noah stopped and looked after his brother, puzzled. "Hey!" he shouted. "What are we going to do?"

Riley turned at the barn door. "I'm going to turn you into a cowboy," he said with a smile. "You've been here all summer, and you still look like a city kid."

Noah looked down at himself. His standard everyday outfit was cargo shorts, tee shirt, shorts, with construction work boots. Riley, on the other hand, hadn't changed much. He had always dressed in a casual western manner. His brother had recently bought himself a new pair of hand-tooled cowboy boots. He alternated wearing a baseball cap and an old straw cowboy hat of Frank's. All he was missing was the big belt buckle.

Riley went into the house and made a couple of phone calls.

Noah and Blue were already in his truck, waiting when he came out of the house, but he motioned them to Frank's truck. "Why do we have to take Frank's truck?" Noah asked.

"Because we need to stop at the hardware store," Riley said truthfully. "Frank wants to paint the outside of the house, so guess what we're going to be doing next week."

Noah and Blue looked at the gray, weather-beaten structure with the new wood on the dormitory structure bright and golden in contrast.

Noah shrugged. "So much for not working."

"We'll head into Murdock first, and on the way home, we'll stop at the Yellow Horse Trading Post. I need to talk to Christian."

They bought ten gallons of a taupe gray-colored paint for the exterior and three gallons of light green for trim work.

Noah didn't like the colors. "Why paint the house if it's going to be the same colors as the boards are now?" he demanded.

Riley shrugged his concern. "Frank let Marissa pick the colors. I didn't know, but he's partially colorblind. He sees colors, but they're different variations than what most people see. She said these colors would match the environment."

"It'll make the place invisible," Noah grumbled. "Why don't we paint it desert camouflage? That would be cool."

"I don't think women are into camouflage." Riley laughed. "Be glad Frank vetoed her first choice, which was pink magnolia. She said it would look pretty against the desert sands."

Noah shuddered at the idea of a pink house. "Yikes! She knows this is Boy's Ranch, doesn't she?"

"Yes, and you should have seen the look of horror on his face," Riley said, grinning as he tossed the last bag of brushes and rollers into the truck bed. "I think she was pulling our leg. Next stop Yellow Horse Trading Post."

When they entered the trading post, Riley went to talk to Christian, and they disappeared as his assistant took over the counter.

Noah enjoyed looking around the Trading Post. Riley suggested he try on new jeans and a western shirt, and he didn't object. His brother was in a good mood, a spending mood, and Noah didn't mind taking advantage of it. Riley sent both Noah and Blue into the dressing rooms to try on jeans and shirts.

He made a big deal of buying Blue, a brand-name western hat. The boy's eyes almost popped out of his head when he saw the price tag, and he couldn't believe someone would give him such an expensive gift.

"Select a good-looking headband for his hat," Riley suggested to Noah.

Noah studied a wall display of hatbands, and he found one he thought was perfect. It was a blue snakeskin band with a hand-tooled silver and turquoise eagle in the middle. It was expensive, though, almost as expensive as the hat.

"Did you find one?" Riley asked behind his brother.

"Yeah, but it's kind of..."

Which one?" Riley interrupted.

Noah pointed, and he knew Riley understood the connection. "Blue Eagle," he said. "Perfect. This is your birthday gift to Blue. He turns thirteen next month. You can pay me later if you ever get an allowance again."

Noah nodded his head in agreement. Sometimes he thought his brother could read his mind.

They slipped the headband on the hat and set it on Blue's head.

"I don't have anything to give you in return," Blue said softly.

"You have already," Riley said. "You've given me peace of mind. You're going to take over the daily care of Kingston, and I know you will treat him right."

Noah turned away. He was blinking away tears, and at the same time, he felt a little stupid. Watching his brother and Blue together made him feel a bit jealous. He would be leaving in a couple of weeks to return to San Antonio and his last year of high school. Riley would be staying in Dry Rock. He knew how he was feeling was stupid because Riley was his brother. His brother was trying to make Blue feel good about himself. Still, it would have been nice if Riley had offered to buy him a hat.

Blue left the hat section and walked outside, strutting a little in his new clothes and hat proudly. Riley tried on a few hats and looked over at Noah.

"I've been wearing one of Frank's old hats most of the summer. I have several good western hats at home. Remind me to call Mom and tell her to bring the rest of my clothes with them. All I have is what was with me on the bus."

Noah looked at the cowboy hats longingly, and he nodded his head in agreement.

"Besides," Riley exclaimed, pulling his baseball cap from his back pocket. "This is more my style." He walked over to the counter where Christian stood, and the man pulled something from behind the counter. Riley tossed it at Noah. "And, this is more your style."

Noah caught the large bright yellow and black object. It was a motorbike helmet.

Noah looked to see Riley with his hands on his hips, looking at him critically. "You know, Noah, cowboy doesn't suit you at all. Follow me. I think I've found something you will like better."

Noah followed his brother outside, and he blinked blindly for a second in the bright sunlight. Then he saw an orange trailer hitched to the back of Uncle Frank's truck with a bright yellow and black motorbike strapped to it. The flame markings on the bike matched the helmet in his hand.

"I'm a few months late," Riley said. "But, I couldn't pass it up. Happy Birthday, little brother."

"It's mine?" Noah breathed, looking at Riley in shock. "You're not kidding? Please tell me you're not kidding!"

"It's yours," Riley assured him. "I cleared it with Mom and Dad, and it's semi-legal. Dad will take care of all the registration stuff when you get home. They have agreed you can ride it on the ranch. The same rules apply here as at home. If you get caught riding without a helmet or showboating, it goes under lock and key."

Christian came outside with a bag and handed it to Riley, who passed it over to his brother. "You can't ride it until we get back to the ranch, but these duds are more you."

Noah looked into the bag, and he was grinning from ear to ear. It was a bright yellow and black set of racing coveralls.

"Those may be too big, but you'll grow into them," Riley said. "They came as a package deal."

"Man!" Noah exclaimed, climbing onto the trailer and straddling the bike seat.

Christian was smiling, and he shook hands with Riley. "You're my kind of customer."

"My house burned to the ground before I came here. I lost a lot of stuff. I'll give you a list of what I'm looking for," Riley promised. "And, I need your advice on who to use as a silversmith."

Marissa, Uncle Frank, and the twins converged on the front porch when Riley drove the truck into the yard, hauling Noah's new bike.

Blue was a little embarrassed as Marissa told him how handsome he looked in his new clothes. Frank took the hat off the boy's head, inspected it carefully, and set it back on the boy's head. "That's a mighty fine looking hat, Blue," he said simply.

"I gotta go change. Noah promised he'd take me for a ride," Blue mumbled.

Uncle Frank eyed the bike as Noah backed it off the trailer.

"Can you ride that thing?" Frank asked.

"Noah's the best rider among us," Riley said.

"That doesn't tell me much," Frank complained. "You all could be lousy riders."

"That's my brothers. Not me," Noah exclaimed, straddling the bike.

"Let me see you take it for a spin before you go putting Blue on the back of that thing," Frank suggested.

Noah adjusted his helmet, started the engine, and got the feel of the cycle's gears before he kicked it into gear. He was off in a cloud of dust.

Marissa was standing on the porch watching. "Isn't he going too fast?" she asked, worried.

Frank and Riley joined her on the porch to get a better view.

"No," Riley said. "He knows what he's doing."

Blue came running from the house wearing his old clothes. "Is it my turn?" he asked, climbing on the porch railing for a better look.

"Oh, honey, I don't know," Marissa worried.

"Noah knows what he's doing," Riley promised. "He's been riding motorbikes since he was about ten."

Marissa didn't look convinced, and she looked worried when Blue climbed on the back of the motorbike behind Noah.

"What about a helmet?" Marissa protested. "Blue is not riding without a helmet!"

A disappointed Blue started to dismount.

"Wait a minute," Riley exclaimed. He jogged over to his truck and rummaged in the toolbox. He returned with a much smaller helmet and snapped it on the boy's head.

"That's not a motorcycle helmet!" Marissa protested.

"No, it's a climbing helmet, for rock climbing," Riley explained. "It's smaller, but it's safe."

"You climb rocks, and cliffs like I've seen on television?" Marissa demanded.

"Yes," Riley admitted reluctantly, seeing the look of worry on her face.

Noah revved the engine, spun in several circles, and checked to make sure his passenger wasn't scared. Then he took off again across the desert.

"I can't watch," Marissa moaned, burying her face in his chest.

"You'll get used to it," Riley promised with a laugh.

Chapter 17

Riley tiptoed from Marissa's bedroom quietly. Everyone in the house was asleep. Noah and Blue were exhausted from spending most of the previous day and evening riding the motorbike. Dawn was barely breaking when he walked sock-footed through the living room and kitchen and headed outside. Riley sat on the porch steps and pulled on his boots. His thoughts were concentrated on what he was going to do.

Marissa awakened to an empty bed, something that was unusual now. They weren't flaunting their relationship, but Frank and the boys were aware of Riley sleeping in her room. They didn't make a big deal of it. She was starting breakfast and getting the twins dressed at the same time. Frank came into the kitchen, and he captured a renegade Jake, pulled his shirt over his head, and set the little boy at the kitchen table. He did the same with Jackson. He broke a banana in half and gave half to each boy to keep them occupied.

"Thanks," Marissa said.

"Are the boys up?" Frank asked.

"They're fighting over the bathroom right now," she said.

Noah whizzed through the kitchen on the way to the barns to start the early chores. Blue was on his heels. A few minutes later, Blue was standing in the doorway with Noah behind him.

"What?" Frank asked.

"Kingston is gone," Blue stated matter-of-factly.

"So is Riley," Noah added. "At least he's not in the barns."

Frank didn't say anything. He walked outside and stood looking into the desert.

Noah ran inside, grabbed a pair of binoculars, and scanned the landscape in all directions. When he couldn't see anything, he climbed on the porch railing, then to the porch roof, and even higher to the very peak of the ranch house roof.

"There he is," Noah shouted. "Wow! You should see him riding Kingston. He's riding like the wind!"

"Who's in control?" Frank demanded.

"Riley, I think," Noah said, handing the binoculars to Blue, who had joined him on the roof.

"Wow! He's riding him!" Blue exclaimed.

Frank squinted towards the direction the boys were pointing, but he couldn't see anything. He went around the side of the house and returned with a ladder. Once on the roof, Frank focused the binoculars on his nephew. Indeed, Riley did look like he was in control, and the horse was responding beautifully.

"He's okay," Frank reported to Marissa. "At least until he gets back. Then I'm going to kick his butt. Blue, don't get any ideas. When and if you ever ride the stallion, I'm going to be right by your side. Understood?"

Blue nodded his head vehemently.

"Okay, boys, we've got chores," Frank reminded them. The boys reluctantly climbed down from their observation posts.

Riley hadn't returned when the chores were done or by the time breakfast was eaten. Noah drove off on the motorbike with Blue in the opposite direction. He'd been warned not to go near the stallion because the motorbike's noise would frighten the horse.

Jefferson Ironheart arrived at his usual time. When he was told Riley had taken the stallion riding, he climbed on the roof to stage his own vigil of watching. He'd been on the roof about forty minutes when Jefferson Ironheart let out a whoop.

"Magnificent!" the old man exclaimed as he climbed down and went inside. He helped himself to a mug of coffee in the kitchen and returned to his post to continue his observation.

Riley didn't ride in until it was almost noon. He rubbed down the stallion, watered him, and tended him.

Frank followed them into the barn and stood outside the stall.

Riley could almost feel the tension radiating from his uncle. "It's okay. I knew I could ride him. I knew Kingston wouldn't hurt me."

"I'm not going to deny you have worked a small miracle with Kingston, but your safety is my responsibility."

Riley looked squarely into his uncle's eyes. "No, I am responsible for myself. I've worked with Kingston all summer. At first, I didn't buy into all the stuff Jefferson Ironheart was talking about. I don't have any mystical power for charming horses. I have a very healthy respect and fear for anything standing sixteen hands high."

"I needed to ride him—just him and me. Our connection is real, and I knew he wouldn't hurt me. This was my payoff for working with him all summer. From this point on, he's Blue's horse."

"I ought to kick your butt," Frank growled. "But, you're not a kid, and you're bigger than me. I'll let you explain it to Marissa!"

"I know when Kingston is dangerous and when to give him space. I know when he'll let me take the next step. I've earned his trust, and now that trust has to be transferred to Blue." Riley stopped in his tracks, staring over at the house. "Why is Jefferson Ironheart sitting on the roof?"

"He's been watching and waiting for you," Frank said. "He's been up there for a couple of hours."

"Is he mad?" Riley asked.

"I don't know," Frank replied. "You're the one who has to deal with him."

Frank headed towards the barns, and Riley headed toward the house. The old man was climbing down the ladder, and Riley expected a reaction from him.

Jefferson Ironheart stood statue-like for a long moment. Then he tipped his hat to Riley. He went to his truck and drove off.

Jake and Jackson both came running outside and tackled Riley around the knees. Tucking a giggling four-year-old under each arm, he carried them to the porch.

"Take us horsey riding," the boys begged.

"Horse, not horsey, and that's Momma's decision," Riley instructed, and he followed them into the house.

Listening to two excited voices at once, Marissa smiled over all the *'Please Mommy's*, and *pretty pleases*, and told them to go sit on the porch to wait for her decision.

"Be careful," she said to Riley.

Riley grinned. "I'll put them on Old Ornery and lead them around. She wouldn't hurt a fly. Uncle Frank only keeps her around to keep from sending her to a glue factory."

"Shush, don't say that around the twins. At their age, they take everything literally." She went to the screen door and called a warning to them. "Don't leave the porch!" She went to the refrigerator, removed a soda and a wrapped sandwich, and handed the food to Riley.

"Thanks," Riley exclaimed, biting into the sandwich. He turned to face her. "Did Jefferson Ironheart say anything to you today?"

She shook her head. "He watched for hours sitting on the roof. Didn't he say something to you?"

Riley shook his head. "No. Maybe he's mad because I didn't wait for him to be around when I rode Kingston."

"After all the work and time you've invested in that horse, I would think riding him would be a major accomplishment."

"It is," Riley exclaimed. "That's why I don't understand why he didn't say anything."

"Well, you can be sure of one thing," Marissa promised. "If Jefferson Ironheart is upset or angry, he'll let you know about it."

Riley nodded and grinned. "That's what I'm afraid of."

Around and around the paddock, Riley led an old mare Frank called Old Ornery. She was gentle and swaybacked, but the twins didn't care. They were riding, and they were excitedly shouting, *'Again!'* after every circle of the corral.

Noah rode in from the desert, stirring a trail of dust in his wake. He was so dirty from the red dust he was barely recognizable. Blue's black hair was reddish-brown from the desert dust.

Noah parked the motorbike. He couldn't wait to talk to his brother. "Riley, we saw you this morning riding Kingston. Was it fantastic?"

Riley pulled the twins off Old Ornery and sent them to the house. He loosened the saddle and pulled it off and slapped the horse on the rump to let her go free into the paddock. He carried the saddle to the tack room.

"I saw you," Blue said simply. "You rode him!"

"Yes, I thought it was time, but I don't want you to try it. You have to have Jefferson Ironheart, Uncle Frank, your Aunt, and possibly John Henry, and Marissa's permission first."

Blue nodded. "I know. Everyone keeps reminding me!"

"Then you'd better listen. You two better head over to the house and get cleaned up," Riley suggested. "As filthy as you are, there's no way Marissa is going to let you anywhere near the dinner table."

"You don't look much better," Noah retorted. "Plus, you smell like a horse!" As the three of them headed toward the house, Noah hung back to walk with his brother. "How was it?" he asked. "How was it riding Kingston? Was Uncle Frank mad?"

"Great, great, and no," Riley answered. "It was terrific. It was the best ride of my life."

"Didn't he try to buck?" Noah questioned.

Riley shook his head. "A four-legged hop at first, but he settled down and responded to the command of the reins. It was amazing. Now I know why the Indian Council wants to race him. He's so fast; riding him is like flying."

"That's really cool," Noah exclaimed. "But you don't like flying!"

"Speed on the ground doesn't bother me," Riley clarified. "How about you? How did Blue's lesson go?"

Noah looked astounded. He opened his mouth to deny it and closed it. "How did you know?" he demanded.

"Blue has grease on his jean leg from kicking on the starter," Riley said. "You shouldn't be teaching him on the motorbike. He's not one of us. He's only been lent to us temporarily, and I'm not sure what the liability would be if he got hurt. That's why Uncle Frank was so pissed at me for letting him around Kingston."

"We were careful," Noah claimed. "Blue's a natural like I was at his age."

"God forbid," Riley said with a grimace. "I remember the skinned elbows and knees, and once you even managed to scrape your entire belly and chest. No more lessons. He can ride as a passenger, but he can't drive it."

After dinner, Riley was feeling a little down, or maybe it was discouraged. He couldn't pinpoint what was bothering him. Most of what Riley was feeling was confusion. Jefferson Ironheart's lack of response to his riding Kingston was puzzling. He had expected a reaction–satisfaction, congratulations–something. Even if he'd yelled at him, it would have been recognition of what he had accomplished.

"Someone's coming!" Noah called out, pointing to the trail of dust in the distance.

Riley was cleaning the interior cab of his truck.

An older model station wagon bumped its way along the lane. Rainey jumped from the car with a wave at Frank and Marissa. She headed straight to Riley.

"Hi!"

Riley smiled. "Hi, yourself."

"I wanted to invite you over to my house. My mom wants to see you, but she's been so busy she hasn't been able to take the time to come over. I thought maybe you wouldn't mind coming over. If you're not busy, of course."

"I'm not busy, and I can follow you over," Riley said. "Would you mind if I invited Marissa to go with us? She'd love to see your mother's work, and Blue can visit with his family while we are there too."

"The more, the merrier," Rainey exclaimed. She stayed for dessert, and as the sun was beginning to set, they set out, a two-car caravan headed for the reservation. Frank volunteered to watch the twins. Rainey was the lead car, and she'd taken Blue with her. Riley was following her with Noah and Marissa.

"Riley, stop at the Trading Post and for ice cream," Noah suggested.

"It's after eight. Christian closes at six," Riley said.

"Somebody is there," Noah said, looking through his side window. "Lights are moving around over there."

Riley looked ahead, flashed his lights, honked his horn, and turned on his turn signal. Rainey understood because she pulled over into the Trading Post parking lot ahead of them. Riley followed her and got out. "Did you see the lights?" he asked.

"Yeah, but they're in the back," Rainey said. "It's probably tourists trying to save the price of an RV campground. They do it all the time. We can ask them to move on."

A chubby young girl of about twelve came running around the corner of the building. She was crying. "Are you here to help? Please, we need help!"

They ran around the back of the building.

There were two large RV trailer homes parked behind the trading post, but the commotion was on the trail to the canyon overlook. Flashlights were being beamed around in the darkness, and people could be heard shouting, "Teddy! Teddy!" One woman was sobbing hysterically.

"What's wrong?" Riley demanded of a man with a flashlight in his hand.

"A little girl is missing. Teddy is only five. Can you get the lights turned on?"

"I don't think there are any outside lights this far away from the building," Riley said. "The Trading Post is closed."

"What the hell," the man exclaimed. "What kind of a place is this?"

Riley almost asked the man what he expected. They were trespassing, but he clamped his mouth shut.

"Noah, Blue, go to my truck. I have a flashlight in the glove compartment, one in my medical kit, and one in the toolbox," he ordered.

The boys went running as Riley, Marissa, and Rainey

joined the small group of people trying to see through the darkness. They were shouting for a child they didn't know as they searched behind rocks and sagebrush.

Noah and Blue ran to them with the flashlights, and a scream was heard.

"Oh, Dear God," Marissa whispered as everyone met at a waist-high wall built along the edge of the canyon rim.

A woman was pointing over the wall with a flashlight.

"Don't move, Teddy," the woman who was sobbing called out. "Baby, don't move!"

The beams of five flashlights spotlighted a small, blonde-headed girl huddled on a small ledge about sixty feet below the rim. A man swung his leg over the wall, but Riley halted him. "No, that's almost a vertical cliff. You'll never survive it."

"We need a rescue team," one of the women screamed.

"Marissa!" Riley said, turning to her. "Drive the truck up the path and park it about twenty-five or so feet from the barrier. "You three," he shouted and pointed at the adults. Use those flashlights and shine them on the trail so she can see where she's going. You!" He pointed to a woman. "Stand in the middle of the path at the white and blue sign! That's where the truck needs to stop. He turned to Rainey and dug into his pocket, and handed her his cell phone. "Call for help, fire, rescue, John Henry, whoever the hell fits this situation."

"I'll have to go to the bluff," Rainey exclaimed. "We're too low to make a cell connection."

"Get help," Riley said urgently. "Hurry!"

Rainey took off running.

"Why don't we break into the Trading Post and call for help?" the same man Riley had spoken to before demanded.

"Because there's no service after hours," Riley snapped. "The Trading Post is too far off the mainline."

"This is a Godforsaken place!" the man exclaimed in frustration.

Riley turned to the tourists. "Don't point the flashlights directly at her. You don't want her blinded," he ordered. "Aim the flashlights a couple feet from her and light the surrounding area. Talk to her, and keep her calm. Tell her not to move!"

Riley saw the headlights of his truck moving very slowly on the path at a tilt. The walking path wasn't wide enough for his vehicle. He saw Noah run to the vehicle and exchange places with Marissa. Noah shifted the truck into four-wheel drive. He kept two wheels on the trail and the other two on rock edges. Marissa had taken his place and was walking in front of the truck and guiding him in. Riley turned to Blue. "Tell Noah to bring the box of climbing gear from the toolbox."

He leaned over the edge and aimed his flashlight in the general area. "Teddy?" he called. "Can you hear me? Nod your head if you can hear me. Don't try to yell or look around, sweetheart. Don't move your arms or your legs."

The blonde curls bobbed, and a plaintive cry of fear could be heard.

"Calm down, sweetheart," Riley called. "I'm going to come and get you, but it's going to take me a few minutes to get ready. Be a good girl, and don't move." He turned to the obviously distraught parents. "Talk to her. Keep her calm if you can."

"Shouldn't we wait for help?" another woman asked.

"Maybe," Riley said honestly. "But, help could be an hour or two away. If Rainey can't get a signal on the cell phone, she may have to drive to the nearest phone, and that's another half hour away."

Blue came running, with Noah following and carrying the cardboard box of climbing gear.

Riley and Noah dug into the box, organizing the ropes and hardware. Noah unfurled the length of rope, pulling it through his hands to make sure it wasn't damaged and measuring it against his height. "There's a hundred and twenty to a hundred and fifty feet here," he said.

"It's enough," Riley said, intent on hooking metal clamps on a harness he was stepping into and pulling over his thighs.

Marissa was watching him with pure fear in her eyes. She forced herself to keep quiet. There was a child's life at stake.

Noah took the end of the rope and crawled under the truck to tie and clamp it to the vehicle's metal frame. Blue was beside him, holding the flashlight. Noah double-checked the emergency brake and jammed several large rocks under both the front and rear wheels.

"If this truck moves an inch, yell, add your weight to it to hold it in place, and shove more rocks in front of the wheels," Noah ordered the men, who were all older than him.

Riley was in the harness when Noah joined him. "The helmet is at home," he warned.

"I'll go without it," Riley said. He looked to see headlights pulling into the parking lot.

Rainey came running. "I drove over to the scenic view, and I got a weak signal. I called Frank, and he said he'd call the authorities." She looked at Riley strapped into the harness, and her mouth dropped open when she realized what he was about to do.

Riley was ready, and he was anxious. It had taken too long to get prepared for his descent. He turned to the seven adults and two teenagers. "I need all of you adults on the ropes, except for her mother and that girl," he pointed to the young girl. "If my brother tells you to do something, don't question it. *Do it!* Blue, I want you, that girl, and Teddy's momma to man the flashlights so I can see what I'm doing. Keep the area lit, but not too close to her."

Noah was demonstrating to the adults how to grip the rope. The young girl, Blue and Teddy's mother, took the flashlights.

"Momma, keep talking to Teddy. Try to use your calm voice," Riley said to the little girl's mother.

He climbed over the wall and stood on the edge of the cliff. He turned his back to the canyon and stood there. Noah walked the line of men and women, checking their grips, advised them on leaning against the rope and for them not to trust the truck to hold the weight, to dig in with their feet, bend their knees, and use the strength of their thighs to hold the weight. He was repeating the instructions he'd been given himself in classes he'd taken. Noah walked to the front of the line. As the first on the rope, he shouted, "Ready!" at the people behind him. He gave his brother a nod.

Riley jumped off the cliff.

Chapter 18

R iley dropped about ten feet on the first jump. It should have been easy, but he wasn't wearing the right gear. The flat, slick leather soles of his boots skidded on the slippery rock, and he stumbled and whacked against the rock with his knees. A shower of pebbles and dust skittered down the cliff.

"Stop!" Riley shouted to Noah, and the rope held steady. Riley fumbled, hanging a thousand feet in the air, and he pulled off his boots. With a mighty heave, his boots were thrown over the cliff wall. He stripped off his socks and dropped them into the blackness of the canyon. He would get a better grip on the cliff rock with his bare feet.

He yelled, "Slack!" upward to Noah to give him a slackline, and when he was ready, he traversed another six feet. This time he landed well. He repeated this pattern of gathering slackline and jumping downward in small increments. He could hear the little girl sobbing, and he began to speak to her softly. He was a good fifteen feet to the right of where she was huddled on a small ledge. One more drop, and he was parallel with her. He slid a few more feet below her to give himself more maneuverability.

"Hold position!" he shouted to Noah and heard his command being echoed above.

Gripping with his feet and toes, Riley moved sideways in little hops until he was positioned only four feet from the little girl. He didn't want to scare her, and he didn't want her to move. The closer he got, the more critical the situation. The child was barely clinging to a soft sandy outcropping. One wrong move and she'd be over the edge. She was chubby and red-faced from crying.

"Hi, Teddy," Riley said softly. "Sweetie, I'm going to make one more jump, and I'm going to be right behind you. Don't be scared and don't move. Please don't move. I'll have you safe in a second."

Terrified eyes looked at him, her eyelashes matted with tears and dirt.

One more horizontal hop, and Riley had the little girl pinned between his knees. He adjusted the rope tension and let himself hang while he lifted her over the rope and against his chest.

"Okay, Teddy," Riley said gently. "I'm your best friend right now. I need you to wrap your legs around my waist and your arms around my neck as tight as you can. Hold onto me, and you'll be with your mommy in a few minutes."

Riley shouted to Noah, and a few seconds later, the rope began to inch upward. Riley didn't try to pull. He kept balanced and held onto the little girl, letting the others on top do the work. He used his feet to dig into tiny rock ridges to walk the cliff.

Foot-by-foot, they were pulled to the top of the cliff face. Riley kept a gentle monolog going for the little girl, and he heard muffled sobs against his chest. The mother, the girl, and

Blue kept pace with their progress, careful to keep the flashlight beams close but not on them.

Riley crested the top of the wall.

"Hold position!" Noah shouted behind him. He removed his hands from the rope and ran to Riley.

"Hold position on the rope until they are both over the wall!" Noah ordered. He grasped the little girl firmly by her forearms, lifting her over the wall, and setting her behind him.

Teddy's mother ran to gather her daughter in her arms. Riley was already pulling himself over the stone wall with Noah's help.

Once he was over the wall, Noah shouted, "Release!" Everyone let go of the rope and surrounded the child and her mother.

Noah gathered the harness as Riley stepped out of it. He coiled the rope and climbed under the truck to release it. He handed them to Blue, who stowed them in the cardboard box and then in the toolbox.

Riley sat on a rock, Marissa sat down beside him, and hugged him silently. Individually each of the tourists thanked Riley profusely. He was pounded on the back, hugged, and kissed on the cheek, but he didn't say much.

"Let's get off the rim," he suggested.

Noah and Blue kicked the rocks from under the tires. Noah took the wheel, backed up a few inches, and they pulled out the rest of them. Noah turned the vehicle around in a dozen short zigzag motions.

Riley was surprised at his brother's driving skills, and he gave him two thumbs up. He let down the tailgate, and he climbed into the bed. Marissa was holding onto him, and she wouldn't let go. Noah slowly drove the path to the parking lot.

The tourists returned to the RVs and turned on their auxiliary lights. Riley could hear a generator running. The little girl's mother was inspecting her under the lights of the

RV carefully. Teddy had a scratch on her cheek, scraped elbows, and knees, but otherwise, she looked to be in good shape.

One of the men pulled out a cooler and offered them drinks. Another opened a few foldable lawn chairs.

Noah brought Riley's EMT kit over and set it beside his chair. Riley was about to offer to check over the child when they heard sirens and saw the flashing blue and red lights speeding toward the Trading Post from both directions. The vehicles turned into the parking lot and pulled directly in front of the RVs. An ambulance crew jumped out and began to examine Teddy.

John Henry slammed out of his vehicle. He was followed by a County Sheriff's vehicle with two deputies. An Arizona State Highway Patrol vehicle was the last to arrive, and those two officers joined them.

Teddy's father explained what happened, and the policemen exchanged glances. The Arizona State officers went to their car, and with a salute, were gone. The County Deputy joined John Henry in interviewing the tourists. The emergency was over, and this must have been John Henry's territory because the officers were deferring to him.

"Are you guys okay?" John Henry demanded with a fierce look on his face.

They nodded, but John Henry was inspecting each of them from head to toe.

"Riley, what's wrong with your feet?"

Everyone looked at Riley's feet. There were dark red splotches on his feet.

One of the ambulance paramedics grabbed one of the lawn chairs, and Riley sat in it as his feet were examined. He was using his kit as a footstool. He hadn't felt any pain, but adrenalin and concentration on the necessary crisis would do that during the crisis. Several shallow gashes were on the bottom of his feet where he'd been cut by the rock on the canyon walls. The EMTs disinfected the cuts.

John Henry came over and inspected his feet. "These cuts aren't deep. You won't need stitches, but they're going to be sore for a couple of days." He turned to the EMT. "Go ahead and bandage these."

He turned back to Riley. "What do your hands look like?"

Riley spread his hands open and looked to Noah. Neither of them had blisters. The hard labor of the summer had callused and toughened their hands. Marissa's hands had several blisters, and they were treated.

"Most of those tourists have blisters too, so you'd better tend to them!" John Henry said.

"I need to find my boots," Riley said.

"I'll do it," Noah said, grabbing a flashlight.

"I saw where they fell," Blue said, taking another.

John Henry went back to the tourists and started demanding information. He inspected driver licenses, vehicle registrations, and insurance information. He started giving the tourists a blistering lecture for trespassing on private property and being stupid enough to let a small child wander around after dark in an unknown area. He was writing citations, but for what, they didn't know.

Teddy's parents came over to Riley and thanked him. Teddy gave him a hug and a kiss on the cheek, and the mother and daughter were taken away in the ambulance. They would be taken to Wolf Springs so Dr. Anderson could sign for their release. Riley saw no need to see a doctor.

Riley and Marissa returned to his truck, and he stowed his medical kit in the toolbox, and they sat on the tailgate. A few minutes later, Noah and Blue returned with his boots. He didn't attempt to put them on. Noah, Blue, and Rainey stood around waiting for John Henry to tell them they could go.

They waited a long time. Finally, John Henry walked away

from the RVs, and the tourists began to load their belongings. The county deputy walked over to them.

"Are you guys okay?" he asked again.

"We're fine," Riley said.

"They'll be escorted out of here in a few minutes," John Henry said, motioning towards the tourists. "I've warned Christian before. He needs to install chains to secure the parking lot at night. This time, I'll see it gets done!

"Those damn idiots almost lost a kid because they didn't want to pay for an RV camp. The jerk in the red shirt is complaining about *unsafe conditions*! He's going to understand a lot more about trespassing laws before he leaves the reservation!"

Furious at the tourists, John Henry switched his attention to his friends. "Do you need us to drive you home?"

Riley shook his head. "Marissa or Noah can drive us, but you need to take Rainey home. She shouldn't be driving alone this late at night by herself."

"I'm fine," Rainey protested. "I didn't do anything but make a phone call. I wasn't hanging from a cliff!"

"I was safe," Riley said. "Noah was lead man on the ropes, and you are upset. Your hands are shaking."

"Okay," John Henry agreed. "Marissa, are you okay to drive?"

She nodded. Riley wrapped his arm around her waist, and she laid her head against his shoulder.

John Henry nodded. "Okay, you head home, and I'll see Rainey gets to hers." He ignored the teenager's protests and asked one of the county officers to drive Rainey home and for the other to follow with her car. He told Rainey he'd stop by her mother's house after the tourists moved on.

Riley's feet were sore; that's all, and he kept insisting the same to everyone who asked. They were painful and slightly swollen. His right foot had a gash under his big toe and another under his little toe. He hadn't felt anything when he'd cut his feet on the rock. Now twelve hours later, they were swollen and painful. He was walking around in an old pair of Frank's slippers. He sat on the front porch swing with Marissa at his side. This wasn't going to be a workday for him. At least not a ranch workday.

He could also use the time to work on his music. Music was part of him. He'd written dozens of songs since they been on the ranch. He had a whole notebook full of melodies and lyrics, finished and unfinished, bits and pieces they might or might not use.

He would always write music. When he and his brothers managed to have one of their *creative* sessions, they usually included disagreements, laughter, and arguing. They had a tight friendship only brothers would understand. Riley called Sully and asked him to bring one of his better keyboards to use until he could purchase a piano.

Noah wasn't an original member of the I-35 band, but he'd been included on the last album released. He didn't sing, but he was pro-level on the drums. McKenna music was shared. It didn't matter who wrote what part, who added, who subtracted, who liked it, who hated it. What mattered was it was done together.

A loud hitting and screaming tussle between the twins required separation and corner time. He and Marissa unrolled the old house blueprints on the kitchen table and went over the plans once again. The changes were substantial. They'd added more bedrooms and more bathrooms, a classroom for homeschooling and/or homework, whatever they decided when it came time for the decision to be made. The boys from the ranch were bused to the reservation schools for elementary and middle school. High school required the forty-mile bus trip to Murdock.

The kitchen had grown in dimension on paper. Marissa wanted more workspace, but she didn't want it open to the living spaces. At the same time, she wanted a kitchen that would maintain the cozy feeling of Frank's kitchen. They would hire an architect to draw the final plans. They had until the following spring before they would begin to take on a full allotment of foster children. One of the reasons for more bedrooms in their house was the discussion of including girls, so siblings wouldn't be separated. Boys would be in Frank's home. Girls would be in the new house, under Riley and Marissa's supervision.

When Marissa needed the table for food preparation, the blueprints were rolled once again. Riley got out of her way. He gingerly walked to the barns. The family was on their way. Somehow, their schedules had meshed, and the McKennas would converge en masse. Sully and his large family would be coming by RV. He'd rather drive than fly, although because of the roles he'd taken in movies, he and his family had been on nearly every continent. His permanent address was San Antonio. There had been broad hints about him taking a hiatus from his movie career. He would be bringing their parents, fresh in from their flights from New York City.

Macy and Lily wouldn't be coming. Lacy had commitments with her ballet company, and Lily wasn't scheduled to return home until a week before school started. Allison, Macy's twin, would undoubtedly be a topic of conversation. A private detective had traced her to Oregon, where she had married a teacher, a woman. Her lifestyle choice was her own. It was only surprising because she'd never hinted that she was gay.

Allison claimed she was clean of all drugs and alcohol, happy, settled, and attending college full-time. She wasn't ready to communicate with her family, and the family would abide by her decision. Allison was reminded that whatever her life choices were, it was okay with them. After years of drama, substance abuse, and criminal activities, the family was genuinely hopeful for their daughter and sister's sobriety and happiness.

Micah was a pilot and shared the expenses of an airplane with an attorney friend. He would be flying his family to the Yuma Regional airport, where an RV would be waiting for him.

Riley kept in touch with his siblings and parents when he could get through to them. Marissa was a little nervous about meeting the mob, and he'd tried to reassure her. His family might be surprised, but they would support his decisions.

Riley heard the sound of Noah's dirt bike and knew the boys were heading into the desert. He went into the dimly lit barn and went straight to Kingston's stall. He led him outside to the corral. Blue was standing outside the barn, looking up at him expectantly.

"I thought you went with Noah."

Blue didn't speak, but he took the stallion's reins.

Riley relinquished them, and he opened the gate.

Blue led the stallion in, but he returned and stood looking at Riley.

"What?" Riley asked.

"When you jumped off the cliff, were you scared?"

Riley shook his head. "No, I was cautious and careful. I've had training in mountain climbing. We've done it many times during daylight hours, although never in the dark."

"I couldn't have done it," Blue said quietly. "I would have been too scared."

"Blue, you're only twelve," Riley said, and he smiled because he knew the boy was going to object. "Until the day after tomorrow, you are still twelve. At twelve or thirteen, I couldn't have done it either." He motioned towards the stallion. "At twelve, I would never have had enough nerve to work with a horse like Kingston like you do. I think you are far braver than I was twelve.

"When I was your age, my brothers and I were thrust into a crazy world of entertainment. There were cameras stuck in our faces and people asking questions. I loved the music we made together. I still do. There were parts of performing I secretly hated. I didn't think I could tell anyone because my brothers worked very hard, and they deserved recognition for their talent. Would you like to know a secret?"

Blue nodded.

Riley swung Blue onto Kingston's back, and the boy patted the horse on the neck.

Riley continued to speak to the boy, and led him into the corral. "As I got older, I got less scared. I realized if music was to be a part of my life, I had to accept what came with it. Everyone has to do that in life. We have to accept what we can't change and continue to move forward to enjoy the rest.

"I've seen you in action, Blue. You have courage and loyalty. When Marissa needed help, you searched every day, and you didn't give up. You haven't abandoned your sisters. You visit every week, and I'm sure knowing you love them, and haven't forgotten them, has helped them a lot. You've had some rough times in your life so far, and they have been hard, but I think you're a terrific kid. You're going to grow up to be a great man. You need to give yourself time to learn and grow."

"I hate school," Blue said quietly.

"I didn't mean that kind of learning," Riley said. "But, since you brought it up, we can talk about it. I know you've had problems in school, but this year should be better. I think you hated school because you were missing too much of it.

You can't keep up if you don't go to school and take the time to study.

"I know you were trying to take care of your mom and sisters. This year you will be going every day, no excuses. You're already reading better, and you have us to help you with the things you don't understand. We've been working with you, using last year's books, and we already have your books for this upcoming year. We're not going to let you get behind again."

Blue nodded. "I'm ready to ride him with a saddle."

"You might be, but we don't know how Kingston is going to react," Riley said. "Let's take this into his stall. He'll have less room to move around. This is just sitting on him, not riding."

Riley saddled Kingston in the stall, but he let Blue tighten the straps. He lifted Blue into the saddle. "Talk to him," Riley said.

"Why can't I ride him, like you did?" Blue asked.

"It's that twelve-year-old thing again," Riley said. "It's probably going to be a thirteen-year-old thing too. You're twelve, but Kingston is only five. Both of you have some growing up to do. You have all those permissions to deal with, and it might be a while before everyone agrees with your riding him.

"I'm giving you fair warning. If you try it without permission, you might be grounded for life. Although that wouldn't matter much, because you wouldn't be able to sit until you were thirty! You do not want to piss off the adults in your life, and we outnumber you. Even I'm a little scared of John Henry and Jefferson Ironheart. Got it?"

"Got it," Blue agreed, and he smiled. It was a full smile, and it warmed Riley's heart. Even though the boy had been warned, he wasn't afraid of them.

A half-hour later, Blue left the barn. He hadn't ridden

Kingston as he wanted and wouldn't because he'd made a promise. He'd sat on the stallion and talked to him for a long time. He had also listened to what Riley said. He wasn't alone anymore, and a bit of the fear that had been lodged inside him for a long time fell away. He had friends and people who were looking out for him.

Riley wanted to ride again, but he wouldn't. He'd turned partial responsibility for Kingston over to Blue. He also didn't want to face Marissa if he tried riding with injured feet.

A little while later, Riley released Kingston into the corral. He was limping slightly. He would have to dig out a pair of sneakers to wear for a couple of days until his feet could heal.

He was sitting on the top rail of the corral when Marissa joined him.

"I thought you were going to take him out for another ride."

"No, I won't be riding him again," Riley said. "I can't get my boots on right now, and I knew if I did, you'd have my head. I think we need to find a few more good riding horses for when the kids come back."

She gave him one of her perfected *Mom* looks. "Blue asked if I would help him understand sixth-grade math."

"Did you?"

"No," she said. "I told Blue, you would have to do it. I was never strong in math. He was talking about ratios and proportions, negative and positive numbers, and pre-algebra. I don't remember being taught anything like that in the sixth grade."

"New math," Riley said. "I can help him."

"Good, you have found a use for your degree in mathematics. Your father called a little while ago from Dry Rock. They should be here soon."

Riley looked over at the woman he loved and grinned. "Nervous?"

"Of course, I am. I'm terrified. What if your family

doesn't like me?"

"They will love you because I love you," he said. He slapped his baseball hat on his jeans and watched the dust fly. "I think I'll try to beat them and grab a quick shower unless you want to join me?"

"Too late," Marissa said, pointing to the plume of dust in the distance. "They're here."

The large RV stopped in front of the house. When the door opened, a tall man stepped from the bus and held his hand out to assist his wife in a faintly old-fashioned and courteous manner.

Noah came bounding from the house. Blue stayed on the porch watching.

Carole McKenna hugged her tall sons, and Daniel did the same.

"Where's Sully?" Riley exclaimed. "Didn't he come?"

"I'm here," A tall and lanky young man stepped from the bus with a little girl in his arms. Passing the child to Riley, he hugged Noah. Riley passed the little girl into Noah's waiting arms as Sully hugged Riley.

Frank stood behind Marissa, and she smiled at him. This was a whole family of genuine huggers. This wasn't polite, pretend affection. This was the real thing. A little girl of about two was being passed between the brothers without complaint. This was little Avery, the latest child to have the whole family wrapped around her little finger. Although all the children seemed to be well loved.

Carole stepped forward and held her arms open for Frank, and he stepped into them and then into his brother's embrace.

Sully introduced his wife, Karina, and his children in order, Alexa, Emilia, Violet, Grace, and Avery. He placed his hand on his wife's protruding belly and beamed with a smile. "This one, according to the sonograms, is going to be Daniel Sullivan. If not, we do have a name selected for her."

"Surprise as a name would work," Noah said.

"It would," Karina said, looking over her shoulder at her husband as they were moving toward the porch.

Riley pulled Marissa forward to introduce her and the twins, hiding behind the porch banisters from the strangers.

Noah looked around and discovered Blue standing away from the reunion. He dragged him into the fray to get his share of attention.

"Mom, Dad, this is Blue Eagle," Noah explained. "I've been telling you about him. He's taught me a ton of stuff, like riding and roping and all kinds of ranching stuff."

"Are you a real Indian?" one of Sully's little girls asked.

"Native American," Noah corrected.

"I am Quechan," Blue said simply.

The little girl stuck out her tongue at her young uncle. "He's K-chun," she said.

"That's the name of his people, his Tribal Nation," Noah explained.

"Don't you two start already," Sully admonished. "Emilia, play nice. Maybe once our new friend gets to know you, he might show you how to ride a horse."

"Really?" Emilia asked excitedly.

"Not right now," Carole interceded. "First, I want a chance to walk around and lose my wobbling travel legs, and I want a little time to get to know my new daughter-in-law to be."

"Good, because I want time to talk to these two," Daniel said, draping an arm over the shoulders of both Noah and Riley.

"Aw, Dad," Noah complained. "Haven't you had Mom to pick on all summer?"

"I do not pick on your mother," Daniel lamented. "But, son, I have all these lectures stored in my head, and there wasn't anyone around to listen."

Riley and Noah were both smiling. Dad's lectures were something they hadn't missed. Daniel led them away from the group while Frank and Marissa guided everyone inside."

Daniel strolled around the ranch buildings with his sons as they gave him the general tour and synopsis of what they had accomplished over the summer months.

"I'm going to move Kingston to his stall," Riley said, excusing himself and giving Noah and his father privacy.

Daniel watched his third son walk away. "Riley looks more..." he trailed off.

"Confident and tanned," Noah said.

Daniel nodded. "Good choices. This summer has been as good for him as it has been for you."

"Have you heard anything from the guys?" Noah asked.

"Your friends, yes. Eric and Brandon's parents paid their fines. Kenny's father hired him to work in his landscaping company, so he's spent his summer doing yard work. Brandon's father bought him a new Corvette to replace the car he wrecked. There was no lesson learned there. Three weeks later, he crossed into the lane of an on-coming car. The other car wasn't hit but swerved into a light pole. Thank God he didn't kill anyone. His blood alcohol levels were two times above the legal limit. Eric was with him," Daniel said, sadly.

"Did they get hurt?" Noah demanded.

Daniel nodded. "Eric shattered his kneecap. Brandon wasn't so lucky. In addition to quite a few bones being broken, he was in a coma for several weeks from a concussion. There were also internal injuries. He lost his spleen and had to have a kidney removed. He will recover, but his rehabilitation is going to be a very long one. His life has changed. He'll never be able to play team sports again. It would be too dangerous.

"Eric won't either, and he was depending on getting a football scholarship. I'm not sure what upset Brandon's father the most, his son being hurt or not being able to play sports."

"Brandon doesn't have a strong family foundation," Noah said. "His father wants to be his friend more than his father. Sometimes I think that's why he pushes so hard. He wants someone to say no, but his father won't, and his mother doesn't live with them anymore. She moved on and has a second family, and he doesn't feel like he's part of it."

"You have done some growing up," Daniel said, dropping his arm over his son's shoulder. "I like it," he said approvingly.

Riley led Kingston into the stall and gave him an ear scratch before shutting the stall door.

"Riley!" Daniel came into the barn with a loud voice, and the stallion reacted instantly. Rearing, Kingston pawed the air.

Daniel stopped and watched as his son stepped inside the stall. His heart all but stopped when he got a good look at the agitated stallion angrily moving around.

Riley mumbled and stroked the horse to calm him.

Daniel made no movement forward. He stood against the door of an empty stall and watched in amazement.

Riley left the stall, and he motioned for his father to come closer.

Daniel shook his head slowly. "Your mother is going to take one look at that monster and kill me for sending you two here," he exclaimed.

Riley laughed. "He scared me at first, but we've agreed to a boss and lackey relationship. He's the boss, and I'm the lackey. Kingston is in charge. Make no mistake about it."

Daniel looked at his son with amazement. "I know what you've told me on the phone, but how did you know you could work with him? You've never been around horses before."

Riley shrugged. "We've been asking the same question from the beginning. Jefferson Ironheart was behind it, and he's a force to be reckoned with, and he rarely takes no for an answer. Wait until you meet him. He's quite a character."

Chapter 19

"Y ou and Noah have had an interesting summer," Daniel said.

Riley looked across the ranch yards and outward to the desert. "It's been a life-changing summer. I've fallen in love with Marissa, and I've discovered what I was meant to do."

"You're serious about working with Frank, here as a counselor and foster parent?"

"As far as I'm concerned, it's a done deal," Riley said. "If we don't work here, we'll open a home of our own for kids."

"What about your music career?" Daniel asked.

"I'll be there as part of I-35, but not as a single," Riley said. "Dad, all the time I spent getting those degrees was about me denying my inner self. I have a need to help people, but I didn't know why or how. Now I know, and I've decided I want to help kids like Blue. Kids who need someone in their lives who will care about them and be there for them."

"And, your music?" Daniel asked.

"Music is part of my DNA," Riley said, shrugging. "It was bred into me. I can make a very nice living writing songs. If I never earn another royalty, Marissa and I are fixed for life. We've decided to establish a new life and a family here."

Daniel looked into the distance of the desert. "It's so isolated out here."

"We missed the conveniences at first," Riley admitted. "It's just a matter of scheduling our time better." He gave his father a grin. "There's no running across the street for a six-dollar cup of coffee, with a fancy name. People around here would think you were out of your mind and incredibly spoiled. After a while, though, this kind of living grows on you, at least it has me. It's not for everyone, but I feel like I've been reprogrammed. I now know what is important to me.

"I've been motivated by living here and accepting what has been given to me. I've been inspired because I'm in love with a wonderful woman and two little boys, who have captured my heart. I belong here. Every time I've tried to fit in somewhere else, I've felt like a square peg trying to fit in a circle. This time I feel like I belong."

"I have suspected something was bothering you for a long time," Daniel admitted. "I don't like to interfere with my grown sons' lives." Daniel held both hands up in a gesture of surrender. "I know, I know. I have in the past, but I learned that lesson with the first two."

"And, we appreciate that you have learned that lesson," Riley said with a tease in his voice. "There's something else I should tell you."

"More secrets?"

"Not so much a secret, but something I've kept private for a while. In addition to having a movie star, music writers, singers, composers, musicians, and ballet dancers in the family, sometime in the future, you might have a minister for a son. I have a Masters in Theology, although I haven't decided yet if I'm going to take the final steps to be ordained," Riley said.

Daniel took the news with a rise of one eyebrow. "I'm not

as surprised as you would think. Your great-grandfather was a minister. His father was one too, and you've been my only son who never complained about having to read church doctrine. Your mother will be thrilled."

They walked from the barn together. Noah was organizing a softball game with all the nieces and Blue.

"Spending the summer here has changed him," Riley said. "Noah has matured. He's practically adopted Blue. He has spent hours and hours helping him learn to read better and get this–teaching him manners! Blue is one lucky kid to have landed here. Uncle Frank and Aunt Katherine ran this ranch as a foster home for years, and with my and Marissa's help, it's going to help even more children."

"Whoa," Sully exclaimed, joining his brother and father. "It's a little aromatic out here."

Riley laughed, and with a put-on western accent, said. "That's country perfume, city boy."

Daniel and Sully laughed.

"You two catch up. I'm going in," Daniel said.

The two brothers walked together.

"I like Marissa," Sully said. "Mom and Karina like her, too. Have you set a date?"

Riley shook his head. "No, we have an agreement. She's still a little spooked after what happened to her in her first marriage. It's an open question, and she'll tell me when she's ready. I won't push her, but she can't delay it too long. We have to be a married couple to be approved as foster parents. It scares me that she might not want to get involved with this mob."

"Not you!" Sully scoffed. "You're the local hero. Blue was telling us about the high-wire act of yours."

"It wasn't a big deal," Riley denied. "All I had to do was traverse and grab her. The rest of them had the hard part of pulling us up."

"Riley! Sully!" Daniel shouted from the porch and pointed. Another RV was leaving a trail of dust on the ranch lane.

Marissa sat in the kitchen talking with Carole and Karina McKenna while most of the children were outside playing. She was surprised by how *normal* these two women were. Riley's mother, Carole, was the mother of seven children. Karina was the wife of a superstar and the financial wizard behind her family's monetary success.

Carole spoke a little bit of surviving cancer and the wonderful time she'd had on the vacation her husband had planned. Karina talked about a change about to take place in her and Sully's marriage. Sully had decided to take several years off from his high-paced career to concentrate more time on their marriage and family. He'd reached a pinnacle of success where he could pick and choose his projects.

When Noah shouted that Micah had arrived, everyone rose from the table to go outside to greet them. The oldest brother Micah unloaded the RV of his wife, Tess, and their children. Tess was quick to tell everyone the paperwork on the newest adoption was progressing on schedule. Katie was their oldest child at ten. Their twins were only two years old.

Frank brought in folding chairs, and the large McKenna reunion continued around the kitchen table and late into the night. Most of the children were bedded down in the new dormitory rooms. The adults continued to catch-up with their lives. There was a lot of boisterous laughter until Frank called it a night.

"Y'all can finish gnawing on the cob," he exclaimed. "We have to rise with the sun for early chores!"

The adults returned to the RVs with the youngest of their children. Marissa was the last in the kitchen with Riley.

"Are your parents going to think we're awful because we are sleeping together?" she worried. "I know they're religious."

"My parents think you are the best thing that's ever happened to me," he responded with a kiss. "I agree with their assessment. I do know one thing. We need to get moving on getting our house built. Uncle Frank has been displaced since we got here. He's slept on the couch, and then he moved into the room I was using. He needs his space back. I was thinking we could buy a good-sized trailer until the house is built. Once we build the house, the trailer could be used as extra housing for counselors. I've seen some really nice ones."

"I've never been in a single trailer. I was in a triple-wide once," Marissa said. "It was twice the size of the apartment I was living in. It's something we can look into."

Noah and Blue were leading, or pulling, Old Ornery around in the paddock with Jake, Jackson, and Grace all sitting in the saddle, one behind the other. Three more nieces were waiting their turn.

"Honey, are you sure that horse is safe?" Carole demanded from behind the fence.

Noah rolled his eyes, silently imploring his brother to do something.

Riley hooked an arm around his mother's arm. "Come on, Mom, you're giving Old Ornery a bad reputation. Nothing is going to happen to the kids. Shouldn't you be inside helping Marissa fix food for tonight's shindig?"

Carole looked at her son with a smirk. "Shame on you. It's supposed to be a surprise!"

Riley raised his eyebrows in mock surprise. "After the fifth cake went into the oven, it was obvious. By now, Marissa and Karina are probably working on pies."

"Casseroles," Carole admitted with a wry grin. "You behave yourself, stay busy, and stay away from the house. See if you can keep your brothers busy for a couple more hours. This is supposed to be a surprise."

"Come get the little kids in about half-hour," Riley suggested. 'We'll saddle a few horses and take the older girls riding, along with my citified brothers. Ask Tess if she wants to come. I know you're not letting her near the stove!"

"She tries," Carole said, fondly with a look of indulgence. "Then, she starts thinking of her patients, and the smoke alarms go off. Those horses will be gentle, won't they?"

"We don't have any other kind," Riley fibbed.

When the McKenna clan of siblings and cousins came in from their horseback ride, there were already a few trucks and cars parked in the ranch yard. Noah, Blue, and Riley took over the unsaddling chores and tending while the girls ran inside to clean up.

After the horses were cared for, the brothers headed inside. Even with two bathrooms, they had to wait in turn. Meanwhile, several more cars and trucks were parked outside.

"Hey, Noah, hurry up!" Riley exclaimed, pounding on the bathroom door. "Give Sully and me a chance to get in there too!"

"This brings back teenage memories," Sully said. "Three boys, sharing one bathroom, and Micah always managed to get in first. He claimed 'oldest' rights."

"Still does," Riley groused.

When they made their entrance into the living room, there were at least a dozen friends and neighbors there, and more were arriving. Rainey and John Henry had spread the word about the rescue and about the McKenna family arriving. An impromptu picnic and barbecue was quickly planned. Everyone who came brought food, portable tables, folding chairs, and whatever they thought might be needed. There was going to be a potluck picnic/supper at the McKenna ranch.

There were a lot of people milling around. Many of the women had Sully's signature written somewhere on their tee shirts and blouses. Riley hadn't met all of the people there, but he knew they were friends and relatives of Frank's, John Henry, and Blue. Blue's Aunt was there along with her children and his sisters. Rainey arrived with two younger brothers and a neighbor she introduced. She promised her mother would be coming later. Uncle Frank and John Henry organized straw bale tosses and three-legged races for the children. One of the neighbors arrived towing a huge barrel contraption. When he parked and pushed the stainless steel sides aside, there was a whole pig roasting inside.

Riley, Noah, and John Henry were trying their pitching arms on a game of horseshoes. They were playing against Jefferson Ironheart, Uncle Frank, and Daniel and were losing badly.

Rainey waited until Riley took his turn, and she whispered something in his ear. He relinquished his place to Christian and left the game. He was hoping his absence would improve his team's chance of winning.

Rainey pulled him toward the front of the house, where her mother had finally arrived.

"Good evening, Mrs. Two Trees," Riley greeted.

"I'm running late, as usual, but I made it," Glenda Two Trees exclaimed with a happy smile. "I have wanted to get over here to thank you, but I've been so busy, I've been spinning around like a top!"

"You don't have to thank me," Riley said. "I didn't do anything except remember your name and how unique your pieces were. You have an unusual style, and it caught my eye." He pointed to the backyard area. "My brother Micah did the research. I'm sorry you were being cheated."

"It was as much our fault as it was Owen Duquette's," Glenda admitted. "We allowed ourselves to be swindled. We walked right into his trap, and we were grateful for anyone who would buy our wares and take on the hard part of merchandising. We didn't investigate his past businesses or business practices, and we paid the price for it.

"In the long run, I think dealing with Owen Duquette was a lesson we needed to learn. The Tribal Council has been very busy. We have selected a committee-within the tribal co-op to set standard prices for our wares. It will protect our silver-smiths, rug, and basket weavers, and it will encourage our arti-sans of traditional wares. We think if we work as a group and team effort, we will stand stronger in the commercial marketplace."

"How does it affect you?" Riley asked.

Glenda Two-Trees smiled broadly. "It wouldn't, since my artwork isn't traditional. It doesn't mean I won't be very involved in the Arts Council. I will. We all will."

"Mom, show him," Rainey interrupted, bored with another lecture about the changes being made within the Indian Council. It had been her mother's favorite topic of conversation for weeks!

Glenda opened the back of the station wagon and care-fully pulled out a large macramé piece. Rainey scrambled around to the backseat and removed a length of white painter's canvas, and she spread it on the ground. Her mother laid the large art piece on the canvas.

The woven art colors invoked the idea of swirling desert canyons in pale shades of sand, peach, turquoise, and sky and clouds of pinks and blues and fluffy white. It was almost mystical in appearance, with a detailed black stallion running across the colors. In the foreground was a western-dressed man.

"I named it *Horse Spirit*," Glenda said, watching the expression of amazement cross Riley's face.

"Adding you into the design was my idea," Rainey offered.

Riley looked over the art piece. "It's beautiful."

"It's my gift of thanks to you," Glenda Two-Trees said.

"No," Riley objected. "Mrs. Two-Trees, it's too much. It would sell in a second at a gallery."

"I didn't make it to sell," Glenda scolded. "I made it for you. Besides, I doubt anyone else would understand the imagery. It fits you and you, alone."

"Thank you," Riley exclaimed. "I can't believe this." He looked to Marissa, who had joined him with genuine pride. "I have a Glenda Two-Trees piece of art. How cool is that?"

"It's beautiful," Marissa said. "It will make a beautiful wall hanging in our new home."

"How lovely," Carole McKenna said, joining them.

"Mom, this is Mrs. Glenda Two-Trees and her daughter Rainey. Mrs. Two-Trees made and gave this to me. Isn't it incredible?"

Carole nodded. "It is. Make sure Micah sees it. But with that cream color, you'd better take it in the house and away from this dust."

Riley and Marissa rolled the piece inside the canvas, carefully carrying it inside and laying it across the bed.

When they returned, Carole had pulled Glenda Two-Trees and Rainey into the picnic area. It was a fun evening. Riley hadn't realized he'd made so many new friends in the area. Noah was saying his goodbyes to the people they had met over the summer months.

As the younger children began to drop from sheer exhaustion, the adults were tucking them into beds in the dormitory rooms they'd used the night before. As the neighbors were saying good-bye, they were cleaning any messes they'd made and packing their vehicles with whatever they'd brought with them and their kids.

Marissa managed to get the twins to sleep as the last of the vehicles departed. Noah yawned widely, but despite his deliberate yawns, he was snagged for trash duty.

Riley went to the barns for one last check to make sure no one had left any doors unlocked or latches unhooked. In the dim light of the low-wattage electric bulbs, he systematically checked the stalls. When he stopped at Kingston's stall, the stallion came over to him.

"I'm going to miss you," Riley mumbled.

"Where do you think he's going?" a gruff voice behind him asked.

Riley didn't turn around. The low gravelly voice belonged to Jefferson Ironheart.

"He's not going anywhere, but I'll be spending less time with him. I didn't see your truck," Riley said. "I thought everyone had gone home."

"I was waiting for you," Jefferson Ironheart said.

Riley turned around. "Why? You haven't spoken to me directly for a while."

The old man looked at him steadily, but his eyes were crinkled with a hidden smile. "I've been busy, and the Tribal Council does thank you for what you brought to our attention."

Riley waited.

Jefferson Ironheart reached over and gripped Riley's shoulder. "I was wrong about this horse, but I wasn't wrong about you. Kingston is not meant for racing. He was meant for special handling, and he chose you for the job."

"He or you?" Riley questioned.

The old man shrugged. "Both of us, and we were right

about you. You were so green you gave us a few laughs, but your instincts are good."

"I've turned him over to Blue. He was supposed to talk to you. Didn't he?" Riley asked.

Jefferson Ironheart shook his head. "Yes, he did. The Tribal Council has met, and we discussed the situation. We believe the stallion belongs to you. We are giving him to you, a gift for a wrong you have set right. By alerting us to Duquette's suspicious activities, you gave us a new focus on what services we should be providing for our people. We also heard what you did by saving the little girl. Had she fallen, it would not have been Christian's fault, but he would have been blamed. The reservation and our people would have been blamed. What you did was an act of bravery."

"It wasn't bravery. I've been trained to scale cliffs. I know the tribal tradition of gift giving is a noble custom of your culture. I am honored, and I certainly mean no disrespect, but I can't accept Kingston. I've decided to stay here at the Boy's Ranch as a counselor and foster parent.

"I have also been working with Blue to transfer Kingston's allegiance to him. Blue has been hurt enough in his short life. I told him, have convinced him he can be Kingston's rider, and I won't take that away. I know he needs to grow a bit, well, truthfully, he needs a lot of growing up, but I believe in him. He can continue to work with the stallion, and he will make all of us proud."

Jefferson Ironheart nodded his head. "Kingston is yours. If you chose to give him to Blue, it's your business. If you do give him to the boy, we can train him at his pace. I agree it will be several years before he would be mature enough to race.

"I would suggest, from a legal standpoint, the ownership of Kingston should be transferred to you until Blue is old enough to claim him. His parents are not what I would call stable guardians. If the boy owned the horse, his parents could sell it, and we wouldn't be able to stop them. In addition, if the horse remains an asset of our tribe, he could be sold. It doesn't happen very often, but I can be outvoted. I'm not saying they would, but it's better to think ahead than be sorry afterward. Plus, someone has to be responsible for his feed bills."

Riley grinned. "Thank you. I'll accept temporary ownership of Kingston. I'll tell Blue in the morning and leave the legal stuff in your hands. We will both be around to help him grow into manhood."

"I heard you and Marissa are joining Frank here at the ranch. That's good. He can use the help." Jefferson Ironheart offered his hand, and Riley shook it. The agreement was made.

The McKennas sat around the kitchen table for their last evening together with the children tucked into beds. They'd been on the ranch for almost two weeks. In the morning, they would be saying their farewells.

Noah came into the kitchen and stuck his head in the refrigerator.

"Noah, you can't possibly be hungry!" Marissa exclaimed.

He grinned, closed the door, and held up his favorite soft drink. "No, and believe it or not, I'm going to miss this place, and you shooing me out of the kitchen."

Marissa opened her arms and hugged him. "I'm going to miss you so much!"

"Me, too," Frank said genuinely.

"You are going to miss the free labor," Noah teased his uncle.

"That too!" Frank admitted, and the men laughed.

Riley and Noah both grinned.

"Sully wants to leave at dawn," Noah said.

Riley looked over to his brothers and their wives. "We'd like you to stay a couple of days longer."

"Why?" Tess asked.

"Yeah, any particular reason?" Noah asked. "You are not planning on getting married, or something, are you?"

Marissa and Riley ignored the gasps of his mother and the smiles from his sisters-in-law.

"Riley?" Carole questioned.

"It's true, Mom," Riley said. "Marissa and I have been discussing marriage. I left the date to her, and she has agreed to marry me. Neither one of us wants a big fuss made out of it."

"Fuss! Riley, it's your wedding!" Carole protested.

"We tried eloping," Micah said, with his wife Tess sitting in his lap. "We were shanghaied later into having a second wedding."

"I really don't want that," Marissa said. "After all we've been through, I feel blessed to have found Riley."

"I feel the same way about Marissa," Riley said. "We want a small wedding with immediate family only, and we'll be married by a Justice of the Peace."

"We can stick around for a couple more days," Sully said. "Give the women time to buy new dresses while we buy suits because I didn't bring one. You can have the small wedding that you want."

"We can pull this off," Micah agreed. "I did bring a suit with me."

"Of course, you did," the majority of the adults said together.

"May I walk the bride down the aisle?" Frank asked.

"Yes, I would love it," Marissa said, stretching on her toes to kiss him on the cheek.

"Well?" Riley asked, looking around the kitchen.

"Who is going to be your best man?" Noah asked.

"I'll have three best men," Riley said, and he turned to Blue. "And, one ring holder."

"And, we'll be the bridesmaids," Karina said. "You get two for one with me!"

"And, between us, we have six flower girls," Tess chimed in. "We can get this organized in a couple of hours!"

"Of course we can," Carole exclaimed. "We'll be in Yuma when the stores open tomorrow."

Daniel looked to his son and Marissa. "You might have been better off if you had eloped."

"We tried that," Tess said. "They would have been better off if they'd pretended to have a fight and waited until we left! Daniel, you'll be the designated photographer!"

Chapter 20

Riley met Noah at the corral at dawn. It was unplanned, but neither could sleep late, now. They were accustomed to rising with the sun. They climbed the corral fencing and looked toward the east.

"I only have a couple more of these sunrises," Noah said.

"The same sun rises in San Antonio," Riley said.

"Yeah, but it won't be the same," Noah said. "The ranch is a special place for me now. Maybe, I'll come back next summer."

"You'll be welcomed," Riley said, and they were both silent as the silent rays of light suddenly burst from the horizon and the beginning of a new day was upon them.

"Is this private?" Daniel asked from behind them.

Both brothers turned around, and smiled at their father. He took it as a cue that he was welcomed.

"I was saying goodbye," Noah admitted.

"For a summer that started as a punishment, you two seem to have gotten the better end of the deal," Daniel said. "I kind of envy you."

"Good, because I'm giving you the barn mucking chore this morning," Noah said.

They laughed.

"What I meant was both of you have grown and changed. Riley will be a married man today. No one expected that to happen," Daniel said.

"Including me," Riley said. "I think I owe Noah big-time for being an idiot and screwing up! If he hadn't, I'd probably still be floundering."

"Yeah, well, I might cash in on that someday," Noah admitted. "I don't think I'd be so stupid as to get in a car with a bunch of drunk kids again."

"Because of what it cost you this summer or because you think it's stupid?" Riley asked.

Noah looked surprised at the question. "Because I *know* it's stupid," he answered. "This summer didn't cost me anything except time. Dad was right. Throwing money at a problem isn't as satisfying as doing something to help."

"My God! He is growing up!" Riley exclaimed, clutching his chest. He was enjoying his younger brother's revelations.

Noah jumped from the fence, hooked a booted foot on one of the rails, and spoke to his father. "When I first starting playing drums at gigs, you would send me on stage and say, "*Have fun, and make yourself proud.*""

"As I-35, we heard it a million times," Riley said.

"You probably did, but Dad told me when his father sent him out to a ballgame or some kind of competition, Grandpa would say, "*Have fun, and make me proud.*" I thought Dad was repeating what his father said. I didn't realize until recently what a big difference there was in those two sentences. Grandpa was telling Dad to 'Make *me* proud' because he saw his son as an extension of himself.

"Our Dad said, 'Have fun, and make *yourself* proud.' Our

Dad was only concerned with our being happy with the results of what we did. Even if we were horrible, and we must have been in the beginning, Dad was happy for us as long as we felt good about it. We've all known from the beginning, all we had to say was stop, and they'd pull us out of whatever we were doing. I think Dad and Mom are pretty special to allow us the space to become the individuals we need to be, so we can be proud of ourselves."

Riley looked over and met his father's eyes. Daniel had tears in his eyes.

"Noah, this whole summer was about building character for both of us," Riley said, jumping from the top rail. Noah followed him, and they turned to their father.

Daniel McKenna smiled, his eyes faintly shimmering with unshed tears and pride of fatherhood. "I think both of my sons passed this summer's trials and tribulations with flying colors," Daniel said. "But, more important, both of you have made yourselves proud."

It was dark and cooler outside, but not too dark as there was a full moon. Everyone was bedded down for the night when they slipped out of the house. They didn't go far, only about five hundred feet where they would build a home for their new family.

"Today, we will lay the foundation for the rest of our lives together," Riley said. "Our home will be here. Our love will grow here, as will our children someday." He handed Marissa a ring box. "Please say you'll marry me."

"I've already said I would," Marissa said. "I also said I didn't need an engagement ring."

"I was listening," Riley said.

Marissa opened the box, and it wasn't an engagement ring. It was a simple silver ring with an open heart and four birthstones.

"It's perfect," she said.

"I know a guy, who knows a guy," Riley said with a smile.

"I don't care who made it. It's beautiful and will bind us together as a family. The ring is perfect, but today is going to be a nightmare of shopping and rushing around," Marissa said. "Who is going to marry us? You don't like the minister of the church in Dry Rock."

"I like Reverend Tolliver. He's an okay guy," Riley said. "I don't like his browbeating sermons. How would you like to be married by Jefferson Ironheart?"

"Can he marry us?"

"Yes, he's a Justice of the Peace. It's only one of the many hats he wears," Riley said. "The ranch is officially on the reservation so, Jefferson Ironheart can officiate. We wanted a simple ceremony."

"Three best men, two maids of honor, six flower girls," Marissa sang the tune of *"Five Golden Rings"*.

"Four little boys and ring holder for good measure," Riley finished, the reworded *partridge in a pear tree part*, and he was laughing. "We'll survive the next couple of days. My family will go home happy they didn't miss our wedding, and we probably won't see them again for six months to a year. We have the rest of our lives to be in love, make love, and show many needy kids how good life can be! When we're ready, we can go into baby production ourselves."

"I'd probably be upset with your family if I didn't like them so much," Marissa agreed.

Later that night, Marissa pushed Riley on his back in the bed, leaned over, and kissed him. "Sometimes, I can't believe I found someone like you. You're gentle and yet so strong. I don't think you realize how wonderful it is to be complimented on the little things that most people overlook. I am so proud to be loved by you and to be in love with you." She could feel him hardening under her, growing with need.

"Why wouldn't I?" he whispered. "You are a beautiful and amazing woman."

"Make love to me, Riley."

He groaned and rolled her to her back. "Your wish is my command."

"I want to feel you inside me," Marissa whispered, and her words were silenced by his mouth. She could feel the length of him as he pressed against her.

Riley positioned himself between her legs. God, he loved the moment when he entered her, and his shaft slid deep into her body. He wanted to plunder, and ravage and he knew Marissa liked it, but... they had family in the house. They could be a loud and lusty couple, as they'd proven the few times when they'd managed privacy. When he built their new home, he was going to make sure the bedroom was soundproof.

While he was in Yuma tomorrow, he would find a company that sold trailers and pay whatever it cost to get a suitable one delivered quickly.

"Easy, sweetheart," he crooned as she moaned and covered her cries with a pillow.

Marissa's eyes looked into Riley's. She raised her legs around him as he sank and thrust into her. He filled her with each thrust, and she rose to meet him. She began to feel an orgasm building, and suddenly they couldn't get close enough. She wanted him to take her harder, and he delivered it stroke after stroke. Her body seized, and Riley groaned into her pillow with relief. He didn't remove himself, not wanting to break the connection between their bodies. He shifted his weight so he wasn't crushing her and ran his hands over her beautiful body.

"In a couple of days, you will be my wife," Riley whispered. "And, someone is babysitting that night because I want to howl at the moon while I'm making love to my woman."

Marissa giggled, and he smiled. He'd never heard her giggle before. He was going to make sure he heard it often.

Epilogue

Momma and Daddy checked on the twins, both sound asleep together in one of their beds. The twins were always put to bed in separate beds, but one or the other would join their twin, and they slept together. The youth-sized beds had been an indulgence, Riley hadn't been able to pass by, and as he told Marissa, the kids were only little once. He had found cowboy beds, one of a covered wagon, the other of a stagecoach. When the boys outgrew them, they could be passed down or moved into another bedroom. They'd already discussed adding to their family in two or three years. They weren't in a hurry, but if something happened earlier they wouldn't mind it either.

It was chilly outside. Winter was coming to the desert, although the lower temperatures rarely dipped to freezing. Every evening they did a walk-through of the new house. Marissa had selected most of the colors, fixtures, and materials. Still, it was Riley the workmen came to with questions. He had surprised her with his knowledge of construction. He was labor when the extra muscle was needed by the building crews. It was taking longer than expected to finish their house, as the project kept growing.

For now, they were living in a triple-wide modular home of over two thousand square feet that would never be moved. It looked like thousands of brick and mortar homes in housing developments across the nation. If Marissa hadn't seen it brought in on flatbed trucks and pieced together like a giant puzzle, she would never have believed it. She'd told Riley they didn't need to build a new house. Still, he claimed they did because the modular home would be necessary to house counselors and a full-time cook when more boys were in residence.

Marissa had realized her mistake too late. She had sent everything from her old house to an auction house. She'd brought a few small appliances from her small-furnished garage apartment in Irvine when they picked up her things.

Riley had only laughed at her regrets. He reminded her he had been reimbursed for all his household goods, lost in a bolt of lightning. They were starting fresh, and neither of them needed any reminders of their previous relationships.

While they had taken the classes they needed to become foster parents, they had spent some time in Yuma furniture stores. They had lived in a borrowed RV belonging to a friend of Frank's. There had been fabulous shopping sprees to furnish the modular home being assembled while they were in class. Some of the furniture would remain in what had been dubbed the Counselor's House. Like the boy's bedroom furniture, some of the furnishings would be moved to their new house when it was finished.

Blue occupied a bedroom in their temporary home. Facilitated by Jefferson Ironheart, it was a permanent placement. His mother and incarcerated father had both signed over custody of Blue to Riley and Marissa. His sisters would probably follow, but the Aunt who had temporary custody hadn't agreed yet.

There were four foster boys already at the Dry Rock Boy's Ranch in McKenna shared custody, and there would be more to come. Mrs. Brockman, a no-nonsense ex-social worker, and Child Protective Agency employee, was in residence at the ranch house. For the time being, breakfast and dinner were prepared and served in Frank's kitchen by Marissa, and lunch was a catch as catch can, as Mrs. Brockman didn't claim to be a cook, and the boys were in school for their mid-day meal.

The adults were teaching the boys responsibility, manners and working with them to untangle the traumas of their young lives. Riley was the official homework tutor, and the first report cards had proven his skills and knowledge. Marissa was the soft mothering touch some of the boys had never had in their lives.

Riley and Marissa walked through the new house construction hand-in-hand.

"It's not going to be long now," Marissa said as she approved of the paint colors she'd chosen.

"The backyard fence is going to have to be moved back," Riley said, looking out a window.

"Why?" she asked, joining him. "What have you added now?"

Riley gave her a sheepish smile. "It will be a separate building."

"What will be a separate building?"

"A music studio and a gym," he said. "Music and fitness are vital to children, and they should be exposed to it."

Marissa smiled. "Frank owes me ten dollars."

"For what?"

"We made a bet," she said. "I told him you'd never make it through the first year without a music studio. I was right."

"You're right about most things," Riley admitted. "It's not a big deal, a few instruments, a few lessons. Kids need to be exposed to different things."

"Most of all, they need to be exposed to love," Marissa said, as Riley's arm tightened around her. He instinctively knew when she was thinking of the past. He wouldn't let her dwell on it.

"The kids who come here will know love," Riley promised. "Although sometimes it's going to be heartbreaking to give them back. We can only hope the parents have learned from their mistakes."

"In the time we do have them, we'll show them love and teach them to have pride in themselves," Marissa said. "Most important, they will witness our love for each other as a good example. There can't be a better lesson they'll take with them."

"Have I told you how much I love you today?" Riley asked.

"Only three times today, but you don't need to say the words because I feel it in every glance, touch, and kiss."

"Yes, I do," Riley said, lowering his lips to hers. "This coyote has mated for life, and I've found my true calling as a husband, parent, and teacher. I'll never take it for granted."

Marissa smiled and tucked herself into his chest as his arms held her tight. It was one of her favorite places to be. Suddenly she snapped to attention. "The light in the kitchen just came on! One of the boys is awake!"

"Let's get back!" Riley exclaimed, claiming her hand and pulling her toward the door. "You know what happened the last time the twins decided they were hungry in the middle of the night!"

Mariella Starr

Hello, this is Mariella.

I've often wondered what makes a writer. I never claimed to be one, because I wrote for myself. Even now, very few people know that I write.

Of the many gifts I received from my parents, the most important one was the encouragement to try things they didn't do themselves. They didn't understand their strange child so different from themselves and her brothers. I had a need to create. My parent's home over the years became a gallery for my artwork. Most of it now resides in the homes of my children and siblings. There hasn't been an empty wall in my home in years.

What fills a child with lifelong inspiration? In my case, it was my parents and two specific teachers. The first, was a grade school teacher who gave me two compliments in one by praising my art on the cover of a written story and the A+ grade was a boost, too. That was in sixth grade.

The second was a seventh-grade teacher who had a reputation for being tough. I was a new student to the school, my family having moved again because of my father's military deployment. I'd heard horror stories from the other kids about this teacher.

I was shocked when the teacher returned my writing assignment with a red copy editing marks all over my pages—something I'd never seen before. I was so embarrassed. I turned it over on my desk so no one else could see it.

My wonderful teacher, though, was walking around the

classroom returning the assignments papers to the students, returned to my desk. He turned over my stapled pages. Without a word, he tapped the top of the page with his finger.

I had missed it. Written across the top of the lined notebook page, in red was:

A+++ Best story I've ever read from a student! Ever! Keep writing!

That single incident has never been forgotten. Mr. Gregory taught me so much that year, but most importantly, he gave me encouragement. I kept writing and I have never stopped.

Posey's Assets
Broken Vows
The Promise
In Search of a Noble Man
Lacy's Rules
Desiree, A Woman of Defiance
Full Circle
Caitlin's Conspiracies
The Awakening of Alexandria
Charlotte's Comeuppance
Teaching Miss Maisie Jane

The McKenna Brothers
The Forever Kind: Sully
Holding Tess

The Overton Saga
Isabel's Independence, Book 1
Britannia's Blaggard, Book 2
Sweet Sarah, Book 3

Connect with Mariella Starr:
MariStarr@outlook.com

Blushing Books

Blushing Books is the oldest eBook publisher on the web. We've been running websites that publish steamy romance and erotica since 1999, and we have been selling eBooks since 2003. We have free and promotional offerings that change weekly, so please do visit us at http://www.blushingbooks.com/free.

Blushing Books Newsletter

Please join the Blushing Books newsletter
to receive updates & special promotional offers.
You can also join by using your mobile phone:
Just text **BLUSHING** to 22828.

Every month, one new sign up via text messaging will receive
a $25.00 Amazon gift card, so sign up today!